MW00588553

A NOVEL BASED ON THE LIFE OF
ANGELA BAMBACE

LITTLE BY LITTLE
WE WON

Peg A. Lamphier, PhD

Little by Little We Won: A Novel Based on the Life of Angela Bambace is a work of fiction. Some incidents, dialogue, and characters are products of the author's imagination and are not to be construed as real. Where real-life historical figures appear, the situations, incidents, and dialogue concerning those persons are based on or inspired by actual events. In all other respects, any resemblance to actual persons, living or dead, events, or locales is entirely coincidental.

Barbera Foundation, Inc.
P.O. Box 1019
Temple City, CA 91780

Copyright © 2019 Barbera Foundation, Inc.
Cover photo courtesy of the Immigration History Research Center Archives at the University of Minnesota
Cover design: Suzanne Turpin

More information at www.mentorisproject.org

ISBN: 978-1-947431-24-9

Library of Congress Control Number: 2019937025

All net proceeds from the sale of this book will be donated to Barbera Foundation, Inc. whose mission is to support educational initiatives that foster an appreciation of history and culture to encourage and inspire young people to create a stronger future.

The Mentoris Project is a series of novels and biographies about the lives of great Italians and Italian-Americans: men and women who have changed history through their contributions as scientists, inventors, explorers, thinkers, and creators. The Barbera Foundation sponsors this series in the hope that, like a mentor, each book will inspire the reader to discover how she or he can make a positive contribution to society.

Contents

Foreword   i

Part I
1911

Chapter One: Doves and Blackbirds   1
Chapter Two: Misery Lane Loves Company   19
Chapter Three: We Mourn Our Loss   39

Part II
1919–1920

Chapter Four: One Small Step   59
Chapter Five: Desperate Times   83
Chapter Six: Red Scare   103

Part III
1926–1927

Chapter Seven: Pulling the Power   129
Chapter Eight: A Losing Battle   145
Chapter Nine: Not Execution, But Murder   161

Part IV
1932–1936

Chapter Ten: A New Deal for Americans   183

Chapter Eleven: Starting Over Again   197
Chapter Twelve: March for Democracy   215

Part V
1968–1972

Chapter Thirteen: Protest and Politics   233
Chapter Fourteen: Who More Special Than We?   247

Epilogue: Angela's Retirement Speech, 1972   257
Take a Bow, Angela   259
Acknowledgments: Drumroll, Please   263
About the Author   265

Foreword

First and foremost, Mentor was a person. We tend to think of the word *mentor* as a noun (a mentor) or a verb (to mentor), but there is a very human dimension embedded in the term. Mentor appears in Homer's *Odyssey* as the old friend entrusted to care for Odysseus's household and his son Telemachus during the Trojan War. When years pass and Telemachus sets out to search for his missing father, the goddess Athena assumes the form of Mentor to accompany him. The human being welcomes a human form for counsel. From its very origins, becoming a mentor is a transcendent act; it carries with it something of the holy.

The Barbera Foundation's Mentoris Project sets out on an Athena-like mission: We hope the books that form this series will be an inspiration to all those who are seekers, to those of the twenty-first century who are on their own odysseys, trying to find enduring principles that will guide them to a spiritual home. The stories that comprise the series are all deeply human. These books dramatize the lives of great Italians and Italian-Americans whose stories bridge the ancient and the modern, taking many forms, just as Athena did, but always holding up a light for those living today.

Whether in novel form or traditional biography, these

books plumb the individual characters of our heroes' journeys. The power of storytelling has always been to envelop the reader in a vivid and continuous dream, and to forge a link with the subject. Our goal is for that link to guide the reader home with a new inspiration.

What is a mentor? A guide, a moral compass, an inspiration. A friend who points you toward true north. We hope that the Mentoris Project will become that friend, and it will help us all transcend our daily lives with something that can only be called holy.

—Robert J. Barbera, President, Barbera Foundation
—Ken LaZebnik, Editor, The Mentoris Project

"The women who worked in our industry in the beginning were great people. They went out, they fought, and they worked very hard to organize— as much as the men—and they were more effective than the men. The key people weren't even thinking of themselves, of marrying and building a family. They just threw themselves into this hope they had of building a better world, a better place for everybody and little by little we won."

—Angela Bambace, 1971

For Oliver Grey
May you be as strong and kind as Angela Bambace

Part I

1911

Chapter One

DOVES AND BLACKBIRDS

"At first, the falling girls had seemed like birds. Bright cardinals, bone-white doves, swooping blackbirds in velvet-collared coats. But when they hit the cement, the terrible truth of the matter was revealed."
—Alice Hoffman, 2014

March 25, 1911

Dinah Lipschitz glanced at the wall clock and felt herself frown. It was 4:45 and quitting time. All she wanted to do was go home and take a bath. Instead she had to deal with an angry sewing machine operator. One of the new girls stood before her, Italian from the look of her, though she was more insistent than most Italian girls.

"They told me $14 a week. Not $12," the dark-haired young woman said. She held her pay envelope out to Dinah. "If it's going to be twelve, I'll give my notice now. I can get $14 at any factory in the city."

Dinah tried not to smile at the woman's tone. She didn't much like Mr. Harris and Mr. Blanck's low wages either. "Your name?" Dinah asked.

The young woman's brown eyes narrowed at Dinah. "Elizabeth Viviano."

"It's just that new girls generally get $12 a week."

"I'm not new. Not to shirtwaists, I mean. Just new to this company. Mr. Blanck said $14 when he hired me. You've shorted me $2."

Dinah admired the young lady's pluck but worked for Mr. Harris and Mr. Blanck, not for these poor girls. Dinah pulled a ledger book out from under a stack of papers and flipped it open. *Yes. There it was.* Viviano, Elizabeth. $14.

After adding $2 to Miss Viviano's envelope, Dinah closed her heavy account books and tucked them into her bottom desk drawer. She pulled a slim gold chain with a key on it from her skirt pocket and locked the drawer along with the cash box. Most days she locked the cash box in the company safe on the tenth floor, but after paying the girls the box contained only $3.

Mr. Bernstein, the floor manager, ran past Dinah's desk. "Fire, fire!" he shouted.

Dinah looked up in alarm. Another darn fire. How many did that make in the last year? They had fire pails all around the room because they worked with cotton, which was even more flammable than paper. The factories that made wool jackets and skirts had it easy compared to shirtwaist factories. Ladies' waists, as they called blouses these days, were made from thin, oh-so-flammable cotton.

Across the room near the windows, she saw their head cutter,

Mr. Abramowitz, throw a pail of sand on a small fire under the cutting table. The flames guttered out, smoked, then seconds later once again burst into angry red flames. It was one of the boxes where the cutters threw their scraps. Mr. Abramowitz repeated the water pail treatment with no better success.

Dinah pushed back her desk chair and stepped toward the fire before stopping herself. There were dozens of male cutters and foremen on the floor. They didn't need a bookkeeper to put out the fire. And it didn't look like much. The nearly two hundred women in the room paid the tiny conflagration no attention at all. The Triangle Waist Company was famous for its periodic scrap fires. Dinah returned to her desk and picked up the phone. She called the company switchboard up on the tenth floor. It rang once, twice, three times. No one answered.

As she listened to the phone ring, Dinah looked over at the fire. Not so little now—it was burning the cutting table and some paper patterns that hung on the back wall. *Where was Mary?* Dinah checked the clock on her desk. It was 4:46 and the fire seemed ten times larger than a minute ago. On the tenth ring, Mary picked up. Dinah yelled "Fire!" into the receiver.

"What?" Mary asked.

"Fire! On eight. Tell Mr. Blanck." Dinah was about to demand Mary patch her into Verna on the ninth floor when Mary hung up. Dinah stared at the phone. She couldn't call the ninth floor directly. All the company calls went through the switchboard. And she couldn't scamper up there. The doors on eight were locked and she didn't have the keys. She'd told Mr. Blanck and Mr. Harris she should have the keys, but they always said no. She thought they liked controlling the movements of hundreds of women, including herself.

Dinah put down the phone and stared at the fire. In the

time it had taken her to make a phone call, it had gone from a small fire to an out-of-control blaze. Off to her left she saw Mr. Bernstein grab the hose nozzle and turn the water valve. His hand turned, then stopped. Nothing happened. He looked across the room to Dinah. Mr. Brown, the floor machinist, ran over to the hose stand. Dinah watched the two men confer. Brown turned the valve again. Still no water.

Bernstein handed something to Brown and ran to the far side of the room for two more fire pails. He ran straight at the fire. *Just like a man*, Dinah reflected. It was brave but not very smart. Fire pails weren't going to put out the fire and they needed to get the girls out of the building.

A handful of the sewing machine operators ran for the back door. They surged around Dinah's desk and piled up against the locked door. Dinah climbed atop her desk as the girls broke against it like a river around a small rectangular island.

Mr. Brown shoved through the tangle of young women shouting, "Make way! I have the key."

She watched as he found some space and fumbled at the lock. He pulled the door open and scrunched himself against the wall. A tide of women flowed past him and down the stairs.

From atop her desk, Dinah stared at the fire. It had taken most of the front of the room. She saw Miss Viviano trapped between the burning cutting tables and the front windows. A flaming shirtwaist pattern landed on her head. Her dark hair smoldered, then burst into flames. Dinah watched in horror as the young woman, so full of confidence just moments before, threw herself at the window behind her. The window cracked and Miss Viviano was gone. Dinah jumped off her desk and joined the exodus down the stairs. It was 4:48.

∼

Yale heard the screech of a fire alarm before James did. Officer James Meehan of the New York Police Department admired his horse for innumerable reasons, but high on the list was Yale's ability to think for himself. Yale wheeled and galloped back down the street, weaving between the dray wagons and omnibuses as he did.

James scanned the sky for telltale signs of fire. A black mushroom-shaped cloud billowed above one of the buildings like a flashing signpost. Seconds later, Yale skidded to a stop in front of a tall brick building, out of which poured a river of lady factory workers. Meehan threw Yale's reins to the first man he saw and bulled his way into the building. A stream of women came down the stairs at the back of the tiny lobby. The stairs looked less than a yard wide. Meehan thought of himself as a strong man, but the tide of desperate female humanity that packed the stairs proved almost too much for him. He turned himself sideways and pushed his way up the stairs, wondering what kind of person would build a building this big with stairs this narrow. He could hear cries of "Fire!" up above, but the women on the stairs were eerily quiet.

He made it to the second floor, then the third and fourth. The clot of women, most of them not older than girls, loosened. At the seventh floor landing he discovered why. A pretty, dark-haired girl lay slumped against the wall, her legs sprawling across the tiny square of space. Astoundingly, the women backed up behind her were carefully stepping over the supine girl's body rather than trampling her in their haste to get out. He grabbed the girl and yanked her up. A man appeared on the tiny landing and wordlessly took the girl from him. The stream of women surged down the stairs, sweeping the man and his burden before them.

Meehan pushed his way up more flights of stairs until he found the doorway that issued all these people. Fire danced and screamed less than fifteen feet from the door, but there were less than a dozen women still waiting to get out. A wave of heat billowed out the door, making it hard to breathe. A man in the grimy overalls of a machinist held the door open, his face red and wet with heat and determination.

Meehan grabbed one of the man's overall straps and leaned into him. "Is that all of them?" he asked. The man shook his head, his eyes as wet as his face, and looked back into the burning room. A girl stood there, between the window and all the flames, her back toward them. Meehan stepped toward the flames before realizing it was hopeless. Flames leapt up and the girl disappeared.

Feeling sick and ashamed, Meehan pulled the man into the stairwell and shut the eighth-floor door behind them. "Is that all?" he yelled over the roar of the fire.

The machinist pointed up.

"More upstairs?"

The man nodded.

A door to the upper floors stood closed behind them. Meehan grabbed the doorknob, turned, and pulled. Nothing happened. "Keys," he yelled at the man.

The machinist leaned in to Meehan and shouted, "No, only bosses have da keys."

Over the flames Meehan heard someone pounding on the other side of the door. Then screams of terror pierced his ears. Meehan hit the door with his shoulder. Once. Twice. A third time.

On the third strike the machinist joined him. The tiny space kept either of them from taking much of a run at it. Meehan stood back and kicked at the door with his booted heels. The door didn't budge. Either the door was made of sterner stuff than a building, or the press of women on the other side was keeping it closed.

Behind them smoke leaked out from under the door they'd just closed. "Time ta go," the machinist yelled. He grabbed Meehan's collar and hauled him back toward the stairs. As they descended, the cries of women behind the locked door drifted away into the smoky air. It was 4:55.

Sara emerged from the dressing room to see Dinah standing on her desk. *That's odd.* Then she saw flames on the far end of the cutting tables. *Damn fires. This is the third one this year.* Mr. Abramowitz, the head cutter, grabbed one of the red fire pails that lined the far wall and threw a bucket of sand on the flames. Black smoke billowed up as the orange-red flames stuttered out. Sara exhaled a breath she hadn't known she'd been holding. Fire pails always came to the rescue.

"Tessa if you don't hurry we're going to miss the first act," she called to her sister. To celebrate the end of the workweek they were going to see show at a nearby vaudeville house. Sara looked back at the fire. It wasn't out after all—it was bigger. She turned and hustled back into the dressing room. "Fire! Everybody out," she yelled. A dozen young women milled around the tiny room, some dressed only in their slips and stockings. *Where was Tessa?* Sara scrambled for the bathroom at the back of the dressing space. "Tess?"

"Give a girl a minute," Tess called out from behind the closed bathroom door. "I've had to go for hours and there was a line."

"There's a fire, Tess. It's not real big, but we ought to get out of here before we get stuck here answering questions like the last time."

Sara glanced back at the dressing room. Rosie and Gussie were nearly dressed, but Margaret, Ethel, and Violet were still in their work clothes, probably waiting for their turn in the bathroom. "Grab your clothes and get out of here," she hollered at them. Why the company didn't put in more bathrooms, she'd never understand. They knew they hired women and they knew women had to use the facilities more than men, but still Mr. Blanck and Mr. Harris insisted one bathroom per floor was enough, though over two hundred women worked on each of the three floors. More bathrooms and the girls would waste time fooling around, Blanck and Harris argued. Sara thought they wasted more time standing in line at lunchtime and after work. But that was their time to waste, so the bosses didn't care. They weren't allowed to use the bathroom between lunch breaks and quitting time anyway.

Tessa emerged from the bathroom with a grin and swept up her bag. "Let's go, slowpoke," she said. The sisters grinned at each other.

They emerged into a room that was different from how Sara had left it just minutes before. Flames engulfed the far corner and screaming girls crowded near the door. Sara froze for a second. Mr. Harris insisted they keep the doors locked during business hours, though she had no idea why. Did he think they'd sneak out and go to Coney Island? Or steal a yard or two of cheap cambric fabric, even though dozens of cutters kept their eyes on the girls?

Sara looked back at the flames. The other stairs lay behind the fire, so that way out was no good. Then she remembered.

She grabbed Tess and yelled at the other young women milling around the dressing room, "Follow me."

She made for a bank of windows on the left side of the room and pushed one up. Or tried to. The window wouldn't budge. She yanked Tessa's purse from her arm and swung it at the glass. Tessa screamed, half in surprise, half in outrage. The glass cracked. Sara swung again and the glass shattered. Pushing the purse at the sides of the window, Sara knocked the shards out of the frame. Just beyond the window stood a narrow fire escape in an L-shaped airshaft created by the way the building came together with the building next door. Sara slung Tessa's purse over her arm and stepped out onto the sloped ladder and began climbing down. She moved as quickly as she could, but Tessa stepped on her hands. She looked up to tell Tess to be careful, only to catch a shower of rusty dirt in her face. Her foot came to a solid place. Sara turned her head and looked down. She was on a tiny platform, no more than eighteen inches wide. Behind it the rusty ladder continued to each floor, meeting another small platform. Worse, the ladders seemed to go on and on. Somewhere, a fire alarm began to bray.

Sara climbed down to the next platform and made a decision. The fire was on the eighth floor and now she was on the sixth floor. Beyond the window stood a cavernous room. The shades were down but Sara could see empty cutting tables through the gloom. Another factory—closed for the day or forever, she wasn't sure. The Triangle Shirtwaist girls arrived at work before everyone else each morning and were still working when everyone else went home. She pulled Tessa's purse from her arm and shoved it at the window. The glass cracked and fell inward.

"This way," Sara screamed up at Tessa. She flung herself over the windowsill and into the empty room. Tessa climbed in right behind her. The two of them helped girls in through the window—first Gussie, then Ethel, and then the others.

The last one in line, a redhead Sara didn't know, looked at her with huge eyes and said, "The whole floor was on fire by the time I got out. No one else could get over this way."

Someone burst into tears.

Someone else wailed, "We're going to die."

"No we are not," Sara shouted. "Listen up. This room is set up just like the ours. So that means there's a door over there." Sara pointed across the empty room.

The young women charged across the room, darting around cutting tables and sewing machine stands to get to the door. Gussie got there first. She grabbed the nob and pulled. Nothing happened. "It's locked," she wailed.

The other girls crowded behind her, the closest ones striking the door with their fists. The doors on the eighth floor opened inward, probably because the stairwell was so narrow. This one probably did too. They weren't going to be able to shove the door open. Someone yelled and then everyone did. Sara glanced at her watch, pinned to her white cotton shirtwaist. Five minutes ago she'd been thinking about vaudeville.

And then she heard it. A sound. Like a knock. Sara took a deep breath and hollered, "Quiet!"

The girls quieted.

The sound came again. Definitely a knock.

"We're locked in," Gussie yelled.

"Get away from the door," a male voice called.

A thump came as someone hit the door. The door shuddered. And then a louder thump and the scream of a doorknob tearing loose. The door flew open, whacking Ethel as it did. She slammed back against the wall without a sound. A uniformed policeman, cheeks ruddy with exertion, stood in the doorframe. Mr. Brown, the man who fixed the sewing machines, stood behind the policeman.

Sara stood back as the girls crowded out the door and followed the policeman down the stairs. Mr. Brown stood aside and waited. Sara came out last. She looked at Mr. Brown and then up the stairs. "Is everyone out?" she asked.

He shook his head. "Most of the girls on the eighth floor are out."

"Most?"

"Three got caught on the far side of the fire." He paused and wiped at his eyes. "Poor wee things."

"And the ninth and tenth floors?"

Mr. Brown shrugged before his face brightened with thought. "Are there more on the fire escape?"

Before she could admit she had no idea, Mr. Brown raced across the room. Sara followed hard on his heels. As they approached the broken window, a monstrous screech of metal rent the air, and then another, as if the building were groaning out its death throes. Terror-filled screams filled the spaces between. Sara stuck her head out the window and looked up. The eighth-floor shutter had somehow come loose and blocked the fire escape. Flames shot out the windows at both the eighth and ninth floors. Dozens of women, trapped on the narrow metal ladder, smoldered and smoked and screamed.

The building gave another horrendous screech as the fire escape tore loose from its moorings. Mr. Brown pulled Sara away from the window, but not before she saw a mass of burning, screaming women plummet past the sixth floor. The machinist grabbed her hand and pulled her back toward the stairs. Behind her, Sara heard the roar of the fire. It sounded like a ravening beast. She supposed that was exactly what it was.

On the ninth floor, Lucia Maltese tried to find her little sister and mother. She'd finished straitening up her workspace at the coveted first sewing machine table, the one nearest the Greene Street windows, when the cry "Fire!" echoed through the room. She pushed back her chair and turned to peruse the room, more curious than afraid. The Triangle was notorious for its little fires. Why, the factory had burned up three times the past ten years, though those fires always started at night. Lucia wasn't alone in thinking Mr. Blanck and Mr. Harris purposefully set fire to their factory to collect the insurance money.

Her eyes found not a neat, easily contained fire, but a whooshing, sucking blaze shooting from the windows at the back of the room, near the bathrooms and dressing rooms. Mamma and Rosarea were back there. Rosarea, just fourteen years old, had a sewing machine near the back of the room, as befitted a new hire. Mamma sat with her to watch over her and help when Rosarea invariably fell behind.

Flames billowed out the windows that let out onto the rear airshaft, caught the nearby sewing tables, and began leapfrogging across the room. Women ran, screaming and pushing. There were 278 sewing machines on the ninth floor, though this morning about two dozen of them had stood empty. As she watched, dozens of women ran for the Greene Street door, just behind where Lucia stood. Everyone knew it was locked, but there was no place else to go.

Fire filled the room with smoke and heat. Lucia climbed up

onto her sewing table and began leaping table to table, heading for the back of the room. She'd get Mamma and Rosarea and try for the fire escape. Or the back stairs. Or the elevator. The bosses didn't let the women use it, not even the pregnant ones, but fire obliterated the rules. Lucia stopped and surveyed the room. *There.* Mamma stood by the dressing room door. *But Rosarea?*

Lucia leaped across the remaining four sewing tables, taking care not to catch her feet on the common drive shaft that ran down the length of each table. When she reached the last row, she jumped down into Mamma's waiting arms. Poor Mamma, she usually looked barely older than her daughters, being only fifteen years old when she'd had Lucia, her firstborn. Now anxiety made her appear decades older. The fire licked down a sewing table toward them.

Mamma pulled her toward the rear door. The area was already crowded with women. "I was going to try the fire escape," she yelled at Lucia over the noise of panicked women and roaring flames, "but I waited for Rosarea and now it's too late." She pointed to the left side of the room, now engulfed in flames. "Just a minute ago, girls got through there."

"Where's Rosarea?" Lucia shouted.

"Bathroom," Mamma yelled back.

"I'll get her." Lucia looked over at the rear door and saw a miracle. The elevator door opened. A dozen women poured into it. Lucia pointed so Mamma could see. "Go. I'll be right behind you." Mamma tried to hold on to her but Lucia shoved her toward the elevator. There was Papà and the boys to think about—they'd fall apart without Mamma.

Lucia snatched up a handful of cut fabric and held it up to her mouth before turning back toward the fire. It had nearly reached the dressing room door, its heat and acrid smoke sickeningly thick. Lucia lunged for the dressing room. Inside the tiny room, a knot of women held each other, some wailing, some pale and silent in the smoking room. She grabbed Bertha, a slim Jewish girl who sat near Mamma and Rosarea. "Have you seen my sister?" Lucia asked.

Bertha pointed at the toilet room.

Lucia shoved Bertha toward the door. "They're taking people out on the elevator."

Bertha turned and yelled at the knot of women, "Head for the elevator."

Lucia headed for the toilets. "Rosarea!" she yelled.

"In here!" Rosarea shouted.

Lucia found her sister in the last stall, cowering behind the white porcelain toilet, rosary beads clutched in her hands.

Lucia stared at her sister. "What are you doing?" she asked.

"Praying."

"Praying? In a fire?" Lucia wanted to shake Rosarea. Fourteen was old enough to have grown some common sense, or at least that's what Lucia thought. "Let's go. Mamma's at the elevator."

Lucia hauled her sister out of the bathroom. Flames filled the doorway, licking at the frame and the interior wall. Rosarea screamed, yanked her hand away, and fled back to the bathroom. One young woman grabbed two of her friends and half yelled, "Hail Mary, full of grace."

As flames ran across the dressing room walls, Lucia nearly laughed. Rosarea had been right all along. Prayer was all they had. She followed her sister back to the bathroom. They were crouched behind a toilet, holding each other, when the fire took them.

∾

When the alarm bell sounded from the street, Joseph Zito and Gaspar Mortillalo were sharing a cigarette and waiting for the end of the day. As the elevator operators, their job was to ferry the bosses and management types from the tenth floor, where the company offices were, to the ground floor at quitting time. They also moved prodigious amounts of freight up and down the elevator, with shipments of fabric, lace, and buttons going up and finished shirtwaists, skirts, and cloaks going down. It was the elevator that had allowed New York to grow so tall.

Gaspar checked his pocket watch to find it was 4:47. The klaxon call of the alarm made conversation impossible. He looked inquiringly at Joseph. Together they stepped out onto the sidewalk. A knot of onlookers stared up at the building. Joseph and Gaspar did the same. Smoke billowed from windows near the top of the building.

Gaspar turned and ran for the elevator. Joseph followed him. They engaged the levers that started the elevator upwards. Less than a minute later they stopped on the eighth floor. The doors opened to a knot of young women. Thick black smoke rolled into the elevator car. Fire raged on the far side of the room.

Women surged into the elevator car. Gaspar pushed women to the back, crowding them together. Ordinarily, the elevator held twelve people or 1,500 pounds, but Gaspar thought it could hold more. More women crowded in, most of them silent. Gaspar figured if he'd been trapped in a burning room, he'd be screaming in fear. Women were tough. Certainly, his own wife was stronger than he was. Look at the way she had the baby and then got up and cooked dinner.

Once the elevator could hold no more, Joseph closed the

doors, assuring the women left behind they'd be right back. In seconds they were in the Washington Street lobby. One woman kissed Gaspar on the cheek before she left. Joseph grinned at his partner and engaged the lever again.

The doors opened again on the eighth floor to find everyone gone. Gaspar saw that the door to the stairs stood open. The fire had engulfed the entire left side and front of the room. The two men looked at each other and silently agreed. The elevator doors closed and they ascended to the ninth floor. When the doors opened again, they found what seemed like hundreds of women. This time the fire raged much closer to the elevator and was encroaching on the dressing rooms. Again they packed the elevator car. When Joseph had counted to twenty-eight, the elevator could hold no more. He shoved a cluster of women back, but they pushed forward. "We'll be back," he screamed.

Gaspar and Joseph took he elevator down, unloaded the women, and went up again. By the sixth or seventh trip, they were loading women whose clothing smoldered from the sparks that swirled just outside the main body of the fire.

On the tenth or eleventh trip, as they were about to go back up, a New York City policeman grabbed Joseph by the coat collar. "No more. It's too dangerous," the policeman yelled.

Joseph pushed the man away and pulled the door closed.

When the doors opened again, both men knew they'd made their last trip. Heat flooded into the already hot elevator cabin. Before them, flames engulfed the dressing room and most of the sewing tables. And still dozens of women crowded before the elevator. Gaspar could see more women, cut off behind the fire, backed up against the windows. They watched as a young man broke one of the windows, grabbed a young woman around the waist, kissed her, and dropped her out the window. The young man watched for a second or two before stepping after her.

Women crowded into the elevator car, piling on top of each other in a desperate attempt to fill the car to its ceiling. When the car could hold no more, Joseph and Gaspar had to shove the remaining women back. Together they closed the doors. Joseph felt a sob wrench out of him as they descended. In the quiet elevator, someone patted his back.

Caterina Maltese watched the elevator go. She looked back across the burning floor, toward the dressing room. Lucia and Rosarea hadn't come out and now she'd waited too long. She looked back over at the windows. Girls and women were leaping from them. The fire roared so that she could barely think. Flames shot out of the dressing room. Her girls were in there. Her babies. She felt heat on her head a second before her dress caught fire. Four women pried the elevator doors open, only to find an empty shaft. One of the girls leaped for the cable, missed, and fell. Another tried it and caught the cable. She began sliding down. Other girls tried. Some caught the cable. Some did not.

And then there was no one between Caterina and the empty elevator shaft. She was the last living person on the ninth floor. Was it better to die in a fall than to burn? Caterina looked across the expanse of elevator shaft at the cable. Did she even want to try? With her girls behind her, what was the point? Caterina looked down at her hands. She was thirty-nine years old, but her hands were worn from twenty years of factory work and New York cold. She crossed herself, said a prayer to the Madonna for her daughters' souls, and stepped into the elevator shaft. The bodies of the previously fallen cushioned her landing, but not enough.

Chapter Two

MISERY LANE LOVES COMPANY

"Our birth is nothing but our death begun, as tapers waste the moment they take fire."

—Edward Young, 1718

March 25–26, 1911

The can jounced down the sidewalk with a satisfying clatter. Angela Bambace watched it bang off a light pole and come to rest in front of Mr. Catiglioni's fruit stand.

From behind a stack of melons, the bald grocer frowned at her. "What you gotta make such a terrible sound for?" he said.

"'Cause I'm mad," Angela replied. She stopped in front of Mr. Catiglioni and picked up her can. Good cans were worth keeping.

"Whatsa matter, then?" He waved his hand out over the melons at the failing light. "No more snow, no more cold; the sun shines, does it not? Is a good day."

"No, it is not," Angela said. She put her hands on her hips and stomped her foot.

Mr. Catiglioni came out from behind his melons and pulled an apple from his apron pocket. He held it out to Angela. "You wanna tell me about it?"

She took the apple and examined it. Its skin was a bit wrinkled and it felt a little soft, but that's what apples were like in March. She bit into it and opened her mouth to tell Mr. Catiglioni her sad story, but he wagged his forefinger and shook his head. Angela chewed, swallowed, and tucked the rest of the apple into her coat pocket.

"Today I was at school, even though it's Saturday, on account of the nuns were handing out parts for the Easter pageant," she said.

"So that is why you not help your *madre* today?"

"Mamma said she wanted me to be in the pageant." Angela tried not to smile. She was still mad, but not at Mamma. Mamma always wanted Angela to do school things, unlike other mothers who wanted their daughters to quit school after eighth grade and go to work. "I know the big girls are going to get all the good parts, like the Holy Mother." Angela paused. "And they want Marie to be an angel, even though she wasn't there today. She's home sick and she gets to be an angel. The sisters like her best. Everyone does. And I wanted to be Mary Magdalene."

Mr. Catiglioni watched Angela's eyes light up at the thought of playing Mary Magdalene. "Is only fair that the big girls play the important parts. Someday soon you'll have your turn. Right?" he said.

She huffed out a sigh and said, "But I'm almost thirteen."

"See? One day some younger girl will be mad at you."

Angela squeezed the can so tight it made a little crunching

sound. "That's not what I'm angry about. I didn't think an eighth grader would get to be a Mary. Not really. But the pageant needs ever so many Roman soldiers."

"And you wanted to be a soldier?"

"They get swords!" she said. "Not real ones, of course, but wooden ones. And they have sword fights. That's so much better than angel wings. The angels just stand around looking holy."

"And the sisters only let boys be soldiers," Mr. Catiglioni said. Angela sighed and nodded.

Mr. Catiglioni led Angela over to an upturned produce crate. He sat on one side, leaving room for her on the other. She sat and laid the now-dented rusty can in the little basket her skirt made between her knees.

"Sometimes we don't get what we want. But you know what I think?" he asked. Beside him, Angela shrugged her shoulders. "We have to be patient with God, because we do not know his plan. What is it the Bible says? The meek shall inherit the earth."

Angela leapt to her feet. The can clattered to the ground, forgotten. "The meek are sheep. That's what the sisters want me to be—a sheep," she said, stomping her foot again. "I don't want to be a sheep. People eat sheep. I want to be a soldier and have sword fights."

As Mr. Catiglioni opened his mouth to answer Angela, a man came running up the street. He stopped in front of Mr. Catiglioni and gasped out, "Phone?"

The grocer stood. "In the back. It takes a nickel."

Sweat stood out on the man's pale face as he jogged to the back of the store. Mr. Catiglioni and Angela watched him dig in his pocket for a change purse, thrust a coin into the phone, and dial a number. Both knew they were being impolite, but neither could help themselves. Phone calls were rare, both because you could buy half a loaf of bread with a nickel and because few people wanted to have private conversations in the grocer's market. Angela had never made or received a phone call, nor had anyone she knew.

"Is she there? Helen!" the man yelled into the phone receiver. "Because there was fire. A bad one. At one of the factories in lower Manhattan."

Mr. Catiglioni raised an eyebrow at Angela.

"I don't know which one. Down by Little Italy. I'm not sure. But they say there's bodies all over the street. Is she there?"

Angela watched as the man sagged like a balloon with the air let out.

"Thanks, Mamma. I love you too," the man said, then hung up the phone and leaned against the wall. His shoulders shook.

Angela looked up at Mr. Catiglioni. He patted her shoulder. After a minute, the man wiped his face and turned to face them.

"Can I help you, young man?" Mr. Catiglioni asked, his tone as gentle as he'd been with Angela.

"My sister. She was home. Thank the Blessed Mother, she was home," the man said, wiping at his face one more time. "You haven't heard? There was a bad fire at one of those damn clothing factories. They say hundreds of girls are dead. No one knows which factory and my sister works at Allied Cloaks."

Angela looked up at Mr. Catiglioni. Everyone knew only the poorest women worked in the clothing trades—and the poorest women in New York were mostly Jewish and Italian. And here they were, standing in Italian Harlem. The grocer gave Angela a little push between her shoulder blades. "Go on home, little one. Your Mamma will be worried."

Angela looked from Mr. Catiglioni to the man and back again. "But," she protested.

"No buts, little one. Go home. Tell your mother what you heard. She'll know what to do."

Angela trudged up the sidewalk for home, thoughts of swords and sheep temporarily replaced with worry. Behind her, the rusty tin can lay forgotten on the sidewalk.

Sometime after supper, Angela heard a newsboy down on the street. She ran to the second-floor window, shoved it up, and peered out into the dark. Her sister, Marie, poked her head out too, even though she'd been home sick with a cold all day. Angela pushed her back. "Mamma will spank you if she sees you out of bed," she said.

Marie stuck her tongue out at Angela, but stepped back from the window. Marie was less than two years younger than Angela, and everyone liked her. She was the good girl. Marie wouldn't have minded being a sheep.

"A hundred forty dead," cried the newsboy. "The *World* has it first."

Angela grimaced. The *New York World* always had the most scandalous news. That meant the newsboy was Silvio Ricci. He lived on the sixth floor with his mother and a half dozen brothers and sisters. None of the Ricci kids went to school.

Mamma charged in from the kitchen, holding a dishtowel. She thrust a penny into Angela's hand. "Hurry," she half whispered. Angela looked back over her shoulder. Papa slumped in his chair like always. *Il Progresso*, a New York newspaper printed in Italian, lay collapsed on his chest. They both understood it was not a good idea to wake Papà. He was a lot older than Mamma, more like one of the many grandpas in the building than the dads, especially with his gray hair and wrinkly skin. And he was sick a lot. With what Angela didn't know, but when he didn't feel good he'd sleep a lot and wake up cranky.

Angela caught up her coat and ran out the door, down the stairs, and out to the street. She thrust her way through the knotted crowd around Silvio and pushed the penny into his hand.

Silvio's face shone with excitement as he handed her the one-page special. "Someone's gonna pay for this," he said with a tight grin.

Angela agreed. Someone would pay. But not the rich men who ran the factory. Those kind of men never paid, not in New York. It was probably the same all over the world, but all she knew was New York City. Sure, she'd been born in Brazil and lived her first year in Calabria, but she didn't remember any of that.

Angela ran back up the stairs to the apartment. At least they lived in a decent building in Italian Harlem. Everyone knew only the poorest and most desperate lived in Little Italy, down in lower Manhattan. It helped that Mamma had only three children and that Papà made good money as a waiter—when he was working, that was. Mamma worked hard too. She did piecework for a hat factory, bringing home cloth that she stitched together at the kitchen table. Angela would wake up in the middle of the night, hear the soft whir of the sewing machine coming from the kitchen, and know everything was all right. When Papà was having one of his dark times, he slept all the time and only worked weekends. Mamma seemed to never sleep at all.

Mamma waited in the hall, holding baby Shelley's hand. Light from the apartment spilled out, making the little boy's dark hair glow. If the nuns could see him now, they'd want four-year-old Shelley to be an angel too. And one day he'd get to be a soldier and have wooden sword fights.

"Here," Mamma hissed and held out her hand. Angela

handed over the broadsheet. The two of them hustled into the kitchen. She gestured Angela to a chair and plopped Shelley into her lap before pulling the gaslight down close to the table. A tiny shard of pride shot through Angela. Lots of kids had parents who couldn't read or even speak English. Mamma could read Italian, Portuguese, and English. Papà could only read Italian.

Shelley squirmed, his weight reminding Angela that he wasn't really a baby anymore, but nearly five years old. Still, he was a little boy, while she was nearly a big girl. Nearly.

Mamma groaned, "It was the Triangle Company. Mrs. DeLuca's sister works there." Mamma straightened and sighed. "Stay here. I have to go see Annie." Mamma hustled out of the apartment and ran upstairs.

Angela wrapped an arm around Shelley, hugging his warmth to her. Marie stepped into the kitchen doorway. She coughed a wheezy, hacking sound and swayed on her feet.

Angela stood, still holding her little brother. "Come on. You should be in bed," she said to Marie.

Angela led Marie into the apartment's only bedroom. Mamma and Papà slept in the living room, their bed pushed up against the far wall. Shelley's cot was in there too. Mamma said the girls got the bedroom because they needed to go to bed earlier and rest for school. School was important to Mamma; she and Papà argued about it all the time. Papà thought it was time Angela went to work, but Mamma said her girls would graduate from high school. "Education is the only way to get ahead in America," she said. Papà thought going to school was a kind of laziness, though Angela wondered what he knew about it. He worked half as much as Mamma and knew half as much too. Angela knew one thing for sure—you didn't get ahead by sleeping in your chair all day.

She got Marie and Shelley tucked into their beds and went back to the kitchen to wait for Mamma. After what seemed like hours, Mamma finally opened the door.

"You should be in bed," Mamma sighed. "Annie wants to go down there. Now."

"Where?" Angela was confused. Where did Annie DeLuca want to go in the middle of the night?

"To the factory. It's down by Washington Square Park."

"Way down there?" Angela asked.

Mamma sighed and said, "Albina didn't come home. Annie thought she was out with friends. You know, how the girls do sometimes on Saturday after work. But she should be home by now. Annie fell asleep and didn't know Albina hadn't come home. What with the baby and all, it's no wonder."

Angela nodded her understanding. Annie DeLuca was a new wife with a new baby. She lived two floors up with her husband, Carlo, and her sister, Albina. And the new baby, Rosina, whom they all called Rosie. Carlo wasn't home, though; he'd gone back to Italy after the baby was born to tell his family there, and Annie's too. He had a good job as a bookkeeper and could afford to travel to Sicily once a year. They'd all thought Annie had been lucky to catch him.

"I want to come with you," Angela said.

Mamma heaved a sigh. "I suppose you should. Marie can watch Shelley. Annie will want to bring her baby with her. If we find, you know, the worst, you can help."

Angela did know. If Albina was dead, someone would have to hold Rosie while Mamma held Annie.

They took the Second Street elevated train south, riding down

Manhattan Island with Central Park on one side and the East River on the other, though it was too dark to see much of anything but streetlights and the occasional wagon. New York City never really slept, but in the middle of the night it got pretty quiet. Annie sat ramrod straight on a bench opposite Mamma and Angela. Angela clutched the baby to her chest, but didn't even look around when they stopped to let passengers off and on. As they traveled south, more people got on the train than got off. By their tense faces, Angela guessed they were all heading for the same place.

They left the train at the Astor Place station and walked the rest of the way amidst a crowd. They walked one block west, one block south, and then turned west again. Tall brick buildings lined the streets, some of them tenement housing, others business buildings gone dark for the evening. Angela smelled the smoke before they turned the corner onto Greene Street and saw the burning building. She tightened her grip on Mamma's hand.

Spotlights illuminated the brick structure, which looked fine at first. It was only when Angela looked up, prompted by all the people around her who were doing the same, that she saw the burned wreckage of the upper floors. She, Mamma, and Annie came to a crowd of people pushed up against a barricade. By the look of things, they wouldn't be getting any closer to the building. Mamma pushed them to the front. Off to the left, another set of barricades ran across a narrow alley between the burned building and its neighbor. A stout policeman, cudgel out, stood at the ready, while firemen and more policemen scuttled in the alley.

Angela strained her eyes, trying to make sense of what she saw. It looked like a monstrous dead spider, all tangled legs and broken parts. She looked up again and realized what it was—the fire escape. It had fallen off the building and now lay in this narrow alley like a dead thing.

Two firemen approached the barrier from the fallen fire escape with something gray and bulky stretched between them. As they came to the mouth of the alleyway, the big policeman drew back the barrier and let them pass. The two firemen had a cloth-wrapped laundry bundle between them. Then Angela realized it was not laundry. It was a person, dead, wrapped in a sheet.

She stared down the alley in horror. According to the newspaper, the fire happened over six hours ago, but they were still removing bodies. How many women had died in this alley for it to take so long to remove them?

Mamma waved her hand at the stout policeman. "Sir? Sir?" she asked.

He looked at her, his eyes narrowed with suspicion. "Yes, Ma'am."

Angela noticed he had an Irish accent. The Irish did not care for the Italians. Mamma said it was because they'd been in America longer and had been at the bottom of the pile for so long that they were happy to have someone else beneath them. Sister Margaret said it was because the Italians would work for so much less and drove the Irish out of the good factory jobs. The Irish had good reason to hate the Italians, or so Sister said. Angela wasn't sure there was such a thing as a good factory job, but some were less bad than others. Also, Sister Margaret was Irish.

Mamma smiled her best smile at the policeman. "I'm sorry to bother you, officer, but could you tell us where we, uh—" Mamma's voice faltered. Behind her, Annie burst into tears.

The officer heaved a sigh that suggested he too would like to cry. "Ma'am, we're moving the dead down to a warehouse on Charities Pier. Do you know where that is?" he said.

"I think so. Down by the Lodging House?" Mamma asked.

"Yes, Ma'am. You go there if you have a missing loved one." Now it was the policeman's turn to falter. He coughed into a dirt-smeared handkerchief. "Worst thing I've ever seen."

Mamma looked down at his nametag. "Thank you, Officer Meehan. I appreciate your help." She grabbed Annie and turned to go.

"God bless you, ma'am," the officer called after them. His voice wobbled in the night air.

For a second, Angela wanted to kick Sister Margaret.

They wasted two hours circling the building, trying to find a way to get closer. Annie, eyes ringed dark with exhaustion, wouldn't take no for an answer.

"Maybe she's just hurt," Annie pointed out. "She'll be in the crowd looking for her friends, just like we are."

Mamma admitted that Annie had a point. The newspaper extra said over four hundred women worked at the Triangle Factory. If 140 of them were dead, that meant 260 of them had gotten out. So they combed the crowd on Greene Street, stopping to ask all the young women if they'd worked in the building and if they knew Albina Caruso.

"She's a little thing," Annie kept saying. She'd gesture at Angela and say, "No taller than this girl."

No one knew Albina. They did meet several people who'd worked in the Asch Building, but no one who'd been on the upper floors, where the Triangle Company had its factory. They tried the crowd on Washington Place too, but with no more luck than Greene Street. At one point they sat on a curb and waited while Annie fed Rosie.

Angela watched the passing people, eyes peeled for Annie's sister. Across the street, the fire truck's ladder loomed in the night sky, reaching only halfway up the building, abandoned as useless.

Albina, or Albie, as she liked to be called, was a lot older than Angela. She'd graduated from St. Cecilia's at least two years ago. Before she finished school, Albie used to walk home with Angela and Marie. Twice she'd bought the sisters ice-cream sodas at the drugstore just down from Mr. Catiglioni's little market. For a big girl, she'd been nice. And pretty, like her sister Annie— tall and slim, with wavy dark hair and big black eyes.

They trudged back to the Astor Place station and took the train back the way they'd come. They got off the train at Twenty-Third Street and walked up to Twenty-Sixth, where they ran smack-dab into Bellevue Hospital. Massive and imposing, the hospital was a complex of interconnected buildings. Everyone in New York knew Bellevue because it took in everyone, even people with no money.

A line of ambulances stood outside the Twenty-Sixth Street entrance, the horses' heads down in exhaustion. Angela figured they'd transported the injured people from the fire, so maybe they should check the hospital for Albie. Mamma and Annie agreed it was a good idea. They turned and headed for the hospital's main entrance on First Avenue, passing through curlicued wrought-iron gates on their way to the front door.

They stood in a line that led to a white marble front counter. The lady in front of them, an older, gray-haired woman with a girl not much older than Angela, turned around to ask, "Did you have someone in the fire?" She had a thick Yiddish accent.

Annie explained that they were looking for her sister.

"I'm looking for my daughter Julia. This is my granddaughter Esther, and I am Mrs. Rosen," the woman said.

They introduced themselves. Two men lined up behind Mamma, Annie, and Angela and joined in the conversation. One said his name was Max Segalowitz and the other Josef Redsky. They were both looking for daughters who'd worked at the Triangle Factory.

"Awful place," Mr. Segalowitz said. He'd pulled his soft cap from his head and was wringing it in his hands. "I wanted Rosie to do piecework at home, but no, she insisted on going out to work. More money, she says, but I think she likes the girls she works with better than the money."

"I know what you mean," Mr. Redsky chimed in. "My Beryl is a real firecracker. She didn't want to stay at home. No fun, she'd said." He chuckled a little. "Did you know she liked to be called Ben? Can you believe that? A girl named Ben? She's a firecracker, my Beryl."

The line moved inexorably forward until it was Mrs. Rosen's turn. The attendant looked at a sheaf of papers and shook his head. She burst into tears and stepped aside. Annie went next, buttressed by Mamma.

"Albina Caruso," she whispered.

"Pardon me? You'll have to speak up," the attendant said.

"Albina Caruso," Mamma repeated in her loud, take-charge voice.

The man checked the first page and shook his head. "Not here. Next!"

They made way for the two men. Angela could see the clerk looking and shaking his head. The seven of them met up at the hospital's front door. Mr. Segalowitz slapped his much-abused hat atop his head and motioned for the doors. "Shall we, ladies?" he said.

Dawn had just begun to lighten the eastern sky when they left the hospital. Mr. Segalowitz walked them to a bakery, where they bought a bag of soft rolls—or tried to. When the counterman learned why they were out so early, he refused to take their money. Then he made them sit down at a table and brought them small cups of espresso, into which he poured spoonfuls of heavy cream. They ate and drank in silence. Annie fed Rosie again before a lady baker whisked the baby away for a change of diapers. Angela could hear the women at the back of the bakery cooing and fussing over Rosie. They dawdled awhile in this safe space, knowing they were in no hurry to arrive at their last destination.

The sun was coming up over the East River when they left the bakery. The walked to the pier, past the nearly new Municipal Lodging House, which served the area's homeless men, to the warehouse that stood at the end of the pier. A line of people had formed alongside one of the warehouse's exterior walls.

They took their place at the end of the line. An ambulance pulled away from the building and another pulled up in its place. Two men in ragged clothes came out of the warehouse, removed a bundle from the wagon, and carried it inside. Another wagon pulled up, piled high with long wooden boxes. More ragged men came to unload the wagon.

Angela realized they were unloading empty coffins. She left the line and walked over to the railing at the edge of the pier. She was standing there, leaning over the railing so she could see the water, when a young man came up and stood next to her.

He tugged the brim of his cap and nodded at her. "You know what they call this place, don't you?" he asked.

"The police officer said Charities Pier," Angela said.

"Ah, that's its name, but that's not what they be calling it. It's really Misery Lane."

Angela turned to look at her companion. He wore round glasses and the studious look of a Yeshiva student. Sister Margaret said the Jews were worse than the Italians, who were at least Catholics. Sister Margaret wasn't a very nice person. Though, to be fair, not all the Sisters thought that way. It was just that Sister Margaret taught seventh and eighth grade.

"Why's it called that?" Angela asked. She had her suspicions, but she wanted to hear what the young man would say.

He waved his arm behind him. "Well, first there's the Lodging House, which was meant just to take homeless men. But there's so many homeless families, the place is full of fear and sadness. Did you see they're using the homeless men to cart the bodies from the fire?"

Angela nodded.

"Can you imagine having to do that for money? And there's all the sick people who get dumped at the hospital." He twirled his finger around his ear. "You know, sick in the head. What a misery that must be, not to have your head right. And those people can't take care of themselves either. And then the city morgue is just up the street. It's where the poor end up, just before they get dumped in some potter's field somewhere. And there's this place." He waved at the warehouse. "This is where they brought the bodies when the General Slocum exploded."

"Huh?"

"It was six, no seven years ago," he said. "You're probably too young to remember. A thousand people died when a steamship caught fire and sank." He jerked his head back at the warehouse. "And then there's Blackwell's Island."

33

Angela looked out over the river, north to the notorious island. The sun had risen, lighting the asylum's spires so they looked almost pretty. "I heard they don't keep the lunatics over there anymore," she said.

"No. It's a workhouse and prison now. Another terrible place to put the poor."

Angela stared at the boy. "How do you know all this?"

He smiled a grim smile. "My rabbi taught me. As a Jew, it's my job to care about the poor and work to fix the world's problems."

Angela gazed out over the water to Blackwell's Island. "That sounds like a good job. You'll always have work."

He barked out a laugh. They talked for a little while longer. His name was Yosef and his mother was in the line too, with Rabbi Weiss. They were looking for his older sister Jessie.

After a while, Mamma called Angela over. They'd made it to the head of the line. Angela waved back over her shoulder at her new friend and walked into the warehouse of death.

The building didn't have any electric lights. Instead, more home-less men held kerosene lanterns over the double rows of bare wood coffins. People were directed to walk down one side and back on the other. A police officer at the door said, "Don't just look at faces. Look for familiar clothing, shoes, watches—any-thing. If you need a better look, one of the men with lanterns will help you." As they shuffled into the haze, Angela heard the officer repeat himself. He kept saying the same words over and over.

As she stepped into the room, the smell hit her. Burned, rot-ten meat. And smoke. And something else. Something mean and miserable that said, "Go away from this place." The warehouse was full of people, policemen, men in suits with clipboards, and all the people in line, but it was quiet. No one spoke above a whisper. They were in the realm of the dead now.

Angela was about to ask Mamma why they shouldn't look at the faces when she saw the first dead girl. Her skull was misshapen and her face was slashed with dozens of inch-long cuts. In front of her, Annie began to sniffle. Mamma took Rosie out of Annie's arms and handed her to Angela. Angela held the baby close, grateful for Rosie's warm innocence. They took small steps past one corpse, then another and another. Angela figured out the first girls in the line must have been the jumpers. The newspaper told how girls, desperate to escape the fire, had jumped from the eighth- and ninth-floor windows. Angela hadn't believed it. The *World* liked to exaggerate—or so she thought then. Not anymore.

About halfway up the line she saw her first burned girl. Or that's what she guessed the charred thing in the box was. It could have been anything, really. It was both worse and better than the girls who still looked like themselves. Some of the burned girls had watches or shoes laying on their torsos, as if the police or someone had pulled identifying items off them and laid them where people could see. The line stopped as someone called out for a lantern. A man came over and held a light over a coffin.

People leaned in. Someone pointed and nodded. Someone burst into tears. Angela didn't know how to feel—was she sorry or happy that they hadn't found their missing loved one?

Some of the girls' hair had come undone and was draped over the top coffin boards. Angela thought doctors or someone must have done this, so people could see the hair. Could she recognize Mamma by her hair? Or Marie? Angela thought so. Dark liquid oozed out of some of the coffins. Blood, she supposed. She tried not to step in it, but then Rosie would fuss and she'd forget to watch her feet or she'd be looking at a girl or a black thing and she'd feel the stickiness on the sole of her shoe.

When a body was identified, the clipboard men would rush over and take the survivor aside. Papers would be filled out while the rest of the line shuffled by. It occurred to Angela that someone ought to have set up some tables in another part of the warehouse for this part of the procedure, someplace more private. *Maybe there were no tables? Why not?* Her brain wandered away from the horror in front of her, thinking about where they might find tables and chairs, when Annie stopped and pointed.

"Noooo," she moaned. One of the lantern men stepped over and cast his light on the corpse. Despite herself, Angela leaned in, careful to keep baby Rosie's head turned away. Even she could see it was Albina. She'd been one of the jumpers. *Was that better than burning? Maybe. But what about that plunge to the street? What did the girls think about? Did it hurt when they landed? Or did they die right away?*

A clipboard man pulled Annie out of the line. Mamma and Angela followed. What was Albina's full name? Date of birth? Religion? Your name? Address? Where do you want her sent? The man listed a half dozen mortuaries. Annie looked helplessly at Mamma. Mamma picked one. The man said thank you and walked away.

They stood there, unsure what to do next. Then Mamma put her arms around all of them and whispered, "Let's go home."

As they left the building, Angela saw that the line had grown, curling down the pier and into the street. A clot of well-dressed young people stood in line, their smiling faces bright with excitement. A pink-cheeked girl blew a bubble of gum, popped it, and laughed. Angela realized they were there to see the dead—not to find a loved one, but for the thrill of seeing something forbidden.

Mamma walked over to them. "This is not a carnival. Look around you," she said, waving her arm at the anxious people in line and the bereaved ones who'd been inside. "You should be ashamed of yourselves."

The bubble-popping girl stared open-mouthed at Mamma. Before any of them could speak, Mamma walked away. Then she did something shocking, something Angela had never seen her do and never would see her do again. Mamma turned back toward the fun-seekers and spat at their feet. As she walked away again, Angela and Annie followed her down the pier. Halfway to the street, Annie burst into tears.

Chapter Three

WE MOURN OUR LOSS

"We all felt that we had been wrong, that something was wrong with that building which we had accepted or the tragedy never would have happened."
—Frances Perkins, US Secretary of Labor, 1942

April 24–26, 1911

Angela heaved back the scratchy wool blanket and crawled out of bed. She stepped over to the window and looked out. Nothing moved out there—no horses, no carriages, no people. East Harlem was asleep, but she wasn't. Even Marie was sleeping. Every time Angela laid down, all she saw were the dead girls and that fire escape. The images flicked behind her closed eyes, like that kinematoscope show she'd seen with Mamma, everything gray and white and jerky. It had been a month since the fire, but still she saw the same images over and over. She couldn't turn them off, even though she was so tired during the day that she nearly fell asleep in school.

She tiptoed to the bedroom door and eased it open. Papà was working the dinner shift at Marino's up by Majestic Hall. He never got home until well after midnight. She should know—he made enough noise when he came in. Men could do that, make a lot of noise. Women had to be quiet and not wake up the men. When she was big, she would make a lot of noise, as much as she wanted.

But not right now. She crept out into the hall, careful to avoid the creaky place on the floor. She passed Shelley's cot, where the little boy slept, curled up like a fava bean.

Mamma was in the kitchen with Mrs. Tosi and Mrs. Altimari. The three of them often sat in the Bambace kitchen in the evenings, swapping work stories and neighborhood gossip, when Papà was out. Mrs. Tosi worked with Mamma at the hat factory and Mrs. Altimari lived next door to Annie DeLuca.

Angela took the five or six steps between her and the kitchen door and leaned her ear against it. Mamma always closed the door after Marie and Angela went to bed. Mamma always said schoolgirls need their sleep—that's why she hadn't told Mamma she couldn't sleep. But she had something she wanted to ask Mamma and it couldn't wait anymore.

She cracked open the door and angled her head through the space. "Mamma? Can I come in?" Angela asked.

"Why are you not sleeping, *cucciola*? Tomorrow's a school day," Mamma said, scooting back her chair and coming over to Angela. She led her to the only empty chair. "Sit, sit."

As Mrs. Altimari and Mrs. Tosi watched, Mamma took the milk jug out of the icebox and poured Angela half a glass.

"Poor baby," Mrs. Altimari said. "Your Mamma says you

went to Misery Lane with her and Mrs. DeLuca. You are a good girl to help with the baby." They women had been speaking Sicilian, but switched to English for Angela. Mamma wanted her girls to be Americans, so she made them speak English as often as possible.

Angela went to see Annie every day after school. She'd watch the baby so Annie could be alone for an hour or so. "I like Rosie," Angela said. What she didn't say was that the only time she felt any peace was when she was holding the little girl. Even Shelley didn't help—he was too big.

"Babies are nice, aren't they?" Mrs. Tosi said, smiling gently at Angela. "They make bad things better."

Angela looked at Mrs. Tosi, wide-eyed. How did she know? Probably because she was a *nonna*. She had a bed in her family's kitchen because there were too many Tosis living in the apartment. They were crowded and poor, but Mrs. Tosi always had a smile on her face.

Mamma patted Angela on the head, but looked over at Mrs. Altimari. "I told you. It was too much," she said.

"You didn't know," Mrs. Altimari said with a shake of her head. "Who would think such a thing could happen?"

"It's all right, Mamma." Angela felt bad that her Mamma felt bad. "I wanted to go. And I'm glad I did." If such things were in the world, it was better to know about them than not.

"It's like the wolf," Mrs. Tosi said. "Whether or not you see the wolf, the wolf is there. And the wolf will eat you if you forget about him."

Angela saw her chance. "I want to go to the funeral mass. The one for the six people who were never identified. Can I go, Mamma? Please?" she asked.

"It's on Tuesday, which is a school day." Mamma reached for

41

newspaper laying on the table. She paged to the middle of the paper and tapped an article. "See?"

"I know, but on Friday Mother Superior said we could miss school for the special mass. For the victims and their families."

"She did, did she?" Mrs. Tosi's eyes widened at the idea. "Isn't the service at Our Lady of Pompeii? Off Bleecker Street?"

"Uh huh," Angela agreed. Mamma gave her a stern look. "I mean, yes, ma'am. It is. So I thought if it was all right with Mother Superior, maybe I could go."

Mamma shook her head. "I can't take a day off work. You know how your father is."

Angela sighed.

Mrs. Tosi leaned over and touched Mamma's arm. "I could take her, Peppina," she said.

Mamma shook her head. "It's not just a mass. They're taking those poor people to a cemetery all the way over in Brooklyn. She'd miss a whole day of school."

Mrs. Altimari tapped the table with her forefinger and said, "What about this? What if Mrs. Tosi and your girls went to the mass and then watched the funeral procession afterwards, but didn't go all the way to the cemetery. They'd miss only half a day. Nonna Tosi shouldn't be walking that far anyway."

"My legs aren't what they used to be," Mrs. Tosi said, smiling at Angela.

Mamma sighed. "Why do want to go, *cucciola*?"

Angela pushed her empty milk glass away and bit her lip in thought. How did she explain it?

"She wants to finish the story, that's what I think," Mrs. Altimari said.

"I guess," Angela said. "But it's more than that. When the

fire first happened, everyone was so upset. It was on the first page of the newspaper every day for a week. And everyone was saying how things had to change and how it could never happen again. But now it's like people have already started to forget."

"And you can't forget, can you?" Mamma said, reaching over to hug Angela. "That's why you're not sleeping."

"You knew?"

"Mammas always know," Mrs. Tosi said. Mrs. Altimari nodded.

"And if I let you do this, do you think you'll be able to forget?" Mamma asked.

"I don't want to forget, Mamma. Not ever. I don't think I could, even if I tried. Could you? Will Mrs. DeLuca?"

Mamma frowned. "No, not ever. If you'll never forget, why do you want to go?"

"So I can see all the other people who won't forget," Angela said.

Mamma stood up and put Angela's milk glass in the sink. "Then it's settled. Mrs. Tosi, would it be all right if Marie went too?"

"Of course, Pina. A girl is never too young to see how hard the world is, especially for women. It's like Miss Schneiderman said in her speech." Mrs. Tosi dug in the pile of newspapers on the table and pulled one out. She rifled through it and found what she was looking for. "Here, see?" She pushed the paper over to Angela.

It was Rose Schneiderman's speech to the rich ladies and gentlemen who gathered at the Metropolitan Opera House to memorialize the dead. Angela scanned the article. Apparently, some of the rich ladies called for fellowship, for cool heads, and for peace instead of protest. Miss Schneiderman took the stage and there, in front of all those rich people, in their very own opera house, she told them off.

"I would be a traitor to these poor burned bodies if I came here to talk of good fellowship. We have tried, and found you wanting," she told them.

Angela grinned at Schneiderman's words and read on:

This is not the first time girls have burned alive in this city. Every week I must learn of the untimely death of one of my sister workers. Every year thousands of us are killed. The life of men and women is so cheap and property so sacred. There are so many of us for one job that it matters little if 146 of us are burned to death. We have tried and we are trying now and you have given a couple of dollars for the sorrowing mothers, brothers and sisters by way of charity. But every time the workers protest against the conditions that kill us, the strong hand of the law presses down heavily upon us. I cannot talk of fellowship to you who are gathered here. Too much blood has been spilled.

Angela goggled at the thought of the courage it must have taken to say those words in that place in front of those people. She looked up to find Mamma, Mrs. Altimari, and Mrs. Tosi all looking at her. She jerked her head once in acknowledgement and went back to bed. She fell almost immediately asleep.

Mamma said Papà didn't need to know they were skipping school. Angela and Marie heartily agreed. Tuesday morning,

Marie and Angela dressed and left the apartment like they were going to school. Instead of taking the trolley to St. Cecilia's, they went upstairs to the Tosi apartment. There they were greeted by the congenial chaos that was the Tosi household. Mr. Tosi took his hat and left not long after the girls arrived, followed by his wife and the children. The two oldest were in the first and second grade at St. Cecilia's. Angela knew because she saw the younger Mrs. Tosi on the trolley with them often enough. Usually, the baby stayed home with Nonna Tosi, but not today. Today she had on her sturdy black lace-up shoes and a black dress. Angela and Marie watched as she whipped her kerchief off her head, revealing wavy, steel-gray hair braided and pinned into a crown at the top of her head. Nonna Tosi pulled a large black hat over her braids.

"You like? I borrowed it from my daughter-in-law," she said.

"You're the prettiest nonna ever," Marie warbled.

Angela didn't know if that was true, but she understood what Marie meant. Mrs. Tosi was built for lap-sitting and hugs, and she made the best pizzelle ever.

"I like your hair," Angela said. "It makes you look like a queen."

Mrs. Tosi chuckled and kissed both of them on the cheek. "You are good girls," she said. She grabbed a huge black umbrella and they left the apartment building.

They took the Second Street elevated train south, repeating the journey Angela had taken with Mamma and Annie a month before. Dark clouds filled the sky while gusty breezes pushed garbage and dry leaves down the streets. They got off the train at Bleecker Street and took a trolley west to the church. Their journey took them through the poorest neighborhoods in New York City. Little Italy lay just to the south of their destination.

45

Papà said Italian Harlem was the first Little Italy, until all the Neapolitans came thirty years ago and settled on the Lower East Side. Papà thought the Neapolitans were the lowest of the low and a lot of Sicilians agreed with him. Angela figured they were just poor and that wasn't their fault.

Papà never tired of reminding Angela and Marie that he'd owned his own fleet of fishing boats in Santos, Brazil. As far as Angela could tell, he'd lost all that money, but he still thought he was better than the people in Little Italy. Mamma still talked about Santos too, but more like she missed her own mamma, who still lived there. Mamma said the weather had been more like Calabria, which was one of the reasons Italians moved to Brazil. Mamma met Papà in Santos after she moved there with her mamma, long ago. But then Papà got sick, lost his boats, and had to move back to Italy. That's why Angela was born in Brazil and Marie was born in Calabria.

Then when Papà couldn't find work in Calabria, and even though Mamma wanted to go back to Santos, he made them all move to a little town on Long Island Sound. He'd heard there was work for a fisherman there, but when they arrived none of it turned out to be true. Angela only knew this from the stories Mamma told, because she was too little to remember it herself. Mostly, Mamma talked about how Papà went back to Italy and left Mamma alone in Port Chester with two baby girls.

Angela once heard Mamma tell Mrs. Altimari she thought Papà had abandoned them. "He said he'd send money, but he didn't. He left me with nothing. And there was no one to watch the girls, so how could I get a job? I didn't even know English then," she had said.

"What did you do?" Mrs. Altimari asked.

They'd been talking in the kitchen with the door open, forgetting that Angela was reading in the living room.

"What could I do? I took in sewing to pay the rent and a nice Sicilian man who owned the market gave me credit for food," Mamma said.

"No. You didn't."

"Yes. Can you imagine the shame of it? Living on credit?"

Mamma's voice had gone all high-pitched while she talked. When Papà finally came back to America, they moved to East Harlem. She'd been five then and she barely remembered the move, but she remembered feeling afraid. After quiet Port Chester, New York City had seemed like a scary confusion of noise and movement. Not anymore, though. Angela smiled to herself. She was a New Yorker now.

There was a crowd outside the church when they arrived, but not a large one. Most New Yorkers wouldn't go into a Catholic Church and many of those who would wouldn't go into this one. Some Catholics objected the Our Lady of Pompeii's largely Italian immigrant members, while others remembered when the church had once been St. Benedict the Moor, the only church in New York that served black Catholics. When black populations moved north, escaping the tide of immigrants that flooded into lower New York, the church had been renamed.

They joined the throng entering the church. Outside the church doors, ladies wearing Women's Trade Union League buttons distributed handbills calling for improved worker safety legislation. Inside the doors, gloved and hatted church ladies handed out funeral cards.

They found a pew about halfway back. After they took their seats, Angela examined the card she'd been given.

IN MEMORIAM

*You are earnestly requested to attend a memorial mass for the
repose of the souls of the departed victims of the
WASHINGTON PLACE FIRE DISASTER
At the Church of Our Lady of Pompeii*

May God in His Infinite Wisdom have mercy on their souls
Rev. A. Demo
Pastor

Six wooden coffins stood before the communion rail, each topped with a white cloth and a spray of roses that looked like blood stains. Angela shivered. Six dead people lay up there—five women and one man. Six people either so burned they were unidentifiable or so alone they had no one to identify them. A priest began the mass. As he droned away in Latin, Angela thought about all the people who loved her, including Mamma, Marie, Annie, Mrs. Tosi, and even Papà, in his own way. She couldn't imagine having no one. Was there anything worse than dying unremembered and unloved?

English words interrupted her thoughts. It was time for the sermon. The priest introduced himself as Father Coppo and began to talk about the tragedy. He spoke of better relations between classes of people, reminding them that Jesus had loved the common man, not the rich man. Sobs from men and women in the pews rang out over the sermon.

When he was done, Father Coppo paused then said, "Though we celebrate this mass for the dead according to the traditions of the Holy Mother Church, we recognize that the dead may not have been Catholic. To honor them all, regardless of their faith, the internment will include burial services presided over by Rabbi Stern, Reverend Osgood from the Episcopal Church, and myself. The Brooklyn Elks Lodge Choir will provide graveside music."

They came out of the church to find it had begun to rain in earnest. Mrs. Tosi looked up at the sky. "God, he cries on such a day," she said. She put up her umbrella and grabbed the sisters' hands. "Stay close, you two. Your mother will have my head if you get sick."

Angela leaned into Nonna Tosi, liking the smell of lavender sachet that came off the old woman's skirts. They walked up Sixth Avenue to Fourth Street. Mrs. Tosi thought they could cut across Washington Square Park, where the procession was scheduled to begin, but when they got there the park was full of people, most of them hunkered down under black umbrellas. They skirted the park's southern border, thinking to make for Greene Street. Marie and Mrs. Tosi wanted to see the Asch Building, but apparently they weren't the only ones with that plan. Finally, Mrs. Tosi pushed her way over to Fifth Avenue, both girls in her wake like tiny tender boats behind a black-clad battleship.

They took up a piece of sidewalk a block north of the park, close enough that they could see the Washington Square Arch. Through the rain and ground fog, it looked about a mile away. Angela liked the arch a lot because it was modeled on the Arc de Triomphe in Paris and she figured that was as close to Paris as she was ever going to get. Also, the park had a statue of the great Italian freedom fighter Garibaldi. Papà had gone on and on about the famous Italian who'd fought for both Italian and Brazilian independence. Angela's favorite part of Papà's story was the Brazilian uprising's name—the Ragamuffin War.

49

Angela's feet grew wetter and colder the longer they waited. She looked around at Mrs. Tosi and Marie to find her sister's shoes and stockings no drier. Angela's stomach reminded her it was lunchtime, then her bladder reminded her she should have used the facilities at the church. After what seemed like sixteen hours—time was different when you were cold, wet, hungry, and had to pee—something finally happened.

A gentleman in a dark felt hat leaned out in the street and shouted, "They're coming."

Angela couldn't help but feel excited. She knew she shouldn't, but it was oddly thrilling to be out here with all these people on a school day. The crowd noise increased to a loud buzz. Angela leaned out and looked up the street. *There. Horses.*

The next two hours were among the strangest of Angela's life. Neither the marchers nor the crowd made a sound. Some of the unions had marching bands, though no one played the black-ribboned instruments. Only the rain had anything to say. Even the white horses that pulled the hearses, each wearing black tasseled harness covers, kept their peace. Two men walked along the lead horses, holding the horses' bridles. Other black-clad men walked alongside the wagon, which held six of the largest flower arrangements Angela had ever seen. She supposed the six coffins were under the flowers and felt glad she didn't have to look at them.

The black-suited men looked like important people, maybe the same city officials who warned that the funeral procession might turn violent. She'd seen the story in *The Call* the previous week. One city official said foreigners were too emotional and unruly to be trusted with a public display of grief; other critics cited the displays of grief down at Misery Lane as proof that immigrants were inappropriately emotional.

Angela remembered how angry she'd been when she read those warnings. Who else could mourn the fallen dead but the so-called foreigners who made up the dead's families, friends, and coworkers? Did the rich turn out to mourn? Was God sad for the unknown dead? Or for the living, who had to live in such a world?

Behind the first carriage came a brigade of female workers, most of them carrying signs. One said "End City Graft Before It Kills Again," while another read "Open Shops so Workers Can Leave in Time of Fire." Others called for workplace fire drills and better fire equipment. The most shocking sign read "Swear on the Bodies of the Corpses to End Fire Traps." The woman who carried that sign had it on a pole so long it stuck out above the other signs. She also had a look on her face that Angela would never forget, one that mixed steely anger with stoic determination.

Mamma said the *New York Times* had claimed loss of life would have been prevented if the immigrant women hadn't panicked in the fire. Women were hysterical by nature, the *Times* said, and immigrant women doubly so. Angela snorted. As if female hysteria locked the factory doors, turned off the water, or made the stairways and fire escape inadequate to the building's human needs. Angela wondered if anyone from the *Times* was here now. What would they say in the face of this eerily silent display of female anger?

The United Hebrew Trades of New York marched by. Angela knew from the newspapers that nearly two-thirds of the dead had been Jewish women, the other third mostly Italian with a few Poles and Germans. Another huge contingent of women marched behind the banner of the Cloak and Tailor's Union, No. 9 banner, and another from the Ladies Waist and Dressmakers

Union, Local 25. That was the union that tried to organize the Triangle Factory two years before. It was also the group that organized this funeral procession. Nearly all the marchers were women. They marched without umbrellas, without overshoes or hats, defiant in the weeping rain.

When the International Ladies' Garment Workers' Union banner came into view, Mrs. Tosi shook both of the girls' arms. "There she is. Miss Clara."

Angela examined the marchers. Did she even know anyone named Clara?

Mrs. Tosi saw her looking. "You don't know Clara Lemlich? What is your Mamma teaching you?"

"Mamma's not our teacher," Marie piped up. "Sister Margaret is. Who's Clara Lemming?"

"Lemlich. She's a Jewish girl," Mrs. Tosi said.

Someone shushed them.

Mrs. Tosi squeezed Angela's hand. "I'll tell you a story about her on the ride home."

After two hours, the marchers started to thin out. People left the sidewalks and joined in the procession. Mrs. Tosi pulled the girls away from the curb and said, "We should go home."

They trudged toward Second Street and the elevated train, Nonna Tosi and Marie looking as exhausted as Angela felt. Angela wondered why Nonna Tosi was dragging them all the way over to Second, when they'd passed a half dozen perfectly good trolley lines along the way—and then she saw the sign for Veniero's Bakery.

Mrs. Tosi squeezed their hands. "We need a hot drink and a bathroom, don't you think?" she said.

Angela's step lightened. They stopped in the front of the store to marvel at the window display of cookies and pastries.

Stainless-steel letters spelled out the word *Pasticceria* at the top of the window.

They followed Nonna Tosi as she pushed open the bakery door. Warmth and the bitter scent of roasting coffee competed with the heady scent of sugar.

"There's a ladies' room in the back," Mrs. Tosi said.

Angela grabbed Marie's hand and scampered for the back of the store. They returned to find Mrs. Tosi sitting at a table, a tiny espresso before her. There was nothing else on the table. Angela bit her lower lip and tried not to cry. From behind her she heard Marie gasp. A waiter pushed between the two of them and set a pot of something steaming hot on the table, along with two empty cups, not much larger than espresso cups, and two—no, three—plates of cookies.

Mrs. Tosi smiled at the girls and said, "When I was little, my favorite thing in the world was *cioccolata caldo*. It is such a terrible day for you girls; you need something sweet to balance the bitterness of sorrow."

Angela watched as the apron-wrapped waiter poured out two cups of chocolate so thick she thought the espresso spoons he stuck in the cups might stand up on their own. Angela seized a butter cookie, dunked it in her chocolate, and took a bite. Heaven flooded into her mouth. Beside her, Marie moaned in happiness as she spooned *cioccolata* into her mouth. Nonna Tosi excused herself for the ladies' room. When she came back, one plate of cookies was already empty. She took an almond biscotti and dunked it into her espresso. She held it there for a moment, watching the girls with the satisfied look nonnas get when watching children eat.

People swirled around them while they feasted. Angela had never been in Veniero's when it wasn't busy, and today was no exception. The place glowed with golden light, made all the mellower by the softly shining wooden beams and wall paneling. Angela wiggled in her bent wood chair, unable to contain herself. Outside it was cold and wet and mean and silent and sad, but the bakery was as welcoming as one of Mamma's hugs.

"I promised you a story," Nonna Tosi said when she'd drunk down her espresso.

Marie poured a little more chocolate, first into her cup and then Angela's. When she was done, Mrs. Tosi leaned toward them and started to talk.

"You know things are very bad for the poor. And it is hardest of all to be an immigrant and a woman. You know this because you are not stupid girls."

Angela set down her cup and grabbed Marie's hand.

"Women like your Mamma and Mrs. Altimari and Mrs. DeLuca, and even me for most of my life, we work hard. And the places we work are not nice. They are dirty and dangerous and the pay is too small. We work all day, every day but Sunday, and sometimes even then. And we must still feed our families and take care of the babies and do a hundred other things. You know this."

Angela nodded.

"They think we are stupid, these bosses and men who own New York. They treat us like animals. But we are not. You know this because you are not stupid girls."

Marie squeezed Angela's hand.

"Remember the strike? Only two years ago?"

"Yes, Mrs. Tosi," the girls said in near unison.

"What you do not know is how it started. It was the shirtwaist workers. You saw them today. The Local 25. There was a meeting. There are always meetings. At this meeting many men spoke. Many men always speak. The speaking went on for hours. And then little Clara Lemlich asked to speak. The men, they did not want her to speak. But there were women in the crowd and they yelled at the men to let Clara Lemlich speak. So Miss Lemlich took the stage. She said she had listened to all these speakers until she had no more patience for talk. She was tired of listening to men speak in general terms. She said they were there to decide, would they strike or not strike? The crowd yelled back at her, 'Strike!' They chanted, 'Strike, strike, strike.' Then Miss Lemlich raised her hand in the air and swore to be loyal to the workers. She said if she turned traitor, her hand would wither from her arm. The next day, twenty thousand immigrant women went on strike because Clara Lemlich spoke that day."

"And she was there today? At the procession?" Angela asked.

"Yes. Because they won the strike, but failed the workers at the Triangle Factory."

"How?" Angela said.

"Four months after the strike began, most of the shops agreed to unionize. Workers got bathroom breaks, better wages, and more safety equipment. But those evil men who own the Triangle Factory would not sign the agreement. And you saw what happened," Mrs. Tosi said.

Angela saw that twisted, blackened ruin that had been a fire escape, and then the coffins of dead girls, women, and men. She remembered the smell of death at Misery Lane. And the six coffins that had rolled down the street just today, six people who would be buried nameless.

Mrs. Tosi tapped the back of Angela's hand. "What is the lesson of Clara Lemlich?"

Angela chewed at her lower lip. "The lesson is this: one woman can make a difference, even if she is a poor immigrant."

Mrs. Tosi nodded once. "That is right. There is much work to be done, Angela. Much, much work."

As they rode home, Angela thought about what Mrs. Tosi had said and all she'd seen today. Someone had to stop this from happening again. Sure, the rich ladies felt bad, but they'd never be the ones to change things. The workers had to do that. Maybe she could be one of those people. Angela remembered Rose Schneiderman's speech: "It matters little if 146 of us are burned to death." But it did matter. Today proved that.

Part II

1919–1920

Chapter Four

ONE SMALL STEP

"It was not a woman's fancy that drove them to it, but an eruption of a long-smoldering volcano, an overflow of suffering, abuse and exhaustion."
—Theresa Serber Malkiel on the 1909 Uprising of 20,000

January–February 1919

The lunch bell cut through the roar of the sewing machines. A second later, all the machines went quiet as the shop foreman cut the power. Angela leaned back in her chair and rubbed her neck.

"It's about time," Ida said. She pushed her chair back with a screech. "I was about to go in my chair. I'll bring our lunches back."

Angela smiled and nodded at Ida, though the young woman didn't see, having hurried off to beat the bathroom rush. They'd been sitting next to each other for nearly half a year, and in that time Ida had grown increasingly large with child. It was hard for pregnant women to wait until lunch or quitting time to use the bathroom, but if they didn't, Mr. Lewis docked their pay. Well, not just the pregnant women—anyone who took an unscheduled break. And when they did, he'd stand outside the bathroom to time them and holler as the seconds ticked by. The last time he'd done that to Angela, he'd made her so nervous she could hardly pee.

Around her the scuffling of chairs and feet signaled women settling in for lunch. On nice days they'd leave the shop and eat outside, lined up on the curb or sitting on crates in the alleys. Angela glanced over at the side window. It was still snowing. In weather like this she was glad they'd taken jobs on the Lower East Side. It meant they could ride the elevated train home, which, unlike the trollies, was enclosed.

"Want me to fetch our lunch?"

Angela looked up to find Marie grinning down at her. "No. Ida said she would," Angela said.

Marie nodded at the empty chair on Angela's other side. "Mrs. Shapiro's not here today?"

Angela shook her head and said, "I saw her handkerchief yesterday. She was coughing up blood."

"Jewish disease." Marie shook her head as she sat in Mrs. Shapiro's chair. That's what they called tuberculosis, on account of the many Jews—particularly factory workers—who ended up with it. Long hours and low pay made for exhaustion and malnutrition, particularly among the married women who were more likely to feed their husbands and children before themselves. And no one could afford to go to a doctor.

They both liked Mrs. Shapiro, much as they liked Ida

Rubinstein. Shop foremen liked to sit Jewish and Italian women next to each other because they thought the Jews only talked to the Jews and the Italians only to the Italians. It was stupid, really. All they had to do was look at the factory floor and see that everyone talked to everyone. The foremen and bosses looked at them and saw foreigners, Jews who spoke only Yiddish and Italians who spoke Italian. They didn't know, or pretended not to know, that most of them spoke English as well any anyone. They were poor, not stupid.

Ida returned with the red tin basket that held Angela and Marie's lunch, as well as her own slim blue lunch box. Angela folded down the double handles of her and Marie's lunchbox, admiring as she did the flowers Mamma had painted on the outside. Mamma made everything more beautiful.

She pulled out two napkin-wrapped bundles and handed one to Marie. Each bundle had two thick slices of bread and some of Mr. Catiglioni's cheese. Ida had a small pile of matzo crackers and sliced onions. Sometimes they traded cheese and onions—some days Ida couldn't eat cheese and some days she could. Angela didn't understand all the rules of keeping kosher but she thought that if she couldn't eat cheese, there'd be no reason for living.

They ate their lunch in silence for a few minutes, all of them ravenous. They started work at 6:30 in the morning and by the time the noon bell rang their stomachs had been empty for hours. Ida kept a few matzo crackers in her skirt pocket and nibbled on them throughout the day. Angela helped her hide the habit from Mr. Lewis, who'd have docked Ida's pay even if snacking didn't prevent her from sewing as many sleeves as the rest of them.

Ida finished her lunch, packed up her pail, and pulled a half sheet of paper from her pocket. She slapped it down on the sewing machine table between Angela and Marie. "Well? Are you coming?" Ida asked.

The paper was an announcement for a meeting of the Amalgamated Clothing Workers of America, or ACWA, all dark ink and yelling words.

Marie nodded. "Of course we'll go."

Angela snatched the piece of paper off the table and crumpled it in her hand. "No we won't. You want to get us fired?" she said.

"Of course not," Ida said. "Mr. Lewis is in the cloak room. I saw him go in there ten minutes ago."

Angela suppressed a shudder. Mr. Lewis was old, fat, and smelled of cheap cigars and he liked to touch the girls. Sometimes it was no more than a pat on the shoulder and a pinch on the bottom, but sometimes he'd do more. The cloak room was his favorite hunting ground, though now all the women knew better than to go in there alone.

Not that it was better anywhere else. An article in last week's *New York Call* said there were over twenty thousand factories in Manhattan employing over a half million people, making everything from women's blouses to cigars. Some factories made wooden furniture, some made metal kitchenware, others woolen coats and hats. If you could buy it in America, someone in a Manhattan factory made it.

But with all those factories and all those jobs, there were more immigrants. Something like fifteen thousand people poured into New York each month, mostly from Eastern Europe and Russia. They were the desperate poor, and the men who ran the city's factories knew it. This shop was the third such shop Angela and Marie had worked in during the last year, and it was no better the two before.

Marie laid her hand on Angela's arm. "Can we, Angela? Please?" she asked.

"It's dangerous, Marie. If we lost our jobs, what would Papà say? And if we get blackballed, Mamma will have to go back to work. Do you want that?" Angela said.

Marie shook her head. "Mamma says we gotta stand up for ourselves. You know she's right."

Ida waved a hand over her swollen belly. "I'm going," she said. "So my baby won't have to do this kind of work. If we made a fair wage, then I could save some. Maybe buy the baby some nice things, or send it to school one day. Maybe even college."

Angela snorted. "People like us don't go to college."

"Well, that's the problem, isn't it?" Ida said, nodding. "We get stuck in these jobs, working too much to improve ourselves. And we're so poor that our children have to work in the same terrible jobs, and it never gets better." Ida checked over her shoulder for Mr. Lewis before she continued. "If we organize, we can win. They need us."

"No, they don't. There's always more poor people," Angela said.

"Not if we all stick together. Don't you see?"

Marie nodded. "Ida's right, Angela. It's the only way."

A short burst from the bell signaled they had five minutes before the sewing machines turned on again. Women milled around the factory floor. Angela pushed back her chair. "I'll think about it. But right now I have to use the bathroom," she said. She walked away, shoulders slumped in exhaustion, and joined a long line for the bathroom.

~

Angela tried not to watch the clock. Most days they worked a ten-hour day, but today was Saturday, and Saturdays they only worked eight hours. Best of all, they had Sunday off. Back before the 1909 strike, some women in the textile trades worked as much as eighty-four hours a week, or twelve-hour shifts seven days a week. She didn't know how they did it. By the time Saturday came, her neck and back hurt so bad she could hardly stand it. And she was only twenty years old. How did the older women do it? Back when Mamma was sewing shirtwaists, she had to peddle the sewing machine with her feet; now the machines were powered by electricity. Of course, this only meant the shop owners could expect them to sew more seams and buy more needles.

She pushed sleeve after sleeve under the machine foot and wondered how it had come to this. She'd stayed in high school like Mamma wanted. Then, the summer after she graduated, she parlayed her mathematics skills into a bookkeeping job with Mr. and Mrs. Ferro. They ran a laundry that handled most East Harlem's restaurant linens. It had been a good job. The Ferros were nice and the work wasn't very hard. And Mr. Ferro said he was going to buy another laundry and he would give her a raise because she'd have twice as much bookkeeping. Angela dreamed of the day when she could go into business for herself, or maybe her and Marie together. They'd be Bambace Bookkeeping.

Just after Christmas, two things happened: Mr. Ferro died from a heart attack while fixing one of the big manglers, and Papà got fired. Every time Papà had one of his episodes and wouldn't go to work, he lost his job. Then Mamma would have to work extra by bringing home sewing. They'd been through this a number of times before, the up and down of Papà's moods, his "sickness" that never really got better.

And they'd been doing so well. Before Christmas, Papà had been working—between his tips and her wages as a bookkeeper, they'd had enough money so that Mamma could quit the hat factory. Which was good, because Mamma was looking worn out these days. The dark circles under her eyes never went away and her hair had more gray than black in it. But then Papà went to bed and Mr. Ferro died and Mrs. Ferro couldn't keep the laundry open without him and Angela lost her job. So she took a job sewing shirtwaists. Worst of all, Marie dropped out of school and went to work with her. Angela tried to talk her out of it, but Marie wouldn't listen.

"If you're going to the factories, so am I," she'd declared. "And with both of us working, Mamma can stay home to take care of Papà and Shelley."

When Marie announced her plans to quit school, Mamma had been mad, but Papà rose from his bed long enough to declare it was about time his daughters started earning their keep. Daughters didn't need an education, he said. Not like Shelley would. According to Papà, Shelley would be a big success and they'd all never have to work again. So that was that.

The year 1918 was bad for immigrant workers, what with all the men home from the Great War and taking the best jobs. One place hired Angela as a seamstress, paying her $16 a week, but all Marie could get was a trimming job, cutting stray strings off finished shirtwaists, for $10 a week. Still, between the two of them, they earned as much as Mamma and Papà ever had, and more than when only Mamma was working.

This place was better than some. It had fire sprinklers in the ceilings and every other Monday they had fire drills to see how quickly they could all get out onto the street. But the bosses harassed them for taking bathroom breaks, slowed down the clocks, and shorted their pay. They had to buy their own needles and sewing machine oil. And the Local 25, the Ladies' Garment Workers' Union, didn't help at all. Despite the fact that "ladies" was in the union's name, the men running the union didn't really care about women workers. The union was happy to deal with the skilled workers—the cutters, tailors, and designers who were all men—but they did next to nothing for the immigrant women who made up most of the textile workers.

And all the unions tended to ignore the Italian immigrants. Back after the Civil War, most of the Italian immigrants had been men. They would make some money and go back to Italy. Not anymore—there was no reason to go back to Sicily or Italy. There was nothing there, not after the Piedmontese took over, cut down the trees, and drove the poor off their land. But still the American union organizers thought of Italians as temporary immigrants, all but impossible to organize. Not like the Jewish immigrants, who'd had centuries of experience fighting violence and oppression in the old countries and were glad to use that experience here in their new country.

So here she was, working fifty-eight hours a week for half of what the male cutters made—less than half, when she figured in the needles and oil. She was tired all the time and Marie hardly ever laughed anymore. She and Marie had saved the family, but damned themselves.

The end-of-work bell rang out and the machines slowed to a stop. Angela dropped her finished sleeves into the basket under the table and pushed herself to her feet. They'd go to this meeting. Maybe Ida was right and maybe she wasn't. No—they'd go because Marie wanted to, and it was little enough to do for her. Little enough.

~

The workers gathered in a sixth-floor walkup on Twenty-Third Street, less than four blocks from the shop. On the walk over, Ida, Marie, and Angela bought a bag of apple turnovers and ate half of them. Ida led them up the stairs, stopping at each floor to catch her breath.

The door opened to an apartment already crowded with people. A short whirlwind of a woman ushered them in and helped them find seats while Ida disappeared into the tiny kitchen. Angela kept Marie close to her, worried about all the strange men in the apartment. If it hadn't been for Ida, she'd have made their excuses and left. It was all well and fine to take risks for herself, but Marie was her little sister and they didn't know these men.

"I'm Dorothy," a woman said, after they settled on a ragged sofa. "Shift over there, Nino. Give the girls some room." A young man with curly light brown hair scooted over to the end of the sofa.

Ida waddled out of the kitchen holding a tray upon which sat a stack of mugs and a blue enamel coffee pot. The young man jumped up. "Here, let me, Ida," he said. "Sit down, now." He took the tray from the pregnant woman and set it on a small side table. He pushed her over to the sofa, where he'd been sitting. "And your feet should be up." He scooped up a small stool and swung it under Ida's feet. Then he poured out the coffee and handed cups around the room.

Ida leaned over and bumped Angela's shoulder. "Isn't he the cutest thing you ever saw?" she asked.

Before Angela could answer, Marie leaned around Angela and asked, "Who is he?"

"That is the great Nino Capraro. He's Sicilian, from the same village as my husband," Dorothy answered.

"You're Sicilian?" Angela asked. "Our Papà is from Leonforte."

"No, I was born in Latvia. I came here nearly twenty years ago. But my husband, August, and Nino are both from Sciacca," Dorothy said.

While they talked, Nino distributed the last of the coffee and then clapped his hands twice and said, "Let's begin, shall we? It's snowing pretty good out there, so we won't be long."

After some general agreement about the bad weather, Nino handed over the meeting to another man, who introduced himself as August Bellanca.

"Most of you know me," August said, "but I see some newcomers." He nodded at Marie and Angela, and at two ladies on the other side of the room.

"I'm here to talk about the 48-54 movement," he continued. "You see, there's been some success with the eight-hour movement, mostly because mill and factory owners are only too glad to cut worker hours these days. But cutting hours means cutting wages. Workers' wages are the same as they were at the start of the war nearly five years ago, but all of you know the cost of living has doubled. The owners argue they can't afford higher wages in the middle of an economic downturn, but we say that's nonsense."

"That's right," Dorothy said. "They're making plenty of money."

Angela agreed. The man who owned the shop they were working in now lived on Fifth Avenue and had a chauffeur. His wife had a fur coat.

"The Department of Labor released its 1918 report just last

week," Nino said. "The existence wage for a family of four is now $1,500."

"That much?" Angela said, then blushed. She hadn't meant her words to be so loud.

"How much do we make, sister?" Marie asked.

Angela did the math in her head. "$1,248, if neither of us misses any work. And that's before we buy needles and machine oil," she said.

"Which is why it's so important you're here," Nino said with a wink.

Angela looked over to see Marie beaming at Nino.

"Right," August said. "48-54 is our way of asking for a wage hike. We're demanding wages for 54 hours of work, but under the eight-hour-a-day, six-day work week."

"We'll never get it," one of the ladies across the room said.

"We might. We won't get anything if we don't organize," August said. "Which is what this meeting's about. We represent the Amalgamated Clothing Workers of America. Unlike the Garment Workers' Union, we want to organize all the workers—not just the men or just the English speakers, or even just the skilled workers. We want all the workers, regardless of sex and nationality."

"It'll never work," a mustachioed man said. "We can't all get along that well."

August shook his head. "That's not what our experience says," he said. "We've been organizing up in Lawrence, Massachusetts, and we have Italians, Poles, Russian Jews, Ukrainians, Germans, and some Lithuanians all working together."

"Don't forget that family of Syrians," Dorothy said.

Angela shot Dorothy a look. Syrians? In Massachusetts? Was she kidding?

Marie bounced on the sofa. "I'll help. I want to help," she said.

Angela sighed. Marie was such an optimist. Time to bring her back to earth.

"Listen, I'm all for making things better, but the way I see it, you have two problems," Angela said. "First, there's no way we're getting more pay for shorter hours in this economy. Second, even if you can get all the workers to cooperate, the established unions won't care. And I've never even heard of this Amalgamated Union you're talking about."

August looked over at his wife and said, "Dorothy, I think it's time you told your story."

Dorothy smiled and stood. "Some of you have heard this before, but I can tell it again."

"It's a good story," Nino said with a toothy grin. Dorothy smiled at Nino.

"I came here from Latvia in 1900," she began, "when my family moved to Baltimore. Like many of you, I didn't speak English. I didn't have anything but a strong back. When I was thirteen, I got my first job sewing button holes in men's coats. For my sixty hours of labor each week, I earned $3. This seemed unfair to me when the men who cut the coats made $25 a week. When I was fifteen years old, I organized the female workers at the coat factory into Local 170 of the United Garment Workers of America. But everyone in this room knows how the UGW is—they don't care about the lowly workers and they sure don't care about the women workers. So five years ago, all the women in my factory joined the Amalgamated Clothing Workers. That's the union we're talking about right now. August and I founded it, along with three other men and four other women. I'm on the Joint Board and now I'm ACWA's first full-time organizer."

Angela stared at the small, round-faced woman before her. She hadn't thought women could be union organizers. Oh, maybe a few famous ones like Miss Schneiderman or Miss Lemlich, but not anyone she knew.

"Thank you, Dorothy," August said with a fond smile. "Amalgamated is simply better at organizing workers because we're anarcho-syndicalists. We believe in direct action and self-management of workers. Workers can't depend on the government to help them, nor can they depend on unions not created by the workers."

"So you're anarchists," Angela said with a shake of her head. "I knew it was too good to be true."

"We are anarchists, but we're not like you've heard," Nino said, jumping to his feet. "The government will tell you that we're all violent Bolsheviks trying to destroy the country. But we're not. What we want is to end the system that makes a few men very, very rich and leaves everyone else poor."

"But Papà says anarchists are bad. So did President Wilson," Marie said, looking confusedly from Nino to Angela.

Nino opened his mouth to answer, but Dorothy interrupted him. "In 1915, President Wilson said that hyphenated Americans—you know, Jewish-Americans, German-Americans, Latvian-Americans—were poison to this country. He said we were all disloyal and that we must be crushed. Do those sound like the words of a reasonable man? He thinks all immigrants are anarchists, by which he means not a political party, but agents of disorder and disruption of the American way of life. But are we that?"

Angela shook her head. She thought of all the women she worked alongside, who worked long hours for low pay and went to church on Sundays mornings or Temple on Saturday evening.

Women who did the laundry, cooked the meals, and raised their children the best they could with not enough money. "Then why does everyone say the anarchists are violent?" she asked.

"It's because we're shaking up the system," Nino said. "The rich need the poor to be quiet so they can get richer. They hate all unions, but they hate the unions that organize the poorest workers most of all. And why? Because poor people make them the most money. That's why."

"It's not just the rich," August said with a shake of his head. "It's the politicians. Look at Tammany Hall here in New York. They don't want change. They've grown fat and rich off the backs of poor immigrants. They pay the police to beat us up, and they pay people to break our strikes. Isn't that violence? But when the government does it, we don't call it violence; we call it law and order. And why? Because they want jobs to go to the people who buy them. Patronage, that's the name of the game. Did you know a police captaincy goes for as much as fifteen thousand dollars?"

"Who'd pay that much for a police job?" Angela asked. What she didn't ask was, who had that kind of money in the first place?

"It's a lucrative position. A New York police captain can make a thousand dollars a month off graft from the gambling halls, houses of prostitution, saloons, and opium dens in his precinct. And another cut from the local crime boss, who's extorting all the local businesses. Both the police and the crime families will use violence to keep the workers from organizing."

Angela knew that was true. The Morellos ran the 107th Street Mob in East Harlem. Back when she worked for the Ferros, one of the Morello cousins used to come into the laundry every Monday morning to collect their protection payment. Everyone knew if you didn't pay up, there'd be beatings.

"But back to your original point," Nino continued. "We're not so much anarchists as anarcho-syndicalists. *Anarcho* is for our anarchist roots, though anarchist is simply a word for anyone against hierarchical political systems. So the anarchist spectrum can range from absolute individualism to collectivism. Syndicalist theory holds that industries would be better run by the workers than the owners, or rather that the workers should be the owners, bound together in cooperatives to determine their own lives as workers and humans."

Angela shook her head and said, "It's a pipe dream. We don't need fantasy. We need better pay, better working conditions, and more opportunities for advancement."

"But we should dream big," Marie said. Angela shot her a look. Marie's eyes sparkled with excitement. Or admiration—it was hard to tell.

Nino grinned at the two of them. "The young miss is right, of course," he said. "Without dreams, we die."

Angela shook her head again. Dreams didn't pay the rent. Before she could say anything, Dorothy spoke up. "They're both right. We need practical improvements now and we need dreams for the future," she said, pinning Angela with a steely gaze. "Will you help us? And help yourself?"

Angela held Dorothy's gaze. She liked this woman. More importantly, she admired her. Anyone who could organize button sewers when she was fifteen years old was worth following.

"I'll give it a try," she said.

They started by knocking on their coworkers' doors in the evening. Ida knew the shop bookkeeper. The bookkeeper was glad to give them a list of employees, but swore Ida, Angela, and

Marie to secrecy. It was an oath they were glad to take, if for no other reason than getting a friendly bookkeeper fired wasn't in their best interest.

Marie and Angela took all the women with Italian last names, while Ida and the two other Jewish ladies at the meeting took the rest. They talked about splitting the Italian list between them, but after one run-in with an irate worker's father, they decided to stay together. The man had accused the sisters of trying to get his wife and daughter fired. He'd hollered at them in a southern Italian dialect they didn't understand and pushed them out of the apartment with more force than they were comfortable with.

When they told Mamma about the trouble, she vowed she'd go with them from then on. True to her word, the next evening after dinner, Mamma put on her coat and told Papà she was going out with her girls. Papà wasn't too happy, but Mamma ignored him and went anyway.

As they left the house, Mamma grabbed her rolling pin. "If anyone gives us trouble, I'll bash them with this," she said.

Angela thought she'd die of embarrassment, what with knocking on strangers' doors and having her Mamma with her, but when they knocked on their first door, the man let them right in. After all, what could be more respectable than two young women out with their mother?

They found they had more success on the evenings Mamma came with them. They took special care to talk to the fathers, on the principle that wives and daughters weren't likely to join the union or strike if the man of the household didn't want them to. The tactic worked pretty well, particularly when they argued that only when they organized could they keep the owners' and foremen's hands off the women. They also got into apartments that other organizers reported as resistant to the idea of unionization. It didn't take Angela long to figure out the difference was that previous organizers had been Jewish. Most Italian-Catholic husbands weren't going to let Jewish men tell them what to do, but they'd listen to an Italian *madre*.

One evening when it was just the two of them, they passed the Local 25's office. Marie stopped to look in the windows of what had once been a storefront for a small produce market. "Angela, maybe we should go in and talk to them. I mean, it's an already established union," she said.

Angela agreed. The International Ladies' Garment Workers' Union had been around for two decades. They'd played a huge role in the 1909 strike, the one everyone now called the Uprising of the 20,000. And it had been Clara Lemlich's local union. She'd married and moved to Brooklyn, where she was working on women's suffrage—but still, Clara had once been a leader of the ILGWU, and that meant something.

They pushed their way into the office and a small bell tinkled above the door. A stout older man sat behind a desk at the back of the room. He peered at them over his tiny round glasses. "Yes?" he asked.

Angela noticed he continued to sit in spite of the fact that two women had just walked in. "I'm Angela Bambace," she said. "This is my sister, Marie Bambace. We're both seamstresses at a shirtwaist factory."

"And?" The man's rudeness flustered Angela.

"Well, our shop's not unionized," she said.

"What shop is it?" When Angela told him, the man pulled a ledger book from his desk drawer and rifled through the pages. "You're incorrect, miss. We have the cutters on the rolls."

Marie stepped forward and said, "But there's only about

twenty cutters, and there's over two hundred seamstresses working the sewing machines. We're not in the union."

He snorted and slapped his book closed. "We've found the foreign ladies difficult to organize. The Italians are worse than the Blacks. You can't organize strikebreakers."

"But you haven't even tried," Angela protested. She could hear her voice go up high as she spoke.

"Oh, we've tried, believe me. But there's no point," he said. "You Italians are either vile strikebreakers or infantile extremists. The moderates capable of organization are too small a group to bother with."

Angela gaped at the man, unable to answer such rudeness.

Marie had no such problem. "But your name says you're the Ladies' Garment Workers' Union. We're ladies. We're garment workers. Isn't it our union?" she asked.

Angela grabbed Marie's elbow and dragged her out of the office. "It's no use," she said once they were out on the sidewalk. "We'll do like Dorothy did. We'll organize the shop ourselves and come back here after that."

"To heck with ILGWU," Marie said with a stamp of her foot. "Why should we come back?"

Angela shivered against the cold night air. "Because they're a big union and they've been around for a while. We'll have better protection with a union like that," she said, hugging her sister. "Come on. I'll buy you an espresso and biscotti."

By the end of January, they had most of the seamstresses signed up for the ACWA. They had their first meeting in a church basement and agreed they'd start with the 48-54 demand. If the shop owners said no, they'd strike. As expected, the shop owner said no to a wage hike, pleading poor shop earnings as his excuse. That night, Angela and Marie had to circle around his gleaming black Meisenhelder Roadster to get to the elevated train.

So in the second week of February, the seamstresses went on strike. They made picket signs that read "We Shall Fight and We Shall Win," or "Employers Are Powerful Because They Are Organized so We Should Organize Too" and "Our Wealth Is Our Power of Production." Angela carried a sign that said "All Clothing Workers Should Be in the Union." The ACWA helped the seamstresses with money for food and rent while they were out on strike, but Angela knew they wouldn't last long. Every last one of them worked because their families needed the money. Still, cold as it was and hungry as they were, the women marched in front of the shop every day. The Jewish women taught the Italians their songs and the Italians returned the favor. Except for the cold and the people who yelled at them, it was almost fun.

Until they were attacked.

It happened late in the second week of the strike, the day before Saint Valentine's Day. A group of young men Angela recognized as members of Tommy Gagliano's crew approached the picket line. Gagliano was an underboss for Gaetano Reina, who used to work for the Morellos, and everyone knew his boys were big trouble. People disappeared when Gagliano's crew came around. None of the men were big, but each had been chosen as a Gagliano enforcer for his toughness.

One of the hoodlums grabbed a sign right out of Mrs. Graetano's hand and pushed her. When she screamed, he knocked her down. She lay there on the sidewalk, white-faced in shock, as the other picketers gathered around. When two of the picketers rushed the man and pushed him back, the other men jumped in. A scuffle of grunting men and yelling women erupted on the street, as sudden and violent as a hurricane. Angela saw Marie go down in the melee. She waded in, screaming like a banshee, and grabbed Marie's arm. Someone punched her in the lower back, but she ignored the pain and dragged her sister down the sidewalk.

Angela left Marie on the curb and ran down to the corner of Twenty-Third and Fourteenth, where she yelled for help. On her fifth or sixth bellow, a policeman finally appeared and followed her to the knot of flailing men and women. He waded in, nightstick flying, with no regard for who he was striking. The women fell back or were pulled away by friends, leaving the four men to confront the policeman.

"Off with ye, now," he shouted in an Irish brogue. "I'll not be seeing you on this street again today, shall I?"

The ruffians agreed he would not and sauntered away, laughing and bumping shoulders. Angela looked around at the picketers. Several women were bleeding from facial cuts and a few had bruises blooming on their arms and legs.

Angela couldn't believe it. She stepped in front of the policeman. "You're just going to let them go?" she asked.

Ida stood beside Angela, her belly sticking out in front of her like the prow of a ship. "They attacked us. Isn't that illegal?" she said.

The policeman slapped his stick against his leg and said, "They wouldn't have done nothing if you ladies weren't making a spectacle of yourselves. If ye were my women, I'd have you home, behaving yourself."

Ida opened her mouth to argue, but Angela caught her by the arm and dragged her away. If there were a policeman in New York who would stand up for a bunch of striking immigrant women, she'd never met him.

When they told Mamma at home, she stood up and buttoned on her coat. "We'll just see about that. Come on, girls." Papà asked where they were going and Mamma said they were going to visit Mrs. DeLuca, who lived in the Bowery these days. Instead, she marched them six blocks south to the Palermo, an Italian working man's bar. Mamma pushed her way into the taproom, Angela and Marie on her heels. The bartender, who'd been polishing glasses, froze, astonished to see respectable women inside his bar.

"Is he in?" Mamma barked at the bartender.

The man jerked his head toward the back of the bar.

Mamma marched down a dark, narrow hallway, past the bathroom to a closed door at the end. "Wait here," she said. She grinned at them. "But listen carefully."

She knocked and entered without waiting. Angela turned to Marie and said, "Keep an eye out and I'll listen."

Marie nodded and turned to watch the hall. Angela pressed her ear against the door. She heard Mamma first.

"Do you know what happened today at my daughters' shop?" Mamma said.

"What happened, *Signora*?" a man's voice answered.

"I think you know, Mr. Gagliano. I think you sent those men."

"Were your daughters hurt?" he asked.

"Not mine, but another woman's daughter was hurt. What difference does it make whose daughter?" Mamma said.

Mr. Gagliano said something indistinct.

Mamma barked a laugh. "Your mamma would be ashamed of you. Where is your honor?"

More indistinct mumbling.

"Well, it's not right. I want you to call off your boys. No more strong-arm tactics. *Non mie figlie, né alter figlie.*" Angela

79

grinned. Mamma had said, "Not my daughters, nor any other daughters."

"I'm sorry, Mrs. Bambace. I hadn't thought it would cause harm to the family."

"Well, it does," Mamma said, yelling now. "Factories are full of Sicilian and Italian mothers and daughters. They only want what's right and fair. Is it any more than what you want? And may I remind you, the girls aren't breaking the law."

Then came a long silence. Angela started to worry. Then she heard Mr. Gagliano once more.

"It is done," he said.

"Give Josephine my best. And thank you, Tommaso."

"It's Tommy now."

"You'll always be Tommaso to me, my dear cousin."

Angela heard Mamma take one step, then another before she had the presence of mind to back away from the door. Mamma emerged from Mr. Gagliano's office as triumphant as any conquering general.

"Cousin?" Angela asked.

"Well, his wife is your papa's cousin," Mamma said. "When we first moved to New York, he got himself in trouble at school. I went with his mother to fetch him from the priests. He was sixteen and nearly grown, but she spanked him like four-year-old right there, out on the street in front of the church. Then she told me spank him too. So I did."

"Spanked him?" Marie squeaked.

Mamma nodded. "He's been afraid of me ever since."

They didn't have any more trouble from the Gagliano gang after that.

A week later, the owners made the unionized women workers

an offer. They could now work five ten-hour shifts a week for the same pay they'd once made for fifty-six hours of work and one paid bathroom break.

Angela always suspected they won the strike because Mamma had once spanked the local crime boss.

Chapter Five

DESPERATE TIMES

"Better to Starve Fighting than to Starve Working."
—A sign from the 1912 Lawrence Strike

April–May 1919

"Please, Angela?" Marie said, plucking Angela's book from her hands and holding it above her head. "Please, please, please."

"Hey, I was reading that," Angela said. She reached for her book, but Marie held it just out of range. She'd picked it up at a used bookstore, a bestseller last year or the year before, *The Hundredth Chance* by Ethel M. Dell. It was a silly melodrama, but she found herself drawn into it nonetheless. "Give it back or I'm not taking you anywhere."

Marie flopped down on the bed beside Angela and dropped the book on her chest.

"Thanks. I was just about to find out if Maud and Jack are going to live happily ever after."

"But that's just it," Marie whined. "Your own sister's not going to live happily ever after if you don't go with me to Lawrence."

Angela propped herself up on one elbow. "What's in Lawrence?" she asked.

"You know." Marie batter her eyelashes at Angela, who laughed.

"Papà would kill us if he found out."

"He's not going to. You won't tell, will you?"

"What about Mamma?" Angela said. "You don't expect me to keep a secret from her, do you?"

"No. Mamma likes Nino. She won't mind," Marie said. "And if you go, Mamma will let me go. You can guard my girlish honor." Marie rolled back and forth on the bed, flinging her arms wildly.

Angela giggled in spite of herself. "What kind of girl goes chasing a man up to Massachusetts? Nino will think you're a floozy."

"Angela!" Marie gasped, swatting at Angela, knocking the book to the floor as she did.

"Watch it, pup. That book cost fifty cents."

"He asked me to come, silly, in his last letter," Marie said. "Carlo Tresca is going to speak for the strike for May Day. Only he'll speak on Friday, which is really May 2. If we left Thursday night, we'd only miss one day of work. Carlo Tresca, Angela. Imagine!"

Angela had to admit the idea intrigued her. Tresca published a well-known anarchist newspaper, *The Plebeian*, until the Feds shut him down. He'd also been an important leader in the 1912

Lawrence Strike, when he spoke out against the jailing of Italian strikers. He was pro–women's suffrage, pro–Irish independence, anti-fascist, and anti-war. He also spoke out against the Mafia's infiltration of the labor movement, a stance Angela thought more organizers should take. Angela was convinced Italian crime families were going to be more destructive to America and to the reputations of Italian-Americans than all the socialists and anarchists combined.

"All right," Angela said. "I'll speak to Mamma. If she says we can go, I'll take you."

Marie squealed and bounced off the bed. "Thank you, thank you, thank you. Oh, I love you forever, my darling big sister. Other girls' sisters bow their heads at their failures compared to you."

Angela reached behind her head, grabbed a pillow, and threw it at Marie. They laughed until Papà yelled at them from the living room to quiet down.

Of course Mamma said they could go. The real problem was that Mamma wanted to go with them, a plan that filled both girls with dismay. She was the best mamma in East Harlem—maybe in the whole of New York—but at twenty and eighteen years old, respectively, Angela and Marie thought they deserved a little Mamma-free adventure.

Luckily, Mamma couldn't figure out a way to square it with Papà. It wasn't like he would get Shelley ready for school and make the boy's dinner. Privately, Angela thought Shelley should be able to take care of himself by now. He was thirteen years old, but Mamma and Papà treated him like a young prince. So Mamma had to stay home and take care of Papà and Shelley.

Angela and Marie each carried a small overnight bag with them to work on Thursday, happy that the day was warm and dry. No one wanted to be lugging a bag about the Lower East Side in the rain. When the quitting bell rang at 5:00, they grabbed their bags and took a trolley up to Penn Station. Though Angela had walked past the gargantuan pink granite station before, she'd never been inside. The three-story vaulted ceiling of the great hall and column-lined walls would have given the place a cathedral feeling, but for the noise and bustle of the crowd. The hall to the northern train lines featured a confection of lacy steel trellises that rose to glowing skylights.

"Have you ever seen anything like this?" Marie whispered to Angela.

"Not even St. Patrick's is this grand," Angela said, pausing to read the sign boards. "There's a 6:30 to Boston."

They bought a pair of third-class tickets and boarded the train. Less than three hours and one quick train switch in Boston later, they arrived in Lawrence. Nino's letter to Marie directed them to a boarding house not far from the woolen mill that was the center of the strike.

Nino met them the next morning. Blue circles under his eyes marred his good looks, though he flashed his wide smile when he saw them. "I'm so glad you came," he said and kissed both of them on the cheek. Angela noticed his lips lingered on Marie's cheek a second or two longer than the quick peck he'd given her.

"You look tired, dear," Marie said.

Dear? When did that happen? Angela wondered.

"Oh, I didn't sleep last night. And I won't until tomorrow," Nino said.

"Haven't slept? Why not?" Marie asked.

Nino looked around the boarding room lobby and said, "I'll tell you the story, but not here. I thought I'd take you over to strike headquarters for breakfast. We have a kitchen there that feeds the strikers."

They walked down Merrimack Street along a sluggish and stinky canal. Slumping wooden tenement buildings sat between brick factories. Black smoke poured from the city's smokestacks, filling the air with a noxious fume that rivaled the worst New York had to offer.

Along the way, Nino pointed out two woolen factories. "Those two are both owned by the American Woolen Company," he said. "They own the four largest mills in Lawrence. The native-born workers are bringing home $25 a week, but most of the foreign-born workers make $13 or less."

"So just like our factories in New York," Angela observed.

"Yes, except the workers here are more diverse. We have people from every nation in Europe here and no one nationality is the biggest. Which is why the mills have gotten away with the pay difference this long. None of the established unions thought Lawrence could be organized."

Angela nodded. "It's like the Italians and Jews at home. Everyone thinks we can't cooperate," she said.

"But we can," Marie said. "We proved that in February when we won our strike."

"Exactly," Nino said. "Here, thirty thousand workers went out in February. Most of the skilled, English-speaking workers have gone back to work—but the bulk of the workers, the immigrants, they've stayed out. And it hasn't been easy. The Lawrence police have been trouble from the start. We've sent letters to Governor Coolidge and President Wilson protesting the police brutality. We're picketing peacefully and we're within our legal rights to do so, but the violence continues. The police have gotten so bad, they started clubbing passing pedestrians and chasing people down sidewalks with horses."

They arrived at the union hall and went inside to find a busy, well-organized soup kitchen. They each grabbed a tray and took their place in line. Kerchief women served them thick lentil soup, a slice of coarse wheat bread, and a cup of coffee. All around them, men and women gathered to eat and talk. Almost all of them looked gaunt and exhausted.

When they'd found their seats, Marie asked, "Darling, why were you up all night?"

Angela sighed and dunked her bread in her soup. Marie was such a romantic.

"Well, it's quite a story," Nino said. "As you know, strikes are expensive. The ACWA has spent nearly $100,000 to support the workers here."

"As much as that?" Angela asked between bites of soup.

"Well, considering we still have twenty-five thousand people out, it's not all that much. And we've been out for nearly three months, so we're running out of money. Worse, the strikers are starting to lose hope. Between the mill owners, the police, and the church, we've faced some pretty stiff opposition."

Marie patted Nino's hand. "What's the church have to do with it?" she asked.

"Ah, well, as you may know, Rome has decided to support the fascists in Italy. There's a new fellow by the name of Mussolini making some waves and the Church likes his ideas. In America, some of the priests follow Rome and some do not. Father Milanese here in Lawrence has come out against the strikers. He's encouraged the police to beat us and denounced his striking parishioners as dangerous." Nino sighed and ate a bite of bread.

"Some people think the mills are paying him, but that's neither here nor there. Anyway, we decided to ask Carlo Tresca to speak to energize the base and shake loose some more funding."

Angela pushed away her tray and said, "He was the hero of the 1912 strike."

Nino nodded. "Yes, he was, but back then city officials ran him out of town and said he'd never be allowed back in Lawrence. I met him in Boston yesterday, me and Dr. Calitri. The doctor has his own car, a Pilot Sedan. We waited until midnight, hid Tresca in the back seat under some blankets, and smuggled him into town. We took him straight to Lexington Hall. He's hiding there now."

"How exciting," Marie said. "I told you, Angela, this is going to be so much fun."

For the sake of peace, Angela agreed, but she was worried. Lawrence sounded like a dangerous place. There was no telling what would happen when the union sprung Tresca from his hiding place.

Nino took them around the city that day, walking them to his favorite shops on Market Street and then to a park down by the river. As they walked, they saw the police searching cars and delivery vans. One delivery driver argued with two policemen and got roughed up for it. Angela thought Lawrence seemed like a clock wound too tight.

After getting lunch from a street-side pushcart, they walked over to Prospect Hill to see the rich people's houses. They strolled past streets of mansions, each larger and more ornate than the last. Angela wondered how the people in these houses lived with themselves. How could you live in such grandeur when people who worked twelve-hour days lived in squalor-filled tenements just across town? She supposed they learned to ignore the poor, or thought of them as a different kind of human. She knew for sure there were people who thought of immigrants as sub-human, particularly Jewish and Catholic immigrants. It was a tricky business, these ideas about who counted as a real human and who did not.

At 7:00, Marie and Angela were seated near the back of the auditorium. Nino tried to get them seats up front, but they'd all been saved for people more important. Nino took the stage, looking dapper in a neatly brushed jacket, hair gleaming with pomade. He stood center stage, hands behind his back, until the crowd quieted. Then, voice ringing across the seats, he called out, "Lock the doors. No one comes in or out."

Angela swiveled her head to see four brawny-shouldered men lock the hall's two sets of double doors and stand before them.

Nino rocked on his feet, letting the tension in the hall build. Finally, he held out his arms and simply said, "Carlo."

Carlo Tresca stepped out from the wings and stood next to Nino. The hall went entirely quiet, as if everyone had frozen in place.

Angela felt the intensity of the moment like a hand pressing down on her.

After a long moment, Nino said, "Company, you may applaud if you want to."

An explosion of clapping and triumphant yells filled the hall. Nino let it go on for a minute before he held up his arms and called for silence. He left the stage and Carlo Tresca began to speak.

Angela never heard another speech like it. Tresca spoke for an hour, exhorting the strikers to hold their ground. He was a small, fox-faced man, but his voice was as big as his ideas. He spoke in English, aware that his audience was not just Italian, but peppered his speech with Italian words and phrases, reminding the audience that, like them, he was a foreigner too.

In striking, he reminded his audience, they were striking a blow for self-determination, for every man and woman's right to control their own life. Everyone, he said, should have freedom and independence, not just the rich. Angela's mind reeled at the speech, overwhelmed with the breadth of Tresca's vision. She found herself swept along with the rest of the crowd, on her feet at the speech's end, applauding as wildly as everyone around her. Nino came back out and stood with Tresca as the hero of the hour took his bows.

Marie turned to her sister, eyes shining with tears. "Isn't he wonderful?" she asked.

"He's like no one I've ever heard speak before," Angela said.

Marie laughed. "Not Carlo Tresca, silly. Nino."

Nino walked them to the Lawrence train station the next morning. Angela pretended to need a bathroom and left Marie and Nino on the platform to make their goodbyes in private. Last night, Nino had found the two of them in the crowd and kissed Marie quite soundly. From the way he looked at her that evening and again this morning, Angela was sure he was as besotted with Marie as she was with him.

All Marie could talk about on the short ride from Lawrence to Boston was Nino. Nino this and Nino that. Angela could only smile at her sister's happy chatter. Sometimes she wished she could be as fearless with her emotions as Marie. But wishing didn't make it so. Mamma said it was because Angela was the firstborn and firstborns were always more serious; Mamma sometimes blamed herself for Angela's seriousness. Mamma also thought she should have protected Angela better, back when she'd been little and they'd been abandoned by Papà, but Angela disagreed. None of that was Mamma's fault; it was Papà's.

As best as she could tell, when you trusted a man and gave him your heart, he tromped on it again and again. Isn't that what Papà did to Mamma's heart—forcing her to leave Brazil for Sicily? Forcing her to leave Sicily for America? Leaving her in Port Chester? And how had he helped Mamma the last fifteen years? But still, Papà thought he could tell them what to do. And Mamma let him because she was married to him and that's what wives were supposed to do. As far as Angela could tell, there was no upside to love and marriage. It was a trap—at least for women.

In Boston, they picked up a couple newspapers while they waited for the train to New York. The *Lawrence Leader*'s headline read, "Where Are the Vigilantes?" The article urged the citizens of Lawrence to round up the strike leaders and run them out of town. Apparently, the city marshal declared he would withdraw all protection from the strikers.

The *Telegram* advised "the common people form mobs and use the lamppost as a remedy for strikers." This one struck terror in Angela's heart. A newspaper was publicly calling for the lynching of strikers. Lynching. As if Massachusetts were no better than Mississippi or Alabama. Maybe it wasn't.

They arrived back at Penn Station Saturday afternoon. Outside the spring weather made a mockery of the ugly words in the newspapers. Mamma greeted them at the apartment door like they'd been gone for two weeks instead of two days. Marie was full of stories of Nino's triumph, as if he'd given the rousing speech, not Tresca.

Angela watched her sister talk to Mamma, wishing she could feel as ebullient about the trip. Their strike in Little Italy seemed small and harmless compared to the Lawrence Strike. And what would happen next? Would they really lynch strikers? People commonly thought that only black people got lynched in America, but it wasn't true. Why, they'd lynched Leo Frank just four years ago, more for being a Jew than for the murder he'd been convicted for. Hadn't a judge pardoned Frank after his death? And what about the eleven Italian men lynched by a New Orleans mob? Sure, it was thirty years ago, but in Italian Harlem they still talked about it.

The blow fell four days later.

They were making their way home from the elevated train and stopped at Mr. Catiglioni's store to buy a small bag of spring plums and a newspaper. Papà only took *Il Progresso*, but it was conservative and printed in Italian. They preferred *The Call*, an English-language newspaper sympathetic to workers and workers' issues.

Mr. Catiglioni handed over the paper with a frown. "Don't you girls know Nino Capraro? That nice young man who writes for this newspaper?" Mr. Catiglioni asked, tapping the pile of newspapers on his countertop.

Marie snatched the newspaper out of Angela's hand, scanned its front page, and moaned.

Mr. Catiglioni came around his counter, grabbed Marie by the arm, and hustled her over to an upturned crate. "Sit, sit," he said. He bustled off to the back of the store, muttering about a damp towel.

Angela snatched the newspaper from Marie's limp hand.

And there it was: "Capraro & Kleinman Kidnapped!"

According to a hotel desk clerk, a gang of white-hooded,

armed men charged past his desk just after 2:00 a.m. They broke down the door to the room Nino shared with Nathan Kleinman, his fellow strike leader, and hauled the two men away. When called to the scene, the Lawrence police refused to investigate, saying the kidnapping was a hoax staged by crazed radicals.

"What if they kill him?" Marie asked. "What if he's already dead?"

Angela looked from the newspaper to her sister's tear-streaked face. Before she could answer, Mr. Catiglioni returned with a damp hand towel. He wiped Marie's face and fussed over her. Angela stood by and watched. She had no idea what to say, no idea what to do. Marie was only eighteen years old, but she loved Nino with all her heart. Angela was sure of that.

When Mr. Catiglioni had done all he could, Angela took Marie home to Mamma. Mamma put Marie to bed and made a milky caffe latte for her. Marie didn't say a word, nor did her eyes focus on anything. She'd gone somewhere else, by the look on her ashen face—a place of heartbreak and fear.

Angela walked over to the Local 25 office, thinking perhaps they'd have news, but the office was closed. Instead she walked to the Western Union office and sent a telegraph to strike head-quarters in Lawrence. She didn't expect an answer, but didn't know what else to do. It must be chaos there and they'd have no reason to answer a telegram from a New Yorker no one knew. As she walked home, the sun fell behind the tall buildings to the west, casting a pall over the streets. Street cart hawkers called out their wares, the trolley clanged by, children played stickball in the street, and no one cared that her sister's heart had shattered.

At dawn, a knock sounded at the door. Angela, who'd been dozing in a kitchen chair, loath to disturb Marie in their bed, jerked awake. She opened the door to find a buck-toothed, bespectacled Western Union messenger boy. Mamma came up behind Angela and pulled the boy into the kitchen. He shook his head but Mamma ignored him, pushed him into a chair, and poured him a cup of coffee. Angela noted that he wasn't any older than twelve, but he looked like he'd been working all night. His shirt collar was dirty and his eyes had wrinkles under them.

Angela tore open the yellow envelope and pulled out a flimsy scrap of paper.

> *Western Union*
> *158 E. 103rd Street*
> *New York, New York*
>
> *Nino alive. Sending him home tomorrow.*
> *A. Bellanca*

Angela thrust the scrap of paper at Mamma. "It's from friends," she said.

Mamma sat down to read the telegram. She smiled and crossed herself, then pulled Angela into a hug. "You take this to your sister. I'll make this young man a sandwich to take with him."

The boy looked back and forth between the two of them.

Angela kissed the top of his head and said, "My sister might get her happy ending after all."

August Bellanca took Nino off the train at Penn Station in a high-backed wheelchair. Mamma, Marie, and Angela watched as Nino's brothers Joe and Diego surrounded the chair. Marie had told Angela that Nino came from a middle-class Sicilian family and that he was the baby of a family with twelve sons. Fifteen years ago, he came to America with his six of his brothers, four of whom now lived in Florida. Nino waved the women over, his pale hand as feeble as an injured bird.

Marie burst into tears. Angela didn't blame her—he looked as if someone had beaten him within an inch of his life. Both eyes were black and blue, and the left one was swollen closed. Someone had wrapped a scarf around Nino's neck, but it didn't cover the red marks just under his jaw. It looked as if someone had strangled him. His right cheek had a red gash deep enough to require five stitches. Angela assumed Nino's clothes hid more injuries and she was glad she couldn't see them. Mamma wanted to bring Nino back to their place, but they all knew Papà wouldn't stand for it. Joe and Diego, both bigger and older than Nino, promised to take their brother to their apartment.

For a week, Marie and Angela visited the Capraro brothers' apartment every afternoon after work. Angela often took walks during their visits to give the two lovebirds some privacy. Mamma and Papà would have been scandalized, but no one could look at Nino's battered body and think he was any threat to Marie's purity.

On their fourth visit, he told his story. Marie sat by his side, holding his hand, while Angela sat in a kitchen chair across the room. Diego was still at work and Joe had gone out to buy dinner.

Nino looked off into space and then said, "You know, I've been in Lawrence for ten weeks now."

Angela opened her mouth to tell him he was in New York City, not Lawrence, then stopped herself.

"The city's under martial law, or it might as well be," Nino continued. "The mayor announced he wasn't going to protect the strikers anymore, which made us all laugh. There hadn't been any protection before, not with all those returned soldiers patrolling the streets. So we had a meeting about it that went until nearly midnight. I went back to my hotel and crawled straight into bed. About an hour later, I guess, someone knocked on my door.

"'Who's there,' I said, more out of habit than anything. I mean, I was half asleep. The bellboy called out, 'Someone to see you, sir.' I asked who and he said he couldn't tell me. I thought it must have been the police, so I got out of bed and opened the door."

"Oh, Nino," Marie said. "Why'd you do that?"

"I figured they'd break down the door if I didn't open it and I hadn't done anything wrong," Nino said, then paused. "As soon as I unlocked the door, a bunch of men rushed in. Maybe twenty of them. They were wearing regular coats and pants, but they had those white hoods the Ku Kluxers wear."

Angela didn't mean to, but she gasped.

Nino nodded. "I know. So a couple of them pushed me back on the bed and punched me a few times. Then they told me I'd be coming with them. Well, I was wearing my pajamas, so I asked if I could put on my pants, but all they let me do was put on my shoes. No socks, even."

Angela snorted out a little laugh. "Socks? You thought socks was your problem?"

Marie glared and said, "It's not funny, Angela."

Nino smiled a small smile. "It's a little funny. One of them went through my pants and grabbed my wallet, address book, and all my money. They started to drag me down the stairs and I figured that if they got me out of the hotel, they'd kill me for sure, so I was struggling and trying to get away and they were hitting me and dragging me down the stairs. I think someone hit my head with a club because things went fuzzy for a few minutes. I came to in the hotel basement. I thought they were going to shoot me in the head and throw me in the furnace, but no, they hauled me out the back door. There were these three black cars there and I figured I'd let them put me in one and then I'd throw myself out of the car when they got going."

"You could have been killed doing that," Marie half whispered. "Jumping out of a moving car? Nino, really."

"I was less worried about jumping out of the car than I was about these white-hooded men. But then they put me between two huge men and I was stuck. They all piled into the cars and started driving."

Nino stopped again. His bruises, which had begun to turn greenish-yellow, stood out against his pale skin like signposts. "Marie, you need to know I wasn't brave. I begged for my life and then I told them I'd leave Lawrence if they'd just let me go. I begged, Marie. I begged and I cried."

Tears slipped down Nino's face. "They asked me if Tresca was still in town. Thank goodness he'd gone already, because I'd have told them where he was. I would have. Then they asked me about the other strike leaders, the ones who helped get Tresca into town. I named names."

Marie grabbed Nino's hand. "You thought they were going to kill you. Anyone would have done the same," she said.

He shook his head and said, "I don't think so. I know men who would have died before they betrayed Tresca and the movement."

"You didn't betray anyone," Angela said. "You're alive and the strike is still strong. How did you get away?"

"We drove out of town, somewhere south, and stopped on a

road with no houses, no cars," Nino said. "They pulled me out of the car and this man came up to me with a rope in his hand. He threw it at my feet and told me to pick it up. I refused. I mean, why should I help them string me up? He pulled a gun out of his pocket and told me to pick up the rope. I don't know, I just went crazy. I started screaming and hitting and kicking and they were hitting me back and it was awful. One of the big fellows that rode in the back seat with me hit me in the head. I fell and nearly fainted. Then something distracted them. I think it was Kleinman. He wouldn't get out of the car and he was screaming bloody murder."

"Kleinman? Who's that?" Marie asked, swiveling her head back toward Angela as if she knew. Angela shrugged.

"Nathan Kleinman," Nino said. "He's one of the Lawrence organizers. They had him in one of the other cars. I don't know how they kidnapped him or what happened to him after. No one will tell me."

"We'll find out, won't we Angela?" Marie said.

Angela shrugged. "I can ask over at Local 25."

"Thanks, Angela," Nino said. "I think he saved my life, even if he didn't mean to. You see, the men who'd been beating me left off and went to help with the other fight. I think they thought I was unconscious. So I jumped up and ran. It was dark, no moon or anything, so I ran across this field. One of my shoes came off, but I kept running. I ran like a drunk person, zigzagging across the field, which wasn't on purpose—it was just that I had one shoe and I was afraid for my life, and blood was getting in my eyes."

Nino touched a stitched cut on his forehead near his hairline. "I ran smack-dab into a stone wall. Flipped right over it. I lay there in the dark and tried not to breathe too hard. I waited there until the sun came up. Nearly froze to death. And while I waited, I swore to myself that I'd get away and tell everything to the police, and I'd go back to the strike."

"Blessed Mother," Marie said. "That's the worst thing I've ever heard."

"He's alive," Angela said with a sigh. "Most of the people the Klan sets out to lynch end up dead at the end of a rope. Remember that."

Marie wheeled on Angela. "There's no reason to be so hard," she said.

Nino laid his hand on Marie's. "She's right, darling. I'm alive while better men than me molder in their graves."

"Humph," Marie said.

"You want to hear the rest?" Nino asked. Marie nodded. "When the sun came up, I saw a farmhouse across the way. I walked over and knocked on the door. The farmer who answered looked none too friendly, so I told him I'd been set upon by thieves. I asked him if I could use his phone, but he didn't want me in the house. He made me wait outside, in my pajamas with one shoe, while he called the police. I could smell coffee and bacon when he opened the door, but he left me on the stoop, shivering and half naked. After a half hour or so, a police car pulled up to the farmhouse. It was the Andover police chief. He was a real decent sort, even after I told him I was with the union. He took me to a doctor and he called the union lawyer for me. The doctor took me to the hospital, which is where Joe and Diego found me."

"What will you do now?" Angela asked.

"I'm going back."

"You can't," Marie said. "They'll find you and kill you."

Nino shook his head. "I was a coward but I'm going to make up for it. I'm going to write up my story. *The Call* will publish it. I think once I do that, they'll have to leave me alone. Nothing makes cockroaches scatter like a bright light."

"But they always come back," Angela said. "As soon as you turn off the lights, they come back."

Nino returned to Lawrence ten days after his brothers brought him to New York. His article, "How the Ku Kluxers Taught Me about American Democracy," appeared on the front page of a May edition of *The Call*. In it, he related the story pretty much the way he told it to Marie and Angela, including how frightened he was and how disappointed he'd been with his willingness to beg for his life. The article also mentioned what Angela had already learned from Rose Pesotta, who ran the Local 25: Nathan Kleinman survived his night of terror as well. Apparently, when Nino got away, the KKK abductors figured they couldn't very well lynch their remaining captive, not with an eyewitness roaming around somewhere. So they drove Kleinman back to Lawrence and dumped him in front of the hotel, where the night desk clerk found him and called an ambulance.

Nino's article garnered the strikers a new wave of supporters and money. Days after the article appeared, the woolen mill owners asked the union organizers to meet for talks. The Textile Workers Union, along with Nino and Nathan Kleinman from Amalgamated Clothing Workers, worked out a deal for a 15 percent wage increase—2.5 percent more than they'd originally asked for. They also got a nondiscrimination clause put into the agreement, so the mills couldn't refuse to rehire strikers.

Angela followed the news in the New York papers, jubilant that the strike had pulled a victory from what had begun to seem like sure defeat.

Nino came back from Lawrence a broken man, as if his return had taken all of his courage and left him with no more to spare. He quit organizing and started writing for *The Call* full time. Angela watched his transformation with more than a little sadness. Why quit when he'd won? Sure, he'd almost been killed, but almost didn't count when it came to murder. Either you were dead or you were alive.

And if getting beat up won the workers a raise, then she thought she'd volunteer for a beating—anything to get the job done. Quitters didn't make the world a better place; survivors did. Late at night, in her bed, Angela made a promise to herself. She'd be a survivor, no matter what.

Chapter Six

RED SCARE

"I am convinced that in your zeal to fight against our enemies, you have forgotten what you are fighting for."
—Julia Child on the Red Scare of the 1950s

April–November 1920

A fat, wet drop landed on Angela's nose. The iron sky rumbled again. And they were without Mamma's big black umbrella. It had been all blue May sky this morning when she and Marie left for work.

"Come on," Marie half yelled and made a mad dash for their building.

Angela ran after her sister and laughed when the sky opened up just as she made it through the main door. Spring rain, strong legs, dinner waiting upstairs after a long day—all made it good to be her.

They came through the apartment door to find Mamma and

Papà in the kitchen with Father Abramo. The men looked grim. Mamma looked scared.

Papà gestured for the two of them to sit. "Father tells me a shocking tale. Is it true, Angela, that you organized a strike at your shop?" he asked.

Angela's mind scrambled. There was nothing to do but tell the truth. "Yes, Papà."

Before she could explain, Papà smacked his hand on the table. "You got in fights in the streets? I hear you and your mother disrespected Mr. Gagliano. You took your sister to another state to sin with a man. And this man gets kidnapped and beaten up. And now you visit him. You infect yourself with this violence. You bring this sin into my house."

"It's not like that, Papà. And Marie didn't do anything wrong. I was with her the whole time. She's a good girl," Angela said.

Father Abramo leaned forward and said, "You have sinned by lying to your father. If you don't make acts of contrition, you will burn in hell."

Papà nodded at the priest. "And your mother, she lied to her husband," he said. "And you, Marie. You were my good girl. But now I hear you're running around with a radical. A liar and a whore, that's what you are."

"Antonio," Mamma gasped.

Papà leaned over and casually smacked Mamma in the face with the back of his hand. "You keep your lying mouth shut. No wonder my daughters are whores, with you for a mother."

Marie pushed back her chair and put her hands on her hips. "Don't you hit Mamma again. Papà, I love Nino and I'm going to marry him," she said.

"Sit down," Papà roared, "and shut up. You will not marry

this man. Do you think I do not read about his kind in *Il Progresso*? Do you think I do not know these unions are dangerous?"

Marie shook her head. "Papà, *Il Progresso* lies. Nino and the union are trying to make life better for working Italians. And I want to help him."

"This ends today. Father Abramo knows a God-fearing man who needs workers. You will work in this man's factory. You will not leave the house except to go to work and to church. Do you hear me?" Papà said.

"No, Papà," Angela said, shaking her head. "I worked hard to make my job better. It was not easy and I won't leave it."

Papà slapped Angela, just like he had Mamma. "I didn't ask you what you wanted. You made a spectacle of yourself on the street. You put your mother in danger. You think I don't know?" he said.

"You listen to your Father," Father Abramo said with a satisfied smile. "He knows what is best for the family."

Marie pushed back her chair with a sob and ran from the room. Angela stood to follow her, but taking one look at her mother's face, she sat back down. Her cheek stung from Papà's slap. Mamma's probably did too. She couldn't leave Mamma with Papà and Father Abramo.

"Get us some more coffee, Peppina. What are you thinking, sitting there like a lump?" Papà said, slamming his hand down on the table.

Mamma flinched and jumped to her feet. Father Abramo folded his hands and smiled in satisfaction.

In that moment, Angela hated both men.

Mamma put two cups of coffee down in front of them. Papà lifted the mug and slurped off the top. He did not thank Mamma.

Angela pushed herself to her feet and left the kitchen. Behind her Papà yelled, but she ignored him. In their bedroom, Marie was throwing clothes in a bag. She jerked her chin at a second bag and said, "There's yours."

Angela shook her head. "I can't leave Mamma. And I have no place to go. Neither do you."

"I'll go to Nino. He's asked me to marry him. We'll go to City Hall. I won't have any priest do it, not after today," Marie said.

"They're not all bad. Remember the mass at Our Lady of Pompeii?" Angela said.

"Nino says the Church of Rome is against the workers. He wouldn't have a priest either."

"He's wrong, Marie. All priests are not alike. You won't really be married if you go to City Hall. You'll be living in sin," Angela said. The idea of a marriage not consecrated by the Church shocked her more than she expected.

"Marriages are legal contracts, Angela. That's why you need a lawyer, not a priest, to get a divorce."

"Who's getting a divorce?" Angela asked.

Marie snapped her bag shut and came around the bed to hug her sister. "No one, silly. I was just saying."

"You can't go."

Marie shrugged. "By this time tomorrow, I'll be married," she said.

"You can't leave me."

Marie swallowed hard and wiped at her eyes with the back of her hand. "I gotta live my own life. So do you, Angela."

But how could she? She couldn't live on her own. She didn't make enough money. And if she left, Mamma would have to go back to one of the factories. Shelley would have to quit school and go to work too. That wasn't fair to him, even if he was a spoiled brat.

Marie snuck out of the apartment in the middle of the night. Angela kissed her sister and wished her luck, but that night she lay in bed worrying. Marie didn't really know Nino. He was good looking and she had this romantic idea about him, but was he really a good man? His Lawrence experience had changed him, or maybe brought out the real Nino. She thought Marie might be making a huge mistake.

A week later she came home from work to find Papà in the living room, which wasn't unusual. But he was sitting on a kitchen chair, which *was* unusual. A strange man had taken up Papà's chair as if he, not Papà, ruled the space.

"Angela, come in here," Papà called.

She hung her hat on the hook by the door and stared at the kitchen door. She was exhausted. Work was even less fun these days, what with Marie and Ida gone. Marie married Nino in a civil ceremony two days after she left the apartment and Ida quit work to have her baby. She'd probably be back in a couple of months, but that didn't help Angela's day much.

She'd talked Papà into letting her keep her job, but he made Mamma go back to the hat factory to make up for Marie's lost wages. She and Mamma worked all day, then came home to make dinner, while Papà napped in his chair and Shelley did his home-work. What Papà had to be so tired about, Angela didn't know.

She stepped into the living room. The man in Papà's chair had swarthy skin and black hair, growing gray at the temples and pomaded back in much the same way Papà kept his hair. He stood up when Angela came into the room and nodded his head. Angela noticed he was shorter than her, and she was only five and a half feet tall.

Papà waved his arm at his guest. "This is Mr. Camponeschi. We worked together at Marino's. He's the head waiter there now. Mr. Camponeschi, this is my eldest daughter, Angela."

"Antonio, I think the girl can call me by my given name, Romolo," the man said. His eyes slithered up and down Angela's body as he spoke.

"It's nice to meet you, Mr. Camponeschi." Angela frowned as she spoke, unhappy with Romolo's frank inspection and Papà's amused tolerance. He should have been insulted to have a man look at his daughter this way.

Though she had not held out her hand, he stepped forward and grasped her right hand between his two hands. His palms were cold and damp, like a three-day-old fish at the market.

He turned to Papà and said, "She's every bit as lovely as you said."

Papà nodded like a priest offering a benediction. "Romolo came here from Rome ten years ago. He has decided it is time to take a wife." Papà exchanged amused glances with Romolo. "We decided together. He will marry you."

"Papà!" Angela gasped. She staggered and reached for a nearby straight back chair to steady herself.

"Now, now, marriage will settle you. If you have a husband and some *bambinos* to look after, you won't have so much time to get into trouble."

"I haven't been in trouble, Papà," Angela said, backing toward the kitchen door. This could not be happening.

Romolo grinned at Angela, and she could see his large teeth were stained with tobacco. "Your Papà tells me of his trouble with his youngest daughter," he said. "She has fallen very far and your Papà, who loves you, would save you from that fate. And I have agreed to ignore your scandalous past and marry you anyway. Your Papà says you are a good worker. You will work hard to make our home."

Angela shook her head. *Where was Mamma? Did she agree to this horrible thing?*

"Mr. Camponeschi will support you and this household as well," Papà said.

"You're selling me to a waiter?" Angela's voice rose as she spoke, unable to keep herself from yelling.

Papà leapt across the room and grabbed Angela by the arm. His fingers dug into the tender flesh at her elbow. "Stop this right now," he hissed into her ear. "You will not embarrass me in front of this man."

Romolo Camponeschi caught up his hat and squeezed past Angela, taking care to pinch her bottom as he did. "I leave for work now. I shall return on Saturday to speak of wedding arrangements," he said.

When the proposed bridegroom had made his escape, Papà shook Angela so hard her head snapped back and forth like a rag doll. "You will marry this man or you will be dead to me. You will marry this man or leave this house and never see your Mamma again. I will not have you fall into sin like your sister," he said, holding her at arm's length. "Do you understand?"

Angela blinked back her tears. She would not cry in front of Papà, but she would not marry this Mr. Camponeschi either.

Or so she thought at the time. Mamma came home and made it clear she'd agreed to Papà and Mr. Camponeschi's scheme.

"I can't go against your father," she'd explained. "I'm his wife and you are his daughter and we have a duty to obey."

Two weeks later, Angela found herself in St. Cecelia's,

wearing a cream, two-tiered gown borrowed from one of the women who lived on the fifth floor.

She cried when she said "I do," but she said it.

And regretted it almost immediately.

Angela poked her nose into the icebox. *Where are those eggs?* Then she remembered. Romolo, who usually ate at Marino's, had insisted she make him breakfast this morning. She closed the icebox door and frowned at the bowl of hot, peeled potatoes. He'd seen her put them on to boil before he left and he'd be expecting gnocchi when he came home. That he arrived home well after midnight did not deter Romolo one bit. A wife should make her husband dinner—that's what he said. That he could easily eat at work before coming home, as he'd done before he married, played no part in his domestic logic.

She brushed her hands down her apron, feeling the firm roundness of the baby and smiled for a moment. A baby would make things better. Romolo would be nicer after his son came. And she'd have something of her own to love.

Angela stepped out the back door and went up the staircase at the back of the house. It was Romolo's house—as he never tired of reminding her—bought before he married her. They lived downstairs, while Marie and Nino lived upstairs. Nino and Marie hated Romolo, but they pretended well enough to keep the peace, as much as anyone could with him.

Anglea knocked once on the back door before opening it. "Marie?" she called.

Marie poked her head into the kitchen. "Oh, I was about to come down, as soon as I got my shoes on."

"You should not be walking down those stairs. You can't even see your feet. I told you, if you need anything, you should bang on the floor with your broom."

Marie stepped into the kitchen, her head about two feet behind her belly. Angela had a cute baby belly, but Marie, with her little body, was all belly these days.

"I'm fine. You fuss worse than Nino," Marie said rubbing her lower back after she kissed her sister. Angela thought Nino didn't fuss enough, but then again, neither did Romolo.

"Do you have any eggs? I need two," Angela said.

Marie opened her own icebox and pulled out a bowl of eggs. She motioned for Angela to sit and fetched a smaller bowl down from a shelf. She laid the eggs in the bowl and sat it in front of Angela.

"I was coming down with the newspaper. I'm restless," Marie said. Romolo didn't allow newspapers in the house. The only news Angela ever saw was courtesy of her visits upstairs.

"We can go for a walk around the block once I get the gnocchi made," Angela said.

"That sounds nice," Marie said with a tired smile. She pushed the paper in front of Angela and pointed to a long article on the left side of the front page. "Salcedo Found Dead. Elia Confesses," the headline read.

Angela read. According to the article, Andre Salcedo leapt from the fourteenth-floor office of the FBI, prompted to suicide by the guilt he felt about informing on his fellow Galleanists. Apparently, the FBI had a list of known associates with the anarchist group.

"He wouldn't," Angela said with more force than she intended.

"I know. That's what Nino says too. They killed him. We know they did. And lo and behold, Elia's suddenly willing to talk."

The FBI had picked up Roberto Elia and Andrea Salcedo in connection with a failed attempt on Attorney General Alexander Mitchell Palmer's life. The bomb exploded before the conspirators could leave it on Palmer's doorstep, killing the man who'd been holding it. Palmer hated leftists like nothing else, and he didn't differentiate between the syndicalist anarchists who believed in passive resistance and the violent Galleanist anarchists who'd been leaving bombs all over the northeast.

Angela eyed her sister. "Do you think they had anything to do with the bombing?" she asked.

"You still think it matters? They're scapegoats," Marie said.

"Then whoever put the bomb at Palmer's house ought to be ashamed. Violence always backfires, and then the workers suffer the consequences while the ideologues hide."

Marie frowned and rubbed her belly. "The government uses violence and gets away with it. Look at the Palmer Raid. They were typical Red Scare tactics, stomping all over democracy while pretending to protect it."

For two months, from December of last year to the end of January this year, a series of raids and deportations had wreaked havoc on unions, leftists, political parties, and anti-segregation organizations. The attorney general put most of his energies and men into breaking the mine workers strike, while his henchman J. Edgar Hoover, the new head of the FBI, took after the socialists and anarchists. They'd arrested over three thousand people in two months, all without legal arrest warrants. Palmer's men had undertaken interrogations so brutal, they'd made even Hoover nervous.

Angela shook her head. "The Palmer Raids were so heavy handed, even Congress objected," she said. "I read that the attorney general asked for $2 million to wipe out the American left and Congress gave him less than $100,000. And they've shut down the raids."

Palmer managed to have just over five hundred legal immigrants deported before the secretary of labor stepped in and put a stop to it, arguing that demands for better wages and working conditions didn't threaten democracy.

"Violence always backfires, for them and us," Angela said.

"Like there is an 'us.' Your husband won't hardly let you out of the house."

Angela patted her round stomach. "Once he has a son, he'll not be so bad. He's bound to get tired of me," she said.

What she didn't say was that Nino wasn't much better. Oh, he talked about equality plenty, but at home he expected his wife to cook and clean and keep her mouth shut.

"Tired of controlling you, you mean," Marie said. She pushed back from the table and stood. She watched her sister's shoulders slump in exhaustion.

"Does it matter? Any of it?" Angela asked.

Marie pulled Angela into a hug. "It does, silly one, but not right now. Right now you should get downstairs and get those eggs into your *patate* before they get cold. You'll have lumpy gnocchi if you don't. Then we'll go for a walk. Fresh air will do both of us good."

Two mornings later, Nino opened the kitchen door and waved at Angela. "Is he gone?" he asked.

Angela looked up from the dough she was kneading and nodded, too tired to speak. The baby had rolled and kicked all last night and she hadn't slept a wink.

Nino came over to her and dropped a light kiss on her cheek. "The chickens have come home to roost," he said.

"Chickens? We don't have chickens."

Her brother-in-law laughed. "No, not that. Remember Elia and Salcedo?"

"Uh-huh." She patted the ball of dough into a neat circle and dropped it into an oiled bowl.

"Elia told Carlo Tresca the truth about what happened on the fourteenth floor that day," Nino said.

Angela nodded and said, "I heard."

Elia told Carlo Tresca that the Feds had thrown Salcedo out the window and threatened to do the same to him if he didn't start talking. So Elia started talking. But after the FBI let him go, he regretted it and went to Tresca, who published the story in his newspaper.

Angela gestured Nino into a chair and poured him a cup of coffee.

"Well, Elia says he gave the Feds four names," Nino said. "And two days later, two of those men were arrested for a robbery and double murder. Someone killed two guards who were transporting some shoe company's payroll. Up in Massachusetts. And of course a witness said the men looked Italian."

"Looked Italian? What's that mean?" Angela asked. "Most Americans can't tell Italians from Greeks or Romanians."

Nino snorted. "You're not kidding. Isn't that a little two coincidental, even for the Feds? Elia names four men and days later two of them are arrested for murder?"

"Who is it? Do we know them?" Angela said, folding her dishrag and setting it aside before joining Nino at the table.

"I don't know them, but Carlo knows people who know

them. Nick Sacco and Bart Vanzetti. Vanzetti was the one working with Carlo on Elia's defense team."

"Are they Galleanists?"

"Tresca says not," Nino said. He bit his lower lip and frowned. "The funny thing is, he hates the Galleanists as much as anyone. He's denounced their violence and they've denounced him. So if Sacco and Vanzetti are violent Galleanists, wouldn't Tresca say so?"

Angela shrugged. "I'm not sure it matters. It's not like anyone in authority is going to care what Carlo Tresca says. One anarchist is as good as another. If they can't pin the Palmer bombing on them, they'll pin this murder on them, don't you think?" Angela said with a sigh. It wasn't like anything she had to say would change anything anyway. "Nino, I have laundry to hang out while the bread rises, so you scoot off to work."

"Oh, Angela," Nino said as he got to his feet. "You were the finest organizer I ever saw. What happened to you?"

You did, Angela thought, but didn't say. *If you hadn't snuck Tresca into Lawrence, you wouldn't have been kidnapped. And if you hadn't been kidnapped, Papà would never have found out about our trip and Marie wouldn't have run away and Papà wouldn't have forced me to marry Romolo.* Angela amended her thought. *You and Papà happened to me.*

Angela peered over the top of the pram at her sleeping baby. She tucked Oscar's tiny hand back under the blanket to protect against the chill before they continued toward the park. Not that a three-month-old baby could do anything at the park, but daily walks gave her something to do besides cook, clean, and wash diapers. Besides, Mamma said fresh air was good for babies.

Romolo wanted to give him an Italian name, but she'd stood firm. It was her baby and she wanted her son to have an American name, so she'd named him after her favorite writer, Oscar Wilde, much like Mamma named her last baby after the poet Percy Bysshe Shelley. Heck, Marie named her daughter Athena. Compared to that, Oscar was pretty tame.

Angela surveyed the park. Two months ago, when she and Marie first brought their babies here, the park had been full of children and mothers. But summer ended and the children went back to school. Now the park belonged to chattering squirrels and falling leaves. And Angela and Oscar.

She'd liked the noise and bustle of the summer park. It provided a contrast to the loneliness of her house, especially now that Marie was so busy with Athena. Part of the problem was that she felt left out and useless. Nino was helping with the defense committee for the men accused of those poor guards' murder. It was good he had something to do; he'd quit union organizing after his kidnapping, or at least after the Lawrence Strike ended. Nino talked a good game, but Angela thought he'd lost his nerve. And he knew it, and knew the rest of them knew it too. It embarrassed him, that's what Angela thought, and sometimes he took it out on Marie. Like most leftist men, Nino was no more liberal with his wife than men like Romolo—men who still had one foot in the old country.

She had to admit, Nino's work organizing the New York branch of the Sacco and Vanzetti Defense Committee had renewed his sense of importance. The committee, which was headquartered in Boston, thought the two-month gap between Sacco and Vanzetti's arrest and indictment proved the weakness of the prosecution's case, but Angela wasn't so sure. She'd agreed to allow Nino to use the house for some meetings, but Nino didn't want Angela or Marie involved, so the sisters contributed only coffee and cookies.

She'd agreed to Nino's scheme, not just because she was bored, but because Romolo was gone all the time. He'd fired two waiters and he'd been working the lunch shifts as well as his dinner shift until he could hire more help. He had a hiring problem because he wanted Italian men who weren't political—they were as hard to come by in the waiter class as they were among factory workers.

Oscar made tiny kitten sounds in his sleep. Angela bounced the pram gently and he settled down. Mamma said babies liked movement and she was right; Oscar certainly did. When he was cranky, she'd put him in his carriage and push him down the street, and he'd be fast asleep before they came to the first corner.

Angela found herself continually amazed that she'd made this tiny creature. The depth of her love for this small scrap of humanity surprised her over and over again. She wondered at Mamma's courage now. How had she ever let her daughters out of the house? The world was such a dangerous place and a mother's love was so big. It was scary, this love business. Angela knew with a certainty that if anything ever happened to Oscar, it would destroy her. But still she felt tired and resentful nearly all the time. She loved Oscar, but it wasn't enough. Did all new mothers feel this way, or just her?

The baby kicked out his feet like a swimming frog and opened his eyes, blinking as if surprised to find himself awake.

Angela stroked the fine black hair on his head, leaned into the carriage, and planted a soft kiss on his forehead. "Time for lunch, huh?" she said, and pushed the pram home.

~

Thump, thump, thump sounded on the exterior back stairs. Angela opened the kitchen door before Marie could knock.

Marie kissed Angela on both cheeks and leaned back to look at her sister. She sniffed the air. "Athena took forever to fall asleep. Is something burning?" she asked.

Angela groaned. "I made a pandoro, but I forgot about it while I was getting Oscar ready for bed and burned it to a crisp. And I didn't want to leave the windows open and have the baby catch a chill," Angela explained.

"It's not a house party, silly. It's a meeting," Marie laughed. "If the men want cake, they can stop at a bakery and buy one, for goodness' sake. Here, we'll put on some coffee and no one will smell anything else."

While Marie bustled around the kitchen, Angela pulled the chairs into the living room. She couldn't help being nervous. If Romolo found out, he'd be furious—but it was just so exciting to have something happening in her house. Marie offered her and Nino's place, but their upstairs apartment was about half the size of the downstairs space, and made smaller by the sloping ceiling. Anglea wasn't very tall and even she sometimes bumped her head on the ceiling—the trick was to stay away from the walls.

"Where's Nino?" Angela asked.

"Oh, he's coming. He went into the city to fetch the men," Marie said. "Some of them wanted to meet at John's or Vesuvio's, if you can believe that. You'd think crossing the East River was the equivalent of traversing the arctic."

John's was John's Spaghetti House. Both it and Vesuvio's

were East Harlem restaurants with back rooms usually filled with leftists and unionists. They were also well known to the police.

Nino arrived less than thirty minutes later with Carlo Tresca and a handful of other men. Angela could hardly contain herself. To think, the great man himself was in her living room in Flushing.

Tresca wore a soft wool coat with matching waistcoat and a gray-dotted bow tie. He kissed Angela's hand and hugged Marie like a sister before turning away to speak to a knot of men standing near the front door. Nino introduced Angela to Aldino Felicani, a small dark-haired man from Boston, and then a round-headed balding man named John Dos Passos.

"John just published a novel based on his experience in the war," Tresca said by way of introduction.

"Any good?" Angela asked with a grin.

Dos Passos threw back his head and laughed. "Critics can't make up their minds. It comes down to how you feel about the war, I suppose," he said.

Angela raised an eyebrow in question.

Dos Passos stopped smiling and leaned toward Angela. "I don't have to tell you we live in an age of compulsory patriotism, backed up by hysteria and fear. But any man who fought will tell you there's nothing grand or noble about war. It's a dirty business."

"So your novel is antiwar?" she asked.

"As would be the novel of any man who fought in the trenches. Only the rich stay-at-homes are pro-war. War costs them nothing and garners them much," he said.

Before he could say more, Nino called the meeting to order.

Aldino Felicani retrieved a worn leather satchel from the

floor near the front door and pulled from it a sheaf of papers. He rifled through them, then looked up and surveyed the room. "I thought Luigi would be here," he said.

"He's coming," Nino replied.

"He's been managing *Il Martello* in my absence," Tresca said, looking chagrined. "I'm afraid my newspaper is a demanding mistress."

"Well then," Felicani said. "I shall begin. As you all know, we are here to gather supporters for the defense committee. New York City has too many committed men to ignore."

"And women," Marie murmured in Angela's ear.

Angela bumped shoulders with her sister in agreement. It was ever thus, that even radical men could speak of equality while ignoring women.

"As some of you know, the Italian anarchists of Boston are loosely organized into the Gruppo Autonomo, of which myself and Tresca are members," Felicani continued. "In response to the Palmer Raids, some of our more radical members split from Gruppo. This faction has been tied to a number of bombings. I need not point out that neither Sacco nor Vanzetti are in this faction, but the bombers' affiliation with Gruppo has stained all Boston anarchists. In the weeks after Sacco and Vanzetti were arrested, we at Gruppo formed the Sacco-Vanzetti Defense Committee. I am the treasurer of that committee."

Angela listened with rapt attention. Nothing this exciting had ever happened in her living room.

Carlo Tresca held up a hand and said, "If I might interrupt for a moment."

Felicani waved at Tresca to signal his assent.

"Most of you in this room don't know Aldino, but let me assure you, his credentials are impeccable," Tresca said. "He came to America only five years ago, fleeing rising fascism in Italy. During last year's flu epidemic, he took over *La Notizia* when its editor died."

"Also, I consider Bartolomeo Vanzetti one of my personal friends," Mr. Felicani said with a small smile. "I have a selfish reason for keeping him out of jail. He sold the best fish in Boston and I love grilled octopus above all things."

Marie bumped Angela and whispered, "Gross."

Angela nearly laughed out loud. Mamma used to serve octopus in a red sauce, which Marie would refuse to eat. She feared the little suckers would grab her teeth and hang on. One night, Mamma left the tentacles in long pieces. Angela bit onto the ends of two such pieces and then chased Marie around the apartment while the tentacles wiggled and bumped on her chin. Papà had been at work that night, so the three of them had laughed and laughed.

Mr. Felicani ignored Marie and Angela and continued. "I've rented an office in the same building as the newspaper. We've collected some money to pay the rent and buy two secondhand typewriters and a file cabinet. I have volunteers typing up letters seeking contributions. It would be helpful if we had something like that in New York because we all know Sacco and Vanzetti's defense is going to take huge sums of money."

"The country's so anti-immigrant right now," Nino said. "As if all immigrants were bomb-throwing killers."

"People are afraid," Tresca said. "Afraid the old order will crumble under the weight of its corruption. Afraid of the violence that may erupt from either side. Afraid, afraid, afraid."

"It is that," Felicani said. "But it is more than that. I'll tell you a story." He paused until all eyes were on him. "We had a phone call only a month ago from a man who said he could free

Sacco and Vanzetti. Naturally, I agreed to meet with this man. He brought with him a young woman who worked as a court interpreter and speaks a half dozen languages. Little did I know, one was the language of lies. At our first meeting, Miss DeFalco said that for $50,000 she could get Katzmann's brother to act as Sacco and Vanzetti's defense lawyer."

"Who's Katzmann?" Angela couldn't help but ask.

Felicani looked startled, as if he'd forgotten the two women were there. He looked over his glasses at Angela. "Oh, well, yes. He's the district attorney in Boston, so he's in charge of prosecuting the case against Sacco and Vanzetti," he said.

"Ah," Angela said. "So if you hired his brother, he'd have to recuse himself."

Felicani smiled at her understanding and said, "Just so, young lady. Just so."

Angela bristled. No doubt he thought she was stupid. Before she could tell the man she had a high school education, Felicani returned to his tale.

"The idea was to hire Percy Katzmann for our side, forcing the case into the hands of the district attorney's lackeys. But $50,000 is a great deal of money. I asked Miss DeFalco to arrange a meeting between myself and Percy Katzmann, but she kept putting me off until at last I became suspicious. One night, I followed her back to her house. After waiting a long while, I saw the district attorney enter the lady's home."

"They were trying to trap you," one of the men said.

Felicani pinched his lips together and nodded. "I asked a friend to wire our office with a microphone and then invited Miss DeFalco for a meeting. I had a stenographer in the basement listening and taking notes, you see. I asked Miss DeFalco about what I'd seen. At first she denied it, but I pressed her and she admitted to everything, no doubt thinking there was nothing I could do about it."

"It's just so byzantine," Angela said. "And illegal, right?"

"In theory," Nino said. He stood up and paced the room. "But of course, when Felicani took the notes to the judge, the judge called in Miss DeFalco, who cried pretty tears and swore the nasty anarchists were making it all up. So who do you think the judge believed?"

Felicani waved Nino back into his seat. "My point is that the case is complicated and expensive. And make no mistake, gentlemen: without money, Vanzetti and Sacco will be executed."

Just then the front door burst open and a man wearing a gray pinstriped suit stepped into the living room. "I'm here," he cried with a wave of his hat.

Felicani stood and hugged the newcomer before ushering him to the chair Nino hastily vacated. As the newcomer took his seat, Nino came over and leaned against the wall next to his wife.

"Who's that?" Marie whispered to Nino.

Before Nino could answer, Felicani spoke. "May I introduce you to my most esteemed defense committee partner, Luigi Quintiliano"

Luigi stood and made a small bow.

Angela could hardly take her eyes off the man. He wasn't very tall, really not much taller than she was, nor was he terribly handsome. He had a fleshy nose and a receding hairline. And yet there was something vital about him, some vibration of unbounded life force. He seemed to take up more space than the other men.

When he spoke, it was with a thick Roman accent. "I am sorry, gentlemen," he said, pausing to spare a glance at Marie and Angela. She could feel his gaze hook her like a fish on a line.

She held his eyes and her breath until he looked back to the men in the room. "And ladies. There is no excuse for my lateness, but for the excuse of work. And I know that no work is more important than the work of the defense committee. What we do is a matter of life and death."

Marie shot Angela a look that said, "Who is this guy?"

As if he'd heard the question, Felicani spoke: "Luigi is my right-hand man in our defense work. I met him while he was working on the Italian Defense Committee, which did much good work in stopping the Palmer Raids."

Luigi held up a hand. "We were also in Charleston after the race riot last summer," he said. "It was our investigation that prompted the US Navy to find five white men responsible for the violence that injured eighteen black men. If we have a result half as satisfying with this committee, we will have succeeded."

Marie slipped behind Angela and backed into the kitchen. Angela heard her sister fooling around with the coffee pot and reluctantly joined her. They made more coffee, picked up dirty plates and cups, washed dishes, and swept out the kitchen while the meeting went on.

Angela watched the clock and became increasingly nervous. Finally, she tiptoed over to Nino and whispered in his ear. Nino looked at his watch and announced an end to the meeting. "The last train to Manhattan leaves at 11:15 and it is a ten-minute walk to the Long Island Railroad terminal," he said.

Angela and Marie were still cleaning up when Luigi came into the kitchen. "I hear we have you ladies to thank for this safe meeting place?" he said.

Marie pushed Angela forward and said, "It's my sister's house."

Angela felt herself blush. "It's my husband's house," she said.

She didn't add that he was due home any minute and she needed to have all evidence of the meeting cleaned up before that.

"Ah, you are married," he said. He stepped up to her and took her hand in his. "All the best ladies are," he murmured and kissed the back of her hand.

It felt to Angela like a bolt of lightning had struck her hand. Heat flushed through her as she pulled back her hand. "Mr. Quintiliano, it was nice to meet you," she said.

He looked into her eyes. "Luigi. You will call me Luigi." He nodded at Marie, turned, and was gone.

That night she thought about that kiss after Romolo fell asleep. She thought about it more the next day. But the days went on, filled with diapers and dinners, and eventually Angela forgot Luigi Quintiliano. At least, that's what she told herself.

But more than that, she thought about how exciting it would be to be one of the defense committee members, doing important work. Not that taking care of Oscar wasn't important. But it wasn't very exciting, was it? Men could be fathers and revolutionaries, but women were supposed to be only mothers.

It didn't seem fair.

Part III

1926-1927

Chapter Seven

PULLING THE POWER

*"Things can be too cheap. I pity the man who wants
a coat so cheap that the man or woman who produces
the cloth will starve in the process."*
—Benjamin Harrison, twenty-third
President of the United States, 1891

November 1926

Angela stood in front of the apartment house, purse clutched
in her hands. She shivered, partly against the November
wind and partly in fear. All this money made her nervous. That,
and he was late. *Maybe he isn't coming at all?* Policemen worked
all hours of the day and night, and even a devoted son might
occasionally miss Sunday dinner with his mamma. Between
work and family, she didn't have time any day but Sunday, and
next Sunday might be too late.

A gust of wind caught the brim of her hat. She clapped a

hand on top of her head and wondered what she was doing here. She should be home with her boys.

A man in a dark suit rounded the eastern corner. Angela took a step in his direction and stopped. Though the man wore a soft cap, she could see he was bald. He doffed his hat as he passed her. She tried to smile but failed.

Initially, she'd planned on waiting for Detective Fiaschetti outside police headquarters on Center Street, but Clara thought she'd have a better chance of success if she approached the head of the NYPD's Italian squad away from police headquarters. Clara Larsen worked for the Local 25 and she knew everyone important in New York, including the detective's mother. From that lady Clara learned about Fiaschetti's habit of taking Sunday dinner at his mother's apartment.

Two older, black-clad women walked by, both carrying baskets of produce. The smaller of the two gave Angela a hard stare, as if she knew Angela was up to no good. Angela straightened her spine and shoulders and tried to look innocent, but her stomach bucked and rolled. *I can't do it.* She turned for the trolley, which would take her to the Long Island train and back home.

And then there he was, just as Clara described. Dark hair slicked back with pomade, shoulders broad, striding toward her with a kind of military precision. She'd chosen Fiaschetti because everyone said he was honest and that he hated the criminals who gave the rest of the Italians a bad name. His checkered career had given him a soft spot for the downtrodden too. Back in the first decade of this century, he'd been second in command of the NYPD Italian Squad, but then his commander died and the Irishmen who controlled the department disbanded the squad, demoted its members to patrolmen, and scattered them across the city. Then Prohibition came and the Italian crime families ran amuck. The new police commissioner reformed the Italian Squad with Fiaschetti at its head.

"Excuse me," Angela said, her voice wavering. She swallowed and tried again. "Please, sir, are you Lieutenant Fiaschetti?"

He stopped in front of her. "I am. I don't mean to be rude, but mother is expecting me and I'm late. If you would come to my office tomorrow, during working hours, perhaps I could help you then?"

"I don't. I mean. It's not." *How did one bribe a respected policeman with a reputation for honesty?*

He saw her distress and led her over to a nearby sidewalk bench.

She took a deep breath and blurted out: "I need some help. Well, the ladies of the Local 22 need your help."

"Hmm. Aren't they out on strike?" he asked.

"Yes, sir. We have a real chance of winning. It's three union shops, you see, and more than fifteen thousand workers out on strike. We've been out for eighteen weeks and the shops are bound to come to the bargaining table any day now."

"Then I don't understand how I can help you." He spoke gently, as if to a child.

Angela sighed. She'd given him the wrong impression. She wasn't afraid of him, but what she was about to ask made her nervous. Charles 'Sasha' Zimmerman, the man who ran the 22, thought he should come with her, but Angela knew a man would be more likely to help a lone, young, attractive woman, particularly if both of them were Italian Americans. Sasha's wife Rose agreed with Angela and that sealed the deal.

"I'm sure you know that the New York Police Department has rarely been on the side of strikers," she explained.

He nodded. "There has been some regrettable violence on both sides."

Uh-uh. We're not playing that game, not even if I don't get what I want, she thought. Then she said, "I'm sure it seems that way to you, sir, but we strikers never instigate the violence. It is not in our best interest to do so. The newspapers say otherwise, but rich men who support other rich men own the newspapers. It is the rich men who pay the police as well, as I'm sure you know. The rich men and their police blame the workers so they can maintain the current system."

"I've run into some of that with my fight against the crime families," he said, nodding. "There are many powerful men who do not want the illegal rum running interrupted. There's simply too much money to be made on the black market."

"Exactly. So, you see, I'm on a picket line at a factory in the Bowery. Each morning the police set up a machine gun on the sidewalk opposite where we're marching and point it at us. And still, we show up. Hundreds of women, some no older than fifteen years old, and we fight for the right for a decent wage and a clean, safe shop. With a machine gun pointed at us."

He had the good grace to look shocked. "And you want me to do something about that? Because I can."

"Thank you, Detective, but there's more. We hear that tomorrow the police will attack us. We're going to pull the power and the owner knows. They always know. Union organizing is a leaky business and someone always informs."

"Pull the power?" he asked. "If that's what I think, then you need to know, young lady, that I won't be part of a criminal enterprise. Violence against property is illegal."

Angela nearly laughed. "Oh, no, it's not what you think. A pull down means to push your way onto the shop floor, turn off the power to the sewing machines, and talk to the strikebreakers inside the shop. Usually, the shop managers try to lock us out, but there aren't many locks we can't get past. But if the police attack us before we get to it, then all would be lost, especially with that machine gun."

Lieutenant Fiaschetti unclasped his hands and rubbed at his woolen suit trousers. Angela took the opportunity to open her purse and pull out an envelope. "I've collected ten dollars," she said.

He stood and glared at her. "Young lady, you mistake yourself. I am not for sale."

Angela rose to look him in the eyes. "I know you are not for sale," she said. "That's why I came to you. But you must agree that some of your brethren are. I collected this money yesterday—ten cents here, fifty cents there—from women who could not afford to give it to me. Women who've been out on strike, not earning wages, so their children will have something better one day. The money is to buy the men from the Fifth Precinct who've been paid to attack us. They won't be called off, not even by you, unless they are paid."

The police lieutenant let out a great gust of air. "I see," he said, and took the money.

Philip stirred in his bed, restless even in his sleep. Angela stroked his head, surprised as she always was at the silkiness of her son's hair. The first two years of his life he'd hardly slept, or that's how it felt at the time. Other three-year-olds took naps, but not Philip, though he did sleep through the night now. He made a small, contented sound and settled again. Angela stepped over to Oscar's bed. While Philip retained some of his babyness, at six,

Oscar was a little boy. She smiled at the memory of him dressed for his first day of school, lunch pail in hand.

Angela pressed a soft kiss to Oscar's cheek. His eyelashes fluttered. "Shh," she whispered. He puffed out a little breath of air and slept on.

She tiptoed out to the kitchen. It wouldn't do to wake Romolo either. He'd come in well after 2:00 a.m., smelling of cooking grease and red wine. The restaurant was still slow, a victim of the proliferation of Italian restaurants and pizza parlors that had sprung up in East Harlem the last few years. When Mr. Conti first cut her husband's shifts back, they'd struggled to pay the bills. But nearly a year ago, when she weaned Oscar, she suggested she go back to work. She'd been sure Romolo would say no, that he'd yell and call her names, maybe even hit her like he did when she really upset him, but he hadn't. Instead he'd said the household didn't need two women sitting around doing nothing while the men worked. He agreed that she could go back to sewing while Marie watched the children.

Angela let the "doing nothing" talk pass without comment. Romolo only ever saw the clean house, the folded laundry, the freshly made food, and not the backbreaking work that led to all the minor domestic miracles he took for granted. She'd wanted to go back to work badly enough that she let him think he was getting his way.

Not that she didn't love her boys—or Marie's girls, for that matter—but the endless work of housekeeping and mothering filled her head with a lumpy gray feeling. And then Nino would sit down to dinner with them and talk about his day at the newspaper and the latest union battle, and all she could think was, "Why not me?" Then the bad dreams returned—the ones with the endless coffins of burned and broken women—and she'd wake feeling guilty and ashamed, though of what she wasn't sure.

Grabbing her shoes and coat, she left her kitchen behind and tiptoed up the back stairs. Marie was pouring a cup of coffee when Angela opened the door. Angela nearly laughed aloud; no matter how quiet she was, her sister always knew she was coming and she always had the coffee ready to go.

Marie held out a chipped white mug. "It's the big day, isn't it?" she asked.

Angela blew across the surface of her coffee before taking a sip. "It is if the Lieutenant succeeded. If the machine gun is there, I'll call it off." She sipped again, then said, "What about you?"

Marie grinned at her sister. "Nothing so exciting as your day, I'm sure. I'll take Oscar and Athena to school and then come home. It's laundry day, so after I hang out the sheets maybe I'll take Philip and Clytia to the park."

Their deal was that Marie watched the four children: Angela's sons and Marie's daughters, Athena and Clytia. Angela split her earnings between the two households, which was only fair, even if it irritated Romolo. The way he saw it, Marie and Nino were taking money from his household. It didn't help that he hated Nino, whom he considered no better than an effete rabble-rouser. But complain as he did, Romolo needed Marie. It wasn't as if he was going to get Oscar to school or do any of the hundred tasks that needed doing every day. "My sons," he always said. "My sons this and my sons that," though he did little for them or with them. To Romolo, the fact that Nino fathered daughters was all the proof he needed that his brother-in-law was a failure. Sometimes Angela wondered how her husband's brain worked.

Angela gulped down the rest of her coffee and slipped on her coat and shoes. "Could you pick up some milk on your way home from the school this morning? We're out and you know how Romolo is about his caffe latte," she said.

"I know. Now go." Marie pushed a lunch pail into Angela's hand and waved her toward the door. "You'll be late for the 7:15 if you don't get going."

Angela kissed her sister and left the house for work. Waged work, she reminded herself. Staying home to take care of the babies was work too, though Marie earned not one penny for it. Angela thanked the Holy Mother for giving her a sister like Marie.

She worked a half day at the shop before leaving for the pickets. She'd been lucky to find this job; she wasn't as fast with a sewing machine as some of the women, but this shop didn't care much about speed. Angela thought the difference was that the shop owner was a woman—a smart woman who used to be a worker. The owner figured out that workers didn't like assembly line work. There was nothing more awful than sewing the same seam over and over, all day long, day after day. Workers who made something from start to finish took pride in their work. Mrs. Benning figured out that her shop could make better dresses, ones she could sell at a higher price than assembly line dresses. And the workers would work for slightly less because it was so fun to finish a garment. Mrs. Benning understood that happy employees worked harder, missed less work, and needed replacing less often.

Plus, Mrs. Benning didn't mind a union shop. She was happy to have weekly fire drills and just as happy to give them bathroom breaks and a decent lunch break. Tired and hungry workers were inefficient workers. All of these things seemed so fundamentally sensible that Angela had no idea why all shop owners didn't adopt them, but most couldn't see past their noses. They'd drive workers like automatons, complain about the cost of shorter hours and safety measures, and not understand that it didn't have to be that way.

Mrs. Benning once told Angela that the problem with American manufacturing was that businesses were selling people the idea that it was better to have more stuff, not better stuff. So American women had many poorly made, inexpensive dresses, instead of two or three well-made dresses.

Mrs. Benning believed in her kind of shop, a union shop that treated employees like humans and made a quality product. Angela worked a half shift, then she'd eat her lunch with the girls before walking a few blocks to the coat factory her other girls were picketing. And the ILGWU paid her a little to do it, so she didn't lose any pay.

Six months ago, the union sent Angela to a factory that made men's coats after someone reported the women workers were making less than the men, though they did the same work. Angela got the coat factory to hire her and then she started talking to the women. It was the only way to talk union with workers. She had to convince them to take the chance, and she did that by showing them she was one of them. No worker in America worked at a terrible job for the fun of it. A good union organizer started by just getting the workers to admit that things could be better.

In some shops it was safety issues, while in others it was wages or breaks or the length of the work week. For the factories that made men's suits and coats, the problem was generally wage equity. Historically, tailors were skilled workers who made good money, but factory-made suits put most tailors out of business.

The tailors ended up working for the same factories that had driven them out of business, but those men never lost their sense of themselves as skilled workers, deserving of a living wage—which was reasonable, except that the women who worked at the same factories made half as much as the men.

After a lot of talking, she'd plan a meeting and get some of the women to agree to come. When the lady coat makers met, they'd been angry, angry, angry. It always surprised Angela how passionate female workers could be about wage inequality. Union officials, who were always men, said women were impossible to organize, especially immigrant women. That wasn't Angela's experience. At their first meeting she let the women talk for over an hour, one woman after another expressing her outrage, before introducing the union idea.

They didn't decide anything at their first meeting, nor at their second. But after the third meeting, some of the female workers went to the boss. Angela hung back, letting the women who'd been at the factory longest take the lead. Miss Mack, a rawboned woman with a Kentucky accent, made their case, but the boss wouldn't listen and threatened to fire them if they didn't get back to work.

Miss Mack stood up to him. "This discrimination must end. Otherwise, we will not work," she said.

Angela loved Miss Mack. A good union organizer didn't lead; she got out of the way and let the workers lead. Or at least, that's how she thought of her job.

Before they'd gone on strike, Angela and Miss Mack tried one more time to reason with the owner. "If you pay the women the same amount as the men, they won't go out," Miss Mack told him.

"Women are not supposed to be tailors," the shop owner

said. "Men's clothing is too technical and exacting for the female mind."

"But you hire women to do the same work as the men," Angela argued. "It's only fair you pay women the same as men."

"I won't do it. My tailors would leave me if I paid the women more."

"What should they care what the women make, as long as their wage doesn't change?" Angela countered.

"But they do care. And if the women don't like it, they can go somewhere else. They don't have to work here," he said.

So the women went on strike, joining the ongoing Cloak-maker's Strike, backed by ILGWU Locals 2, 9, and 22. And though by trade she was a dressmaker, which is what they called anyone who made women's clothes, she joined the picket lines with the cloakmakers, or the makers of men's clothing. Luigi Antonini, who was a big shot with the union, didn't like the dressmakers supporting the cloakmakers on the principle that it was too revolutionary, but Angela knew he was wrong. Most Americans didn't care what a worker was called, nor did they care what local the workers joined. Some people were pro-union and some were not, and that was that.

Most of the male Italian union leaders agreed with Antonini, but the Jewish men did not, probably because Jewish men and women had a long history of resistance to oppression. Angela had to wonder: what good was a union that wouldn't organize half the workers? Or agreed with the owners that women should earn less than men? That's why the union was so divided these days. The traditional unionists only wanted to organize skilled workers, which was a polite way of saying they only wanted to organize native-born men. The socialists and communists wanted to organize everyone, male, female, black, and white.

Angela didn't much care about politics and who was in and who was out. She'd decided long ago that she'd align herself with anyone who was for all the workers, not just the ones at the top of the pile. Those poor women at Misery Lane had been at the bottom of the pile, which is why they ended up dead.

When Angela finally arrived at today's strike site, she found over thirty women on the picket line. Miss Mack pointed across the street. "Did ya see?" she said excitedly.

Angela hollered back, "I did!"

The sidewalk across the street was empty. No policemen, no machine gun. Lieutenant Fiaschetti had come through.

Rose Zimmerman came over and kissed Angela on the cheek. "We're on?"

"Yes, we are" Angela said, nodding. "Where's Sasha?" Though technically Sasha Zimmerman managed Local 22, in reality he and his wife Rose were co-managers. Rose was the one who'd helped Angela convince Sasha to let her organize without him. Angela liked both of them a lot, admiring the way their partnership was both professional and personal. Plus, they were both so dedicated to fairness and equality. Sasha was working on getting the Local 22 to organize black workers and though he hadn't had much luck, Angela thought he had the right idea. As long as unions refused to organize black Americans they'd be used as cheap labor, to the detriment of themselves and union- ized workers.

"He thinks it would be best if this was just the women," Rose said.

Angela agreed. If there were even one man in the group of fifty women, the shop owner would assume that man was the leader and would talk only to him.

"Gather round, everyone," Angela called to the picketers. "Put your signs down and gather round!"

When all the women had circled around her, Angela spoke again. "All right, ladies. If we can get the scabs with us, then we'll break this shop and you'll all get raises. Are you ready?"

A chorus of assents rose up into the cool fall air.

Miss Mack spoke up. "We're going to push in and pull the power," she said. "We will succeed."

"That's right!" Rose yelled. "The Push In and Power Pull are time-tested strategies, used by organizers for decades. We push—we do not get pushed. But if we are met with violence, we do not react with violence."

The ladies cheered again. Miss Mack and Angela led them to the building's front door and up the stairs. The coat factory took up the fifth and sixth floors, with the owner's offices on the sixth. They rounded the stairs on the fifth floor and were halfway to the sixth when a man appeared in the shop doorway, his shirtsleeves rolled up to expose bulging arms. Angela knew if she faltered, the women behind her would falter as well. She met the man on the landing, bolstered by the crowd of women behind her.

He took another step, bringing himself right up in her face, and said, "Go away. You commies are not welcome here."

Miss Mack stepped back, but Angela held her ground. "We're not commies," Angela said. "We're women, like your mothers and sisters and wives. We want to talk to the workers inside."

"It's a closed shop," he roared. He shoved Angela so hard that she felt her feet leave the ground. She flew backwards, and before she had a chance to feel fear or panic, she landed in the arms of the women behind her. Rose and Miss Mack set her back on her feet.

Rose ran up the few stairs to the landing. "You should be ashamed of yourself," she half yelled. "What would your mother say if she knew you were pushing women?"

To his credit, the man's face reddened. "The boss says you can't come in," he said.

Angela stepped up beside Rose. "You can keep pushing us, but we are many and we're coming in one way or another," she said.

The man looked down the stairs at all the women. He stepped forward and in a soft voice said, "You're going to have to make it look good or the boss won't pay me. I got kids to feed too."

"Let's go, girls," Angela cried.

A cheer went up as the women pushed past the man into the shop. Once on the factory floor, someone found the power switch and pulled it. The roar of the sewing machines went quiet. Less than a third of the sewing machines had women sitting at them, while a full cadre of male cutters lined a table at the far wall.

Angela climbed onto a table. The pale faces of women at the sewing machines looked up at her in wonder. "You are working for half the wage of the men over there," Angela said to them, waving at the male cutters.

"You think any job, even an unfair job, is better than no job, but I'm here to tell you that if you stand with us, you can have both. A fair job. And you men, you should want that too. One day, the underpaid worker might be your daughter."

The picketers behind her cheered.

Miss Mack hollered, "Discrimination is an abomination."

When Angela told the women at the sewing machines that the union would cover their wages, most of them pushed back their chairs and joined them—not all, but most. As they marched off the shop floor, the owner came out of his office and stared at the women strikers.

Angela felt that old, wild feeling. There was no tougher job for a woman than union organizer. You talked until your mouth went dry and worked to keep workers from changing their minds about a strike, but in moments like this, it was all worth it.

They marched down the stairs, the fifty-plus picketers and the two dozen who'd just joined them. When they stepped out of the building, a pair of policemen stood on the sidewalk.

The older of the two thwacked his billy club against his thigh and asked, "Okay, who's the ringleader among ya?"

Miss Mack started to step forward, but Angela held her back. "I am," Angela said with a defiant lift of her chin.

"You're under arrest, ya guinea wop," the policeman said.

"On what charge?" Angela asked.

"Disturbing the peace. And trespassing."

He grabbed Angela and cuffed her. As he dragged her away, she yelled over her shoulder, "Someone call Nino."

They hauled her to the 5th Precinct house and threw her in a dank jail cell that smelled like old socks and cat pee. She laid awake all night, worrying about Philip and Oscar. She'd never been away from them overnight before, not until now. The next day, the police took her before a judge. The judge wouldn't let her speak in her own defense and no one offered her a lawyer. She got thirty days in jail and the judge wouldn't let the union bail her out. He said she'd have to serve her sentence, so she'd learn a woman's place was in the home.

They took her back to the large cell at the precinct and left her there. Each day that passed seemed like a year. At lunchtime, three women in face paint and gaudy dresses joined her, and later in the afternoon the doors opened to admit a pair of black women and a white, yellow-haired woman with an Appalachian accent.

On her second night in jail, one of the black women came over and pointed at the painted ladies, who were crowded around a deck of cards. "They have the clap," she said, "so stay away from them."

Angela wondered if she had a choice, but none of the women ever showed the slightest interest in her, except a for group of immigrant women who taught her a Hungarian card game. After twenty-two days, the police let her out. For good behavior, the jailer said.

Marie and Nino met her outside the precinct house and took her home.

Romolo hit her a few times before dinner, but not very hard. After dinner, he more fully expressed his displeasure at her arrest and imprisonment. Once he left for work the next day, she packed a bag for herself and another for the boys, and left the house with them. She never went back.

Chapter Eight

A LOSING BATTLE

*"The perfect woman, you see, is a working woman, not
an idler, not a fine lady, but one who uses her hands
and her head and her heart for the good of others."*
—Thomas Hardy, 1891

May 1927

Angela used her borrowed key to unlock the door to Clara
Larsen's apartment. Clara would say it was *their* apartment, but it didn't feel that way. Angela didn't know where she
belonged. Not in the house in Flushing with Romolo, that much
was for sure, nor with Papà and Mamma on East 103rd. Not
that Papà would allow her to move home, even if she wanted
to. Thank the Blessed Virgin he let the boys stay there. Mamma
could take care of them so she could earn the money to support
them, money Mamma badly needed now that Romolo wasn't

helping anymore. Angela didn't think she could live apart from her boys much longer, but for now they were all safe and happy.

She hadn't realized how hard it had been for all of them to live with Romolo until they didn't anymore. Papà, who'd never seemed all that fond of his children, thought his grandsons could do no wrong. The boys laughed more now and played like little boys, unworried about waking their own Papà or upsetting him in any of a number of mysterious ways.

Her low heels click-clacked across the floor, echoing in the empty apartment. *Was there a meeting today?* Deciding there wasn't, Angela pushed open one window, then another, letting in the cooling late-afternoon air. She knocked lightly on the bedroom door, just in case Clara or her husband, Christian were home. He was hardly ever home—which was one of the reasons why Clara asked Angela to stay with her. He'd been organizing silk mills in Patterson, New Jersey, the past year and the empty apartment gave Clara the willies.

Angela pinned her hat and sailed it across the room so it landed on a trunk she and Clara found in a secondhand shop. They'd laughed themselves silly dragging it up the three flights of stairs and now it served as Angela's makeshift closet. Before she could do more, the door flung itself open with such vigor that it bounced off the wall.

"Honey," Clara called. "I'm home." She trip-trapped over to Angela on spiky heels, as quick as a hummingbird, and kissed Angela on the cheek. "I'm just dying for a drink, and I don't mean noodle juice. After the day I've had, I intend to get spifflicated."

Before she met Clara, Angela had thought flappers existed only in the movies. Then she'd met the small blonde and learned differently. Though, for all her slang, she was a top-notch union organizer.

Angela grinned at Clara. "How about we go down to Russo's? They have the best bourbon Manhattans."

Clara pulled a bottle from her purse and waved it around her head. "Anything but that. I'm all out of cabbage, but one of the girls at the 25 gave me a spiffing bottle of giggle juice—something her pop makes in the bathtub. Oh, that reminds me. I ran into a delivery boy downstairs. He said this was for you," Clara said, pulling a large brown envelope out of her purse and handing it over to Angela. "It's too hoity-toity to be union stuff."

Angela had to agree. The upper-left corner was printed with a lawyer's return address in a stiff, formal script. Nothing good ever came from lawyer's offices.

"Go ahead. Only a dumb Dora would ignore something that looked like that," Clara said. She bustled around the apartment, pulling out glasses and genially creating chaos.

With a sigh, Angela ran a thumbnail under the envelope flap and slipped out the papers folded within. They had the kind of official look that confirmed they'd come from a law office. The first page said Romolo Camponeschi was suing Angela Camponeschi for divorce. No surprise there. In fact, the divorce papers were kind of a relief. She'd been afraid Romolo would try to force her back to him. Then she read on. Her knees buckled. Angela reached out and grabbed the back of a kitchen chair.

"What's wrong, darling?" Clara asked. She sat a bottle on the table with a thunk and grabbed Angela by the elbow. "Sit before you fall down." She pulled out a chair with a scrape and pushed Angela down.

Angela looked down at the papers. Her stomach heaved. She took a deep breath.

"What is it?" Clara leaned over Angela, her voice as soft as a lover's.

Tears blurred Angela's vision. He couldn't. He didn't hate her that much, did he? Her stomach heaved and rolled. She made it to the sink before the contents of her stomach came heaving back up. She retched until her stomach was empty, then retched again. Clara stood behind her, patting her on the back.

When she finished, she returned to her kitchen chair. Clara poured a glass of water and offered it to Angela. She waited while Angela took a tiny sip, then another. "What's got your knickers in such a twist?" Clara asked.

Angela held out the sheaf of papers. "Read the second page."

Clara took the papers and sat next to Angela. She read. She gasped. She looked blankly at Angela. "Why would he do this to you?"

Angela shrugged. "I suppose his pride is hurt. I embarrassed him by leaving."

"I thought you said he wasn't interested in the boys."

"He wasn't," Angela said. "He liked that he had two sons, but he ignored them when he was home. He never changed one diaper or got up with them in the night. He never fed them or played with them or took them anywhere."

"It's horrible. You're not unfit. You're working your fingers to the bone to support them and he's not given you a plug nickel." Clara dug in her purse for a packet of cigarettes and lit one. She held the packet out to Angela. "Have a gasper? It might settle your nerves."

Angela took one with shaking hands. She stared at the legal papers. Her husband was not just suing her for divorce. He wanted full custody of the boys. On the grounds that, as a union organizer, she was an unfit mother.

"Can he do it? Can he take your sons from you because you're working to support your sons?" Clara asked.

"What do you think? It's not like the Red Scare disappeared," Angela said with a laugh.

"Phony baloney! He has a job. Who does he think will take care of the boys while he's at work? Wouldn't the court see that?"

Angela barked out a harsh sound, half sob, half laugh. "It's not the same and you know it. It's another version of the system that pays women half what it pays men for the same work." Angela said. She reached for the bottle and poured them each a shot.

Sasha Zimmerman handed her a newspaper. "Read that. I think it'll help with your child custody problem," he said.

They were in the back room of the Local 22's offices, waiting for a meeting. Like all the union's meetings, this one was starting late.

Angela took the paper. The headline read, "Special Committee on Prohibition Testimony." She lowered the paper and cocked an eyebrow at Sasha. "Are you kidding me?" she asked.

"Just read it."

"'It is impossible to tell whether Prohibition is a good thing or a bad thing. It has never been tried in this country,'" Angela read aloud with a laugh. That much was sure true. "'There may not be as much liquor in quantity consumed today as there was before Prohibition, but there is just as much alcohol. The percentage of whiskey drinkers in the United States is now greater than in any other country in the world. At least one million quarts of liquor are consumed in the United States every day. This enormous traffic in liquor is carried on with the knowledge of officials entrusted with the enforcement of the law. At least a million dollars a day is paid in graft and corruption to federal, state, and local officials. Such a condition is not only intolerable, but dangerous to democracy.'"

Angela wondered where these statistics came from. Was there some government agency that counted glasses of whiskey all over the world? Angela turned to Sasha to ask him why he'd given her the article.

"Look at the bottom of the page," he said.

In fine print it said, "'The above is the testimony of Congressman Fiorello La Guardia of New York before a special committee on Prohibition.'"

Angela rattled the newspaper. "And how does a speech on Prohibition corruption help me?"

Sasha sighed. "You need a lawyer and you can't use a union lawyer, not if your husband's using your union work against you."

"I can't afford a lawyer. I'm just going to explain it to the judge. No one wants to take children away from their mother."

"That's not going to work," Sasha said, shaking his head. "Your husband can prove you're working for a union with socialist membership and fraternizing with Jewish union organizers—you know, me and Rose aren't too popular with the powers-that-be right now."

Angela shrugged. "I still don't see what Prohibition has to do with it."

"Not Prohibition," Sasha said. "La Guardia. Fifteen years ago, he was congressional representative to East Harlem. And he's half Italian."

"Only half?"

"His mother is Jewish," Sasha explained. "I don't think he's observant or anything. In fact, I think he's an Episcopalian."

"And you think he can help me?"

Sasha nodded. "His parents were immigrants. He put himself through law school working for Immigration Services. When I met him, he was doing free legal work for garment workers, back before the Triangle fire. And he's worked against child labor and for women's suffrage."

"It'll never work. He's too busy to take on little old me and my divorce case," Angela said.

"Probably so," Sasha said. "But we go way back. My sister and his mother used to go to temple together. And he took some union cases back when I was working for Amalgamated. So I'll write you a note of introduction and you'll go see him."

Angela thought it sounded like a waste of time, but she didn't want to tell Sasha that. Then she thought of an out. "It says here," she said, pointing at the newspaper, "that he was testifying before a special congressional committee in Washington."

Sasha laughed. "He takes the train home every Friday afternoon and spends Saturdays in his old law office, up on Lexington."

Which is how, two days later, Angela found herself standing before the man who would propose marriage to her.

For someone who'd accomplished as much as he had, Fiorello La Guardia was surprisingly ordinary looking. For one thing, he was barely over five feet tall, and quite stout. He wore thick, dark-rimmed glasses and put too much pomade in his hair. Angela quickly learned that the "Little Flower," as he was known in Italian Harlem, didn't let his size or apparent ordinariness stop him from doing anything. He knew everyone and nothing scared him.

She met with him on a Saturday in his East Harlem office.

"My husband is suing me for divorce and full custody of our two boys. He alleges that my union work makes me an unfit mother," she explained to him.

Fiorello leaned forward in his chair so he could see her legs. "A gorgeous and grand woman like yourself? Unfit? Never."

Angela found herself momentarily speechless. Men liked her and she liked men, but most of them were nowhere near as bold as this man. "I don't think my husband would agree with you," she said.

"Ha! Your husband is a fool. I've heard about your work with the unions. You're on the side of the angels, as my dear mother would say. I assume you're looking for a lawyer."

"Yes, sir."

He jerked his head to the side. "I'll have none of that. You'll call me by the name my sainted mother gave me: Fiorello."

Angela wondered briefly what Mamma would say about the congressman's familiarity, then decided she didn't care. She needed help and a little flirting wouldn't hurt. Still, she might try teasing him a little.

"We'll see about that. If you can't help me, you'll stay Mr. La Guardia," she said.

"I can help you, but only by sending you to a different lawyer. My work for the people of the Twentieth District means I cannot represent you in court, though I'd very much like to," he said. "Your case provides an excellent opportunity to argue for the benefit of unions and the equality of women. Plus, if I were your lawyer, I might get you to go to dinner with me." He winked.

Angela felt herself blushing. "I'm still married. I'm sure the voters wouldn't approve."

He sighed and folded his hands. "I'm afraid you're right. Perhaps when we've gotten you this divorce, you might consider."

They stared at each other. Angela had no idea what to say.

Fiorello dug in his top desk drawer. "In any event, I have just the man for you." He pulled out a card and slid it across the desk. "Vito Marcantonio. He ran my congressional campaign two years ago. No, three years ago."

Fiorello came around his desk and sat in the chair next to Angela. He patted her hand. "Before you get too excited, I have to tell you he only just graduated from law school a year ago," he said.

"But he's working as a lawyer now, isn't he?" Angela asked.

"Yes, he is. Walter Nelles hired him right out of law school. In fact, he was Nelles's right-hand man in the formation of the American Civil Liberties Union."

"To fight the Palmer Raids," Angela said, mostly so he'd know she wasn't ignorant of left-wing politics.

The congressman bobbed his head. "And all the other Red Scare foolishness. Nelles got his start representing conscientious objectors during the war, and when the Lusk Committee declared all pacifists enemies of the state, he really went to work. Imagine thinking one couldn't be an American and anti-war at the same time."

Fiorello stared across his office, as if remembering something, then shook it off. "Anyway, that's neither here nor there. You need a lawyer and Vito needs experience. He's new, but he's eager and he's smart. And handsome, though not as handsome as myself." He winked again.

Angela tried not to smile as she stood to go.

Fiorello popped to his feet and clasped Angela's hand in his. He held it for a second, saying nothing.

She looked down at him, finding herself drawn to him in spite of his size. Unlike a lot of men, it felt like he really saw her as a person with a right to a life beyond what society said women should do and have.

"I think it's very brave what you're doing, trying to be a mother and a working woman at the same time," he said. "My only child, Fioretta, died six years ago after she caught spinal meningitis and her mother—my dear wife, Thea—died not long after. The doctors said tuberculosis killed Thea, but I've always thought she died of a broken heart. You can't separate mothers and their children, not through death and certainly not like your husband's trying to do. Children need their mothers in a way they do not need their fathers. Don't you agree, Mrs. Camponeschi?"

"I do, Fiorello," she said. "I think you may call me Angela."

The Little Flower smiled the smile that made his name ring true. "I hope to see you again, Angela. Perhaps once your divorce is final, I might take you to dinner. If you'd like that?"

Angela thought she might like it very much indeed.

The divorce hearing took less than a day. Romolo's lawyer started the morning off by calling Angela's husband to the stand. Romolo testified to her unfitness as a wife and mother, particularly in the last year of their marriage.

"You're saying that even though you could support your family, she insisted on leaving your young sons and returning to work?" the lawyer asked.

"That's right," Romolo barked. He looked around the courtroom and added, "I tell her she must stay home, but she no listen to me."

Angela seethed at his lies. He'd been only too happy to have her go back to work, particularly after he lost the lunch shift.

Romolo's lawyer turned toward the judge and asked, "And what about the children? What happened to them when she went back to work?"

"She leave them alone. Poor babies," Romolo said.

"I did not," Angela hissed into Vito's ear. "Marie took care of them."

"I know," Vito whispered back. "I'll take care of it."

The judge glared at the two of them.

Vito patted her arm and whispered, "Shh."

"And what kind of work does your wife do?" Romolo's lawyer asked.

"Bah," Romolo said. "She couldn't just go to work making dresses like a decent woman. She had to join the communists making trouble."

"What kind of trouble?"

"With the union. No good woman should be doing that. She used to invite communists and socialists and anarchists and all sorts of bad men right into my house. She thought I didn't know. But I knew. A husband always knows."

Angela leaned over to tell Vito she'd never been a communist, but he shushed her. It went on like that for a while. The lawyer asked leading questions and Romolo made it sound like she was running with Lucky Luciano's gang.

When Vito cross-examined Romolo, he forced him to admit that the children had been under the care of his wife's sister, who lived in the same house with them, but he had less luck with the anti-union talk. "Can you prove the people your wife works with are doing anything illegal?" Vito asked.

"Everyone knows they are," Romolo insisted. "I don't need no proof." The judge seemed to agree.

Romolo's lawyer next called a scarecrow of a man to the stand and asked him to identify himself.

"My name is Frank Miller. I work for the Pinkerton Detective Agency. Camponeschi hired me to investigate his wife," the man said.

Angela couldn't believe her ears. Romolo'd had her followed? What kind of man did that?

Frank flipped open a notebook and began to read from it: "She regularly spends time at two union offices, the Local 22 and 25 of the International Ladies' Garment Workers' Union. At the 22, she interacts with notorious communist Charles Zimmerman. At the 25, I saw her on numerous occasions in close conversation with a woman I later identified as Rose Pesotta, a woman known as an anarchist." Miller had information on Nino and Marie too, insisting the two of them were dangerous anarchists.

"Do you mean the same Marie who is Mrs. Camponeschi's sister? With whom her own lawyer says she leaves Camponeschi's sons?" Romolo's lawyer asked, feigning shock and dismay.

Vito tried to undo the damage in his cross-examination, but with little success. Once again, he asked if the witness had proof that any of Angela's work friends were breaking the law, and even though the answer was no, that wasn't the point and everyone in the courtroom knew it.

After a short recess, it was the defense's turn. Mamma came to the stand first and testified that the boys currently lived with her. "But, Angela, she visits every day. And she is paying the rent so I don't have to work anymore," Mamma said. She held up her hands, which were clearly twisted by arthritis. "She is a good daughter and a good mother," Mamma insisted.

Romolo's lawyer asked Mamma if, in her experience, good mothers generally lived apart from their children. Mamma said no and tried to say more before he stopped her.

"But, judge," she said. "You don't understand."

"You are dismissed, Mrs. Bambace," the judge told her, his face sternly disapproving. "Please take your seat."

Marie came next and Vito walked her through the years they'd lived together in Flushing. Marie talked about how hard both of them had worked to make a nice home for their husbands and babies, how they'd stretched dollars by making their own pasta and bread, how they'd taken turns with the laundry and made sure the children learned to speak English as well as Italian.

Vito next asked her questions about her connections to anarchists and socialists. "It's not what everyone thinks," she explained. "People think anarchists are all bomb-throwing murderers, but that's wrong. An anarchist believes that all governments are oppressive to the people because governments, by their very nature, are controlled by the rich and powerful who protect their interests. I am an anarchist because I believe people, all people, have the right to live with dignity, to work for a living wage, and to make real choices about their lives."

In spite of her reasonable tone, the courtroom buzzed with shock at Marie's admission that she was an anarchist.

Marie pivoted to talking about how Romolo treated Angela. "He criticized her constantly. Nothing was good enough. And sometimes she had bruises on her arms and face. She'd lie and say she fell or ran into a door, but I knew."

"Did she ever tell you the truth, Mrs. Capraro?" Vito asked. He was trying to close the door she'd left open, the one where Romolo's lawyer could say there was no proof he'd ever hit his wife.

"Oh, yes, she did. It was right after Oscar was born, about four years ago. She needed help with the baby, so she had to tell me he beat her. She could hardly get out of bed for three days."

Angela's face burned in embarrassment. That people should know this about her marriage shamed her more than she could say.

On cross-examination, Romolo's lawyer asked Marie if Romolo had done anything illegal. "Isn't it within a husband's legal rights to correct his wife?"

"Well, I suppose so," Marie admitted. "But it's still wrong."

"Says a woman who consorts with radicals of the worst sort," the lawyer retorted. After that, he grilled Marie on Nino's work. He managed to connect Nino to the now-infamous Sacco and Vanzetti trial and make it seem like the Capraro household ran a halfway house for murderers and bank robbers.

After Marie's testimony, they had no more witnesses. Angela and Vito had discussed calling some of her friends to testify to her good character, but in the end decided against it. All her friends were allied with the union and most of them were socialists. The problem was that in New York there wasn't much choice. The massively corrupt Tammany Hall controlled the Democratic Party and was as anti-union as the Republicans. If you wanted workers' rights in New York, you had to belong to one of the small, leftist parties. Which wasn't going to do Angela any good in a courtroom controlled by a Tammany Hall judge.

The judge ordered a one-hour lunch break, saying he'd render his verdict when they came back.

Vito took Angela, Marie, and Mamma to lunch at a Jewish delicatessen three blocks from the courthouse, but none of them could eat a bite. Mamma, who couldn't abide wasting food, had the waiter wrap up their sandwiches for later.

Back in the courtroom, Angela took her seat next to Vito and bowed her head to pray. It wasn't something she did very often. In her experience, God helped those who helped themselves and praying felt too much like begging for a handout.

They got to their feet as the judge entered the room, then sat again. Angela straightened her spine, pushed her shoulders back, and lifted her chin. She would not cower before these men, even if the worst happened.

Then the worst happened. The judge declared Romolo and Angela Camponeschi divorced and gave full custody of Philip and Oscar Camponeschi to Romolo Camponeschi. He said Mrs. Camponeschi had forfeited her right to motherhood by spending her time with radicals, organizing immigrant workers into troublemaking unions instead of staying home and obeying her husband, as her marriage vows and God commanded.

Angela sat in her seat, hands clasped tightly in her lap, through the judge's lecture. She called up the image of the silently marching protesters she'd seen all those years ago at the Triangle fire funeral procession. If those people could stand it, so could she. *You will not make me ashamed of myself for doing the right thing. I will not cry at the injustice of this. Not here. Not now.*

The crying came later.

Chapter Nine

NOT EXECUTION, BUT MURDER

"Never in our full life can we hope to do such work for tolerance, for justice, for man's understanding of man, as we now do by accident."
—Bartolomeo Vanzetti, 1927

August 1927

"Here, let me," Mamma said. She pushed Angela away from the stove, where they were cooking meatballs. "You're going to burn them." Mamma took the wooden spoon from Angela and started pushing the meat around in the pan. "Shoo, go talk to your friends. Or see what the children are up to."

Angela pulled her apron over her head and gave Mamma a grateful hug. "Thanks, Mamma," she said. "With all the noise and the phone, I can't seem to concentrate. It's a good thing we made the cake yesterday."

For Oscar's birthday, she and Mamma made a three-layer sponge cake, soaked in sweetened rum and layered with chocolate pastry cream. Mamma splurged on blanched almonds and pressed them to the outside of the cake, making it as pretty as any cake from Veniero's.

The phone rang again. Luigi Quintiliano ran for it, hollering, "I'll get it."

Angela had to smile at the sound of Luigi's voice. She'd sworn off men after the divorce, or she'd intended to. But Luigi kept popping up in her life and she couldn't help it—she felt drawn to him like he was magnetic. She guessed he was, at least for her. He ought to be up in Boston with the rest of the Sacco and Vanzetti Defense Committee, but he said he wanted to be here for Oscar's birthday party, which was sweet even if his last-minute machinations had turned Oscar's day into an early wake.

She left Luigi to his phone call and stepped outside and surveyed the backyard. Her boys and Marie's girls were digging in the garden. A longtime city girl, Mamma wasn't much of a gardener and Angela surely didn't have the time, nor the inclination, to grow tomatoes and peppers. Instead she let the boys turn the patch of dirt into a small town, complete with pebbled roads, twig houses, and many, many excavations.

She watched the four of them, two seven-year-olds and two four-year-olds, and thought about how much her life had improved in the last year. That day in the courtroom, she'd thought her life had come to an end. Then Mamma explained her plan.

It took them a few months, but eventually Mamma found a house for rent less than a block from the Flushing house Angela had lived in with Romolo. The move had twin benefits: it put Angela close to her boys and got Mamma away from Papà, who moved in with a cousin in Little Italy. They rarely saw him these days, though Angela told him he could visit anytime.

Angela was about to step off the back stoop and inspect the children's work when a scream came from the depths of the house. She scrambled back inside.

Luigi stood by the telephone table in the house's tiny front hall. He stepped toward Angela and said, "The governor says he won't sign a stay of execution."

Aware that they were surrounded by people who didn't know about their secret relationship, Angela could only pat Luigi's shoulder. "I'm sorry. I know you hoped he might."

His shoulders slumped for a moment before he caught himself and straightened up. "It's looking grim, but we have a few more things to try," he said, looking toward the living room.

"Go talk to Nino." Angela pushed him out of the hall.

She watched him go, marveling at the connection she felt with Luigi. It had never been this way with Romolo. She knew she ought to stay away from men, especially this one. He was a hothead, though only about politics rather than domestic matters, and for all his talk about women's rights, he liked a home-cooked meal as much as the next man. And as a union organizer, he was never going to have two nickels to rub together. Still, she couldn't help what her heart felt. And she could support herself and her boys without any help from a man, thank you very much.

The smart choice would have been Fiorello. If she'd married him, she'd be living in a big apartment on the Upper West Side and hobnobbing with the congressional wives in Washington. And there was talk of the Little Flower running for mayor, though there'd never been an Italian mayor of New York City. The mayor's wife, imagine that. He'd taken her to dinner a half dozen times and asked her to marry him twice. The first time she'd put him off, and the second time she said no. She'd not been able to muster up anything more than affectionate admiration for Fiorello. Still, she struggled with the decision. Becoming Mrs. Fiorello La Guardia would have made her life easier. Her sons could have gone to the finest schools and colleges. She could have had a closet full of new clothes every year, instead of remaking her blue serge over and over again. But it wouldn't have been right. Maybe if she'd liked him a little less she'd have married him, but a man like Fiorello deserved a wife who loved him more than anything or anyone else. And that was never going to be her.

She was about to join the crowd in the living room when she saw Mamma setting the dinner table. They had a dozen people to seat tonight, including the four children. Thank goodness Nino and Marie brought some extra chairs, or they'd have had people standing up to eat. Angela went to help Mamma—she wouldn't let the Sacco and Vanzetti gloom in the crowd infect her little man's birthday dinner.

They sat down to a feast of meatballs and sauce with a big bowl of rigatoni, veal parmigiana, green beans with pancetta, and a platter of crusty bread. Nino filled wine glasses again and again with a Sicilian Primitivo. Even Oscar had a little glass of watered-down wine, seeing as it was his seventh birthday, though little Philip had only water. But after he fussed about wanting to be a big boy, Angela took pity on him and added a drop of wine to his glass, which satisfied his need to keep up with his big brother.

After the plates emptied and everyone insisted they could not eat another bite, Mamma brought out the cake. Luigi fetched two bottles, one Marsala and one Grappa. Both were hard to find in Prohibition America, but Luigi and Nino both knew the sort of people who had access to black-market Italian wine.

Talk at the table turned repeatedly to the Sacco and Vanzetti case. Leaders from around the globe, including fascist dictator Benito Mussolini, had telegrammed Governor Fuller asking for clemency. Mussolini' s request had both delighted and enraged members of the Sacco and Vanzetti Defense Committee, all of whom were dedicated anti-fascists.

"I heard Mussolini's worried about the reaction in Italy if they're executed," Marie said.

"I don't know why," Nino said. "He's been murdering and jailing leftists since fourteen minutes after declaring himself supreme leader. And speaking of supreme leaders, the Pope's weighed in as well. He called the trial an injustice and urged clemency."

"Say what you will about the Church," Marie said. "It's always been against the death penalty."

Luigi poured another tiny glass of Grappa and said, "There's been demonstrations in Geneva and Paris."

"I heard there was a thing in Australia somewhere," Sasha Zimmerman said.

"Sydney," his wife, Rose, replied. "I'm sure they have Italians there too."

Mamma raised her glass. "May I suggest a toast to Oscar, who is seven years old today."

Angela smiled gratefully at Mamma. It was nice that all these people had gathered at their house, and terrible that those poor men's execution was scheduled for midnight—but a boy only had one birthday a year and they'd been ignoring him all night. All the children, really.

Oscar raised his glass, which had barely a tablespoon of wine in it. "To Sacco and Vanzetti. May they live to see their next birthdays too."

The table erupted in cheers and good wishes for the condemned men and Oscar alike.

Angela wiped tears from her eyes. All the turmoil in little Oscar's life hadn't made her boy mean or sullen. She felt exceedingly proud to be his mother.

After presents, Mamma walked the boys down the block to their father's house and put them to bed. Romolo didn't get home until after midnight, so she'd stay there with them. Romolo hadn't been particularly happy when Angela moved in down the street, but even he had to admit that he couldn't take care of two little boys and still go to work. It was an odd family situation, but it worked out for everyone and the boys didn't seem to differentiate between the two households. Both were home.

No one else left the house, though it could hardly be considered a party anymore. With the boys gone, there was no reason for anyone to keep up a pretense of jollity. As ten o'clock ticked past, the talk turned toward last-minute appeals.

"I hear Elizabeth Evans is going to try to get in to see the governor," Nino said. A number of socially prominent women had taken up Sacco and Vanzetti's cause, including Evans.

"She is," Luigi agreed. "What good it will do them. For all their social power, they've been discounted as class traitors because of their part in this. But she won't get in. And even if she does, Fuller won't listen to her. He didn't even blink when the *Boston Herald* changed its tune and called for a retrial."

Sasha ground out his cigarette and rubbed his face. "When I read that editorial, I thought, 'Now they'll have to admit the judge was biased,' but no. I mean, if the crusty old *Herald* could change its mind, doesn't that say something?"

Marie patted Sasha's knee. "It says plenty. But not to the people who need to hear it." She turned toward Luigi and said, "So you don't think the society ladies will change the governor's mind?"

"No," Luigi said. "The governor will not be swayed by sentiment or morality. Only the law will work now. Musmanno's got an idea. He's going to try an argument that electrocution is cruel and unusual punishment, and even more so given the conditions in that prison."

"Musmanno?" Angela asked from the kitchen doorway. She and Rose had just finished the dishes, while the men relaxed in the living room. For all their progressive ideals, Angela would have bet her right arm that none of them saw anything wrong with the women cleaning up.

Luigi glanced up at her. "Michael Musmanno. He's a war veteran and he's political. He volunteered to be our appellate attorney when Fred Moore had to go back to California."

Fifteen minutes before midnight, the phone rang again. Luigi looked over at Angela, who was now sprawled on the floor with a pillow under her crooked arm. She waved languidly at the hall, signaling him to answer the phone.

Luigi spoke into the receiver for less than a minute, then sat the phone gently into its cradle. He stepped into the living room and shook his head. "They wouldn't even see Musmanno. Mary's standing by the phone in case anything happens," he said. Mary Donovan was the Defense Committee's secretary and one of its few full-time employees.

Angela snorted. "Of course he wouldn't. He didn't want to go on record saying electrocuting men isn't cruel or unusual."

"It's not unusual, that much we can be sure of," Rose said. Everyone agreed.

The room fell silent as the clock marched toward midnight. Luigi paced in the hall, his heels hitting the floor, providing counterpoint to the ticking clock. Then it was midnight. No one said anything.

At ten past, Sasha said, "Medeiros is surely dead by now." Celestino Medeiros had confessed to the murder of the two guards and testified that neither Sacco nor Vanzetti had been involved. The judge and jury hadn't cared.

After another ten minutes, Sasha opened his mouth to speak again, but Rose settled her hand on his leg and he said nothing. At 12:35, the phone rang for the final time that night.

Luigi answered it, listened, and hung up. "That was Mary. It's done. They've been executed."

Angela stood and grabbed Luigi's hand. "That wasn't an execution. They were murdered," she said.

The next morning, Angela came downstairs to find Mamma had picked up a box of pastries from the local bakery and made coffee. She handed Angela a newspaper and set a mug of steaming caffe latte on the table in front of her.

Angela shook out the newspaper's folds and read:

Sacco and Vanzetti Executed Early This Morning
Sacco Cries "Long Live Anarchy"
Vanzetti Insists on His Innocence

Charlestown State Prison, Mass., Tuesday, Aug. 23

Nicola Sacco and Bartolomeo Vanzetti died in the electric chair early this morning, carrying out the sentence imposed on them for the South Braintree murders of April 15, 1920.

Sacco marched to the death chair at 12:11 and was pronounced dead at 12:19. Vanzetti entered the death room at 12:20 and was declared dead at 12:26. Each man protested his innocence until the end. Celestino Medeiros, who confessed he was present at the Braintree murders and that Sacco and Vanzetti were not, was executed first. Medeiros walked to the chair in a stupor and was pronounced dead at 12:09.

Warden William Hendry found himself nearly overcome by the event, particularly after Vanzetti shook his hand and thanked the warden for his kind treatment of them. The warden pronounced the sentence in a voice so whispered that official witnesses could not hear him.

There was more but Angela couldn't bear to read the descriptions of the men's last meals, their walks from their cells to the execution chamber, their last words. These details served only to break the heart. Hers certainly broke—for the men murdered by the same government that said murder was wrong, for the men's families, for their friends, and for the men who had to carry out the sentence. Wasn't that always the way of it? Rich and powerful men wanted Sacco and Vanzetti dead, but other men did the killing for them and had to live with the deed afterwards. She wondered how a man ended up a prison warden and in charge of killing three men in one night. And what did that do to a man's soul? Even if the warden and his men thought the execution was legal and fair, wouldn't presiding over killing three men stain a man for life?

Then Angela's eye caught a sidebar article:

Police Break Up Crowds

Just before midnight, five hundred Italians and several thousand more people met before the Bunker Hill Monument and threatened to hold a demonstration if Sacco and Vanzetti were executed. The excited crowd blocked pedestrian and vehicle passage on Salem Street in the North End. Mounted police charged the crowd. Several persons were crushed under the iron-shod hooves of police horses. Fifty patrolmen were called out, armed with machine guns, gas and tear guns, and pistols to control the crowds. Forty more mounted police were deployed down side streets to drive the hysterical crowds back.

Angela wondered how much traffic there'd been to obstruct at midnight and how the newspaper knew five hundred of the protesters were Italians. And what had the people done to warrant such violence from the police? The article said they "threatened to hold a demonstration." So did they? And when had demonstrations become illegal in America? And why did some variation on "excitable" or "hysterical" always follow the mention of Italians in the press?

In the midst of these dark thoughts, Marie stumbled into the kitchen, rubbing her eyes.

"Where's Nino?" Mamma asked.

"He tossed and turned all night. I told him to stay in bed," Marie said.

Angela pushed the newspaper over to Marie, pointing to the article about the police.

"I'll never understand why people are hostile about anarchists, who are rarely violent, but not hostile about the police, who are violent all the time," Marie said after reading it.

"Well, to be fair, the police's job is to maintain public safety," Angela said.

Mamma sat down at the table. "How is attacking peaceful protesters maintaining public safety? And all the times they've attacked you on a picket line—was that public safety? Remember the machine gun last year?"

Angela didn't think she'd ever forget it.

Marie poked the newspaper again. "Several persons crushed. What does that mean? After the excruciating detail about the execution, all we get about the protest is 'several people crushed.' It makes me so mad."

Angela sighed. "Me too, I guess."

"You guess?" Marie asked.

"What good does my anger do?" Angela said. "The Boston police are no better than the New York police. Should we stop the presses? This is the world we live in. So I'm asking, what can we do?"

Angela felt Mamma drop a kiss on top her head.

Marie pointed to the bottom of the article and said, "Right there."

Angela read the last paragraph. "'The two men's bodies will be turned over to Mrs. Sacco and Miss Vanzetti later this week, with a funeral planned for Friday, August 28.'"

She looked up and grinned at Marie and Mamma. "Let's go. We'll take everyone. Luigi, Nino and Marie, the Zimmermans, and anyone else we can think of."

"Not me," Mamma said. "I'm too old for such a trip. And who would watch the *bambini*? You girls go for your mamma and make her proud."

Angela pushed back her chair and wrapped her arms around Mamma. Marie joined them and together they made a circle of love against a world of last meals and executions.

The train to Boston was packed with anxious and angry people. Angela and Marie were traveling by themselves the morning of the funeral. Nino and Luigi left the morning after the execution, right after Rosina Sacco called to tell Luigi the prison refused to release her husband's body. Against the widows' wishes, they planned to donate all three bodies to Harvard Medical School. The lawyers stopped it, but as members of the defense committee, both Luigi and Nino thought they should get back to Boston.

Marie and Angela waited in the unseasonable pre-dawn cold for the train to Boston. Marie carried Mamma's umbrella and Angela had a small basket with sandwiches and a thermos of coffee. As they sped north, the sky lightened to reveal a gloomy, gray day that threatened rain. A telegram from Nino the previous day told them to come first to the defense committee's headquarters, where Sacco and Vanzetti's bodies would be before the funeral procession.

They arrived at 256 Hanover Street to find total mayhem.

Thick crowds of people lined the sidewalks and milled in the streets. Angela pushed her way to the defense committee's office, only to find the front door boarded over.

"The police did that yesterday so no one could get in," said a man in a dark overcoat. "The nasty buggers." He said the bodies were at the Langone Funeral Home, just two blocks away.

Marie and Angela headed in that direction, pushing their way through unmoving clots of people. The day felt more like November than August, making the street scene all the more surreal, as if summer had gone into mourning for the executed men. When they arrived at the funeral home, they could see two gleaming black coffins through the front window. A tall, lean, dark-haired woman holding a sign stood between the coffins.

Marie gasped. "She's not!"

"She is," Angela said.

The woman was Mary Donovan, the defense committee's secretary, and the sign she held was the same one she'd been arrested for displaying in a park several years ago. It read, "Did you see what I did to those anarchistic bastards?—Judge Thayer."

A police van pulled up in front of the funeral home, bulling its way through the crowd. Three uniformed officers jumped out of the van and shoved their way into the funeral home. The largest man seized Mary and dragged her from the room, while one of the other men tore the sign from her hands and whacked it against a coffin until it broke.

Once the policemen had Mary out on the sidewalk, several bystanders tried to help her, but the third policeman pulled out his cudgel and swung it at their heads.

Someone yelled, "What's she being arrested for?"

"For inciting a riot and distributing anarchist propaganda," one of the policemen yelled back.

"Inciting a riot? There weren't no riot until you lot showed up," a spectator called.

Another hollered, "How's a quote from Judge Thayer anarchist propaganda? Is he an anarchist now?"

Angela nearly laughed out loud at that question, though it did no good. Reason didn't stand a chance when hysteria ruled the day—not among the masses, nor the police.

Angela and Marie tried to get into the funeral home, but to no avail. No one believed Marie was married to a man on the defense committee.

The sisters found an empty storefront and perched on the front window's sill. While they ate their sandwiches and drank coffee from a shared cup, four men carrying a wreath that must have been eight feet across came walking down the center of the street. Pairs of men followed them, each carrying wreaths about half the size of the first one. A small handful of women and children followed, each carrying smaller wreaths or baskets. They stopped in front of the funeral home. The women carrying baskets distributed red armbands to the crowd. Angela and Marie each took one. "Remember Justice" was stitched on the band in black. The woman who handed one to Angela said, "Did you hear the police let Mary Donovan go?"

"Probably afraid of what would happen if they didn't," Angela said.

"That's what everyone thinks," the woman said. "Take that arm band off when we get to Scollay Square." The women repeated this sentence over and over again. Angela had no idea why the armbands had to come off there, but she made a mental note of it. Not long after, two gleaming black hearses pulled up in front of the Langone's, parking side by side in the street. A third closed car pulled up behind them.

"Here we go," Marie whispered to Angela.

Angela felt a drop of water hit her cheek. As suddenly as it began to rain, she was back in New York at the funeral procession for the Triangle fire victims. She shook the memory off and got to her feet.

Six men carried a coffin out to the street. They struggled as they negotiated the curb before slipping the coffin into the hearse. The next coffin came out, carried by another six men. Marie nudged Angela. Nino and Luigi were in the second set of pallbearers. They pushed that coffin into the waiting hearse. A man who could only be Mr. Langone, the funeral home director, stepped forward and closed the rear doors for each hearse. Two women and two children stepped out of the building and into the closed car. Angela knew it was Sacco's wife, their two children, and Vanzetti's sister.

Through it all, the crowd kept eerily quiet. Angela thought that if she closed her eyes, she could imagine she was on the street alone. Somewhere, a high, sweet voice began to sing "Amazing Grace." People joined in and the sound swelled. Marie pulled two handkerchiefs out of her coat pocket and offered one to Angela.

Up the street, the wreath bearers began to walk. Though it was drizzling, dozens of men removed their hats from their heads. The hearses began to roll, but slowly, so people could walk alongside and behind them.

Angela looked for Nino and Luigi but found neither man in the crowd. As they joined the mass of people walking up the street, it began to rain in earnest. "It's just like Triangle. Remember?" Angela whispered to Marie. Marie nodded. "Even God is crying today."

Marie snorted. "He ought to. This is the saddest thing I've ever seen."

Angela remembered that Marie hadn't gone with them to Misery Lane. Nothing could be sadder than that day—not even today.

As they approached a widening in the street, the word came back through the crowd, whispered from marcher to marcher: "Armbands off."

Angela crooked an eyebrow at the man next to her.

"Scollay Square is in a different police precinct than where we started. The police captain here forbid the wearing of armbands." He shook his head. "We don't want any violence. Not today. So armbands off."

It didn't work. As they entered the square, a dozen or so mounted policemen rode in from side streets. They ran their horses at the marchers, knocking down men, women, and children with indiscriminate zeal. People fled before them, running down the same streets from which the policemen had come only seconds before.

Angela and Marie managed to avoid most of the violence by pressing themselves up against a building. A young man, blond and blue-eyed, stood in front of them.

He turned and said, "I should have stayed home. I don't even care about this stuff. But my mother would have my head if she knew I left ladies in danger."

A policeman rode up to the young man and yelled, "Hey, you, get away from those women and run."

The young man looked back at Angela and Marie, eyes wide.

"Don't move," Angela whispered. "He'll run you down if you move."

The young man pressed his back against the sisters. "I don't want any trouble, officer," he said.

"Run, I told ya," the policeman yelled, swinging his cudgel

at the blond. "Run and keep on running." He swung again. Only the young man's quick reflexes kept his head from being split open.

The boy looked left, then broke right, running like a rabbit with a wolf on its heels. By the time the policeman spurred his horse in that direction, his quarry had disappeared.

Angela and Marie stayed where they were for a few minute more. Fallen men and women littered the square. Policemen ran through the crowds, grabbing people and hauling them into waiting paddy wagons. One man swore in his astonishment and was arrested for public indecency. Angela found herself shivering, though whether from cold or fright she could not tell.

Their young blond rescuer suddenly reappeared in front of them. "Now I know what you're fighting for," he gasped out. Then he ran off again.

Minutes later, enough marchers had entered the square that they firmly outnumbered the police. Some of them linked up arms and made their way through. Angela grabbed Marie's hand and they joined the line of linked marchers.

Open cars came up through the crowd and the wreaths were laid inside them. The procession picked up more speed, but not so much that walkers couldn't keep up. After a while the rain stopped and the sun peeped cautiously through the clouds. Angela and Marie shrugged out of their coats and carried them.

They walked and walked and walked. Angela remembered how Mrs. Tosi hadn't let them join the Triangle fire funeral procession to the cemetery, arguing that it was too far for an old lady and two little girls. What would Mrs. Tosi say if she could see them now?

The sidewalk crowds thinned as they walked, but never entirely disappeared. At one point they walked through a neighborhood of brightly painted houses so big they could only be called mansions. Marie and Angela stared at them as they walked by.

"What must it be like to live in a place like that?" Marie asked.

Angela shook her head. "We'll never know. But if we keep fighting, maybe someday our children or grandchildren will know."

"I wouldn't want any child to be rich," Marie said.

"Not all money comes from abusing workers," Angela said. "Look at my boss at the dress shop. She's a good woman. Or La Guardia—he has loads of money."

As they talked, the procession began to slow again. They passed through iron gates set in large stone pillars. They'd finally arrived at the cemetery. In front of them stood a two-story granite cemetery chapel. It was big enough to count as a church, though it would not be big enough to contain the crowd that had just walked eight miles.

"Let's stay out here," Marie said. "Nino said Mary Donovan is going to speak from the chapel steps after the service. We can have front-row seats for that."

Angela agreed. They found a low tombstone just across a small dirt road from the chapel and perched themselves on it. They watched as a priest clad in the robes of a monsignor entered the chapel. The car containing the dead men's families pulled in front of the chapel behind the hearses. The coffins stayed where they were as people crowded inside.

"Are they leaving them there?" Angela asked.

Marie shrugged. "I guess so. No—here comes Mr. Langone."

The funeral home owner, as dignified as a pontiff, opened

the rear doors of the hearses. Men stepped up and carried the coffins inside.

It began to rain again. Marie put up her umbrella. All around them people did the same, turning the cemetery into a sea of black. They waited. Some of the ladies made a protective circle behind one of the larger crypts so they could relieve themselves.

Finally, a line of men carrying the two coffins exited the chapel. The monsignor followed them, swinging a smoking thurible. The smell of incense wafted across the road. People filed down the chapel steps and milled around the cemetery grounds.

Then Mary appeared, surrounded by the men of the defense committee. To her left stood Luigi and Nino. She stepped forward, unfolded a piece of paper, and began to speak. Her voice, clear as a bell, rang out over the cemetery grounds:

"Nicola Sacco and Bartolomeo Vanzetti, you came to America seeking freedom. In youth you came as workers searching for that liberty and equality of opportunity heralded as the particular gift of this country to all newcomers. You centered your labors in Massachusetts, the very birthplace of these ideals. And now Massachusetts and America have killed you—murdered you because you were Italian anarchists."

She next spoke of the Salem Witchcraft Trials, comparing the hysteria that condemned so many women to hang to those who demonized the left today.

"The sham of these old acts of barbarism can never be wiped out, but the men who burned witches were blinded by superstitious fear. Sacco and Vanzetti were killed in deliberate cold blood. Their killers allowed class pride to blind them. They cared more for wealth, comfort, and institutions than they did for truth. Your long years of torture, your hours of supreme agony are the living banner under which we and descendants for generations to come will march to accomplish that better world based on a brotherhood of man for which you died. In your martyrdom we will fight on and conquer."

Angela watched Mary speak, proud of this woman who had the courage to spit in the eye of authority and the strength of character to stand up for what she believed. An America that would let Mary Donovan deliver such a fiery speech was an America worth fighting for. She'd try to remember Mary Donovan and not Scollay Square, because it was better to fight *for* something, rather than against something.

Afterwards, Angela and Marie found Nino and Luigi and begged a ride back to the train station. As they rode the night train home to New York, Angela thought about Mary's words. She was right. This miscarriage of justice would be like a siren, calling America to do better, just as the Triangle fire had done. They would continue to fight. She would continue to fight. And one day workers would have safe places to work, a work week that didn't crush the soul, and wages commensurate with their labor. All the workers—not just the men or the people born here, or the whites, but everyone. They would have equality and justice *for all*.

Part IV

1932–1936

Chapter Ten

A NEW DEAL FOR AMERICANS

"But with the slow menace of a glacier, Depression came on. Everyone tried to get out of the way."
—Frances Perkins, US Secretary of Labor, 1934

April–November 1932

"They're never going to respect you. You have to admit that, Angela." Sidney Hillman gave her his patented genial grin. He had a space between his two front teeth and he knew the gap made him look like a rambunctious sixteen-year-old, all energy and innocence.

"But Amalgamated is leaking members faster than the Titanic leaked water," Angela argued. "At least the ILGWU still has some punch. And punch is what we need these days."

They were having this politely heated discussion outside a dressmaking factory Angela was trying to organize—

unsuccessfully. With a quarter of Americans out of work, the ones who still had jobs didn't want to cause any trouble. The union organizers all agreed, from the radicals like the Zimmermans to the moderates like David Dubinsky, who now headed the ILGWU, that the Depression was a disaster not only for Americans, but also for unions.

Angela grabbed Sidney's wrist and looked at his watch. "I have ten minutes before my lunch break is over, and I haven't eaten yet," she said.

"Ten minutes is all I need." He lightly touched her elbow and steered her down the sidewalk to a trolley bench.

Angela sat, pulled a sandwich from her pocket, and unwrapped it.

While she ate, Sidney pulled a pamphlet from his pocket. "Have you seen this? It's from those fuddy-duddies at the ILGWU."

Angela swallowed and took the pamphlet with a sigh.

"You read Italian, don't you?" Sidney asked.

"Yes, but I didn't know you did."

"I don't need to. I know almost as many Italians as I know Russian Jews." He pointed to the third paragraph on the pamphlet's front page and said, "Read that. Out loud. In English."

"It's a good thing I like you, or I'd sock you in the nose right now." Angela peered at the paragraph. "'We turn to you women because you help your men with the sacred work of redemption and emancipation and progress. Support and encourage them with your serene and sturdy faith in the success of the cause of justice and truth.'"

"See?" Sidney asked, his thick glasses making him look just pop-eyed enough to seem harmless. "They think the woman's place is in the home, supporting her striking husband. It's like they don't know the words 'Ladies Garment Workers' make up the bulk of the union's name and that women make up the bulk of garment workers."

Angela swallowed a bite of her sandwich. "The men don't believe in female organizers either, or in Italian organizers. But it doesn't matter if they believe in me. I get shops organized. Or I did, before the Depression. The last few years have been impossible. Workers don't want to upset the bosses. Take this shop," she said, waving her arm at the building behind her. "No one wants to come to a union meeting. They don't even want to listen to me."

"So come back to Amalgamated. We're the real radicals now. The ILGWU has thrown out most of the anarchists and socialists."

Angela shook her head. "That's just it. I don't care about politics and I never have. I want to organize workers for better wages, safer conditions, and humane working hours. And I'm beginning to think fringe politics, no matter how well intentioned, isn't going to get that done, especially during a depression, when everyone's frightened of losing their job."

"Are you making progress here?" Sidney asked, gesturing back to the building. "Getting any support from the local union?"

Angela glanced at Sidney's watch again. "I have to go." She stood up, ready to go back to work. She'd keep talking to the women sitting around her. Maybe one or two of them would see reason and encourage the rest of them.

Sidney popped to his feet and with both hands grabbed her right arm. "Come work for me," he pleaded. "Three months. I'll send you over to New Jersey. There are some shops in Elizabeth ripe for organizing, but the workers are Italian women. They're not going to listen to Jewish organizers. Because you're right—Amalgamated Clothing Workers is leaking. Last time I looked at the rolls, we had fewer than twenty thousand members. In the meantime, the shop owners are getting away with murder. And you know I'm not being metaphorical here—you know women die in these badly run shops."

"Women die in Los Angeles too. Want me to go there? That's what Rose Pesotta did—she's in L.A. organizing Mexican-American women. Apparently, the shop owners pay those poor women a quarter of what they pay the white workers. It's important work, but I have two sons, you know. I can't pack up and leave. I'm not single like Rose."

A smile filled Sidney's face. "New Jersey's not California. You can go back and forth on the ferry." He paused and chewed his lower lip. "We'll pay you 15 percent more than whatever you're getting now."

Angela crumpled her sandwich paper into a ball and pushed it into her dress pocket. She stood and walked away from Sidney. As she joined the line of women heading back to work, she called over her shoulder, "Be at your office Monday morning or else I'm coming back here."

Sidney spun his hat by the brim and tossed it into the air. "You won't be sorry," he called.

Angela stifled her laugh. After a decade and a half of organizing shops in Lower Manhattan, it would be an adventure to go somewhere else. Even if it was only New Jersey.

~

"Did you hear? Franklin Roosevelt's heading west. He's speaking at Penn Station tomorrow before his train leaves," Mamma said, handing Angela a wet plate.

Angela wiped the plate dry and added it to the pile on the counter. They'd had Marie, Nino, Athena, and Clytia over for dinner. With the boys, Mamma, and Angela, that made eight people. Par for the course, the moment they'd finished eating Nino insisted his family go home, leaving Mamma and Angela with all the dirty dishes. Oscar and Philip had cleared the table, but afterwards she sent them back to their father's house so she could talk to Mamma in private.

"Like it matters who the president is. One silver-spooned blue blood or another, they're all the same," Angela said.

"I don't know," Mamma mused. "This one might be different." She grabbed a handful of flatware and swished it through the soapy water before dropping it all in the rinse water.

"I doubt it," Angela said as she dried the forks and knives. "He's a New York Democrat. You know what that means. It'll be politics as usual, though I suppose anyone would be better than Hoover."

Democrats in New York were the bedrock of the Tammany Hall political machine. Though ostensibly pro-immigrant, Tammany Hall hated unions almost as much as it hated the Italian Mob. Both organizations interfered with the machine's ability to assert complete control over everything and everyone in New York.

Mamma pulled the stopper on the sink and watched the water swirl away. "Did you see Hoover's speech where he said Americans would be stronger once the weak had been weeded out? As if all economic disaster was caused by the poor and not by the rich men on Wall Street."

"He's a Social Darwinist," Angela said. "They think helping the poor will make it easier for them to reproduce, and that will be the ruin of America. What did you expect?"

"A little human decency, I guess," Mamma said. She wiped out the sink and rinsed out her washrag.

"Ha. From a politician? You can't be serious about this Roosevelt fellow. I bet he's no better than President Hoover—these guys are all the same. I thought you really believed in all that revolution talk Nino's always spouting."

Mamma leaned on the counter and laughed. "Have you ever noticed the men who talk revolution rarely do anything about it?" she said.

Angela dropped the clean utensils into their drawer and motioned to the kitchen table. "Let's sit down for a minute, Mamma. My feet hurt. This Franklin Roosevelt is as rich as they come. And he's related to President Roosevelt. These people think the presidency is something you inherit, like a throne."

Angela watched as Mamma lowered herself into a chair. She'd turned stout and her hair was shot through with silver, but she still had her fire, even after Papà died last year. Or maybe it was because he died. These days, Mamma seemed like a woman freed from a tremendous burden.

"Franklin Roosevelt is leaving for a whistle-stop tour of the West this Saturday. How about you and me go see him—see what he has to say," Mamma said.

Angela didn't want to hear a rich man's speech, but Mamma did and that was a good enough reason to go. "Marie could use a day away from Nino," she offered.

Mamma nodded but didn't say anything.

Angela didn't want to say her next thought out loud, but she figured she had to. "Mamma, did you see the bruises? She had marks on her arm like someone grabbed her really hard. And it looked like someone choked her. There were dark marks under that scarf she had tied around her neck tonight."

Mamma snorted. "Someone. You know who is doing this to her."

Angela did. Nino wasn't strike organizing anymore and only occasionally wrote for one of the newspapers. Mostly he worked on his translation of *Don Quixote* and talked about moving upstate to live on a farm. The young revolutionary Angela met in 1919 had turned into a dour, unsatisfied man who took out his frustrations on his wife.

"There's nothing we can do," Mamma continued. "She won't leave him. She won't even admit there's a problem. I understand it, but it makes me sad. Not every woman has your strength, *cucciola*. Look how you singlehandedly organized that strike in Elizabeth last summer and still managed to get home to your boys every weekend."

"Only because of you, Mamma." Angela leaned over and hugged her mother. "I don't know what I'd do if you weren't here to help."

"When Shelley left for college, I didn't know what to do with myself." Mamma's smile turned into a frown as she thought of her youngest child. "And he doesn't come home much. I suppose being a doctor keeps him busy."

"He's not a doctor yet, Mamma. He's in training. The army didn't pay for him to go to medical school so he could visit his mamma and nonna all the time. Anyway, if you want to go see this Roosevelt fellow, let's take Marie too. Maybe we can talk some sense into her."

"I doubt it," Mamma said. "But we can have a nice day anyway."

The day dawned cold and clear. Angela sent the boys on into the city to spend the day with Nino so Marie could meet her sister and Mamma at Penn Station. As far as Angela was concerned, having Nino watch all four children while they had an adventure would make the day all that much more fun.

Mamma tried to bail out of their outing by claiming it was mean to wake the boys so early and put them on a train. "They need sleep, the poor *bambinos*. And they shouldn't be alone on the train."

Angela thought twelve-year-old Oscar slept plenty and he was old enough to ride the train without his mamma or nonna. And nine-year-old Philip would be up at the crack of dawn regardless, though he'd probably sit in bed and read. He'd been reading a set of novels about a wild man who lived with the apes and he could hardly put them down to sleep. Last night he'd been reading *Tarzan the Invincible*.

"You ought to read it, Mamma," he told her, eyes shining with excitement. "Tarzan's fighting the Russians."

Why an ape-man was fighting Russians, Angela was afraid to ask, but she was glad Philip liked to read. She wanted her boys to go to college like Shelley did, and reading would help them get there, even if it was only silly ape-man books.

They waited for Marie outside the station's main entrance. Angela pulled the lapels of her coat close against her chest, glad she'd worn gloves. Fall in the city could be glorious, but one never knew when the weather would turn cold. The nasty weather they'd had for Sacco and Vanzetti's August funeral proved that.

She saw Marie coming down the block, her too-thin cloth coat blowing open where she'd failed to button it. "Why don't you buy yourself a decent coat?" Angela said by way of a greeting. She kissed her sister's cheek and tugged her toward the building's neo-Romanesque interior. Mamma hugged Marie and admonished her for being too thin.

Marie waved a hand in the air. "Nino says there's no money. Oh, the boys arrived just before I left. Nino says he'll take your boys and our girls down to the wharf for hot dogs if they do their homework first. Why's Roosevelt kicking off his tour here if he has to take a ferry to cross the river?"

Mamma shrugged. "I suppose the ferry terminal's not grand enough for the man who's going to be the next president of the United States. And he will be president, even if we don't like his speech."

Angela had to agree. Last summer, twenty thousand war veterans gathered in Washington to ask Congress to pay their army bonuses. Back in 1924, when the government figured out it couldn't afford to pay all the men who'd fought in the Great War, they'd made a deal to pay the veterans twenty years hence, saying they'd add in a bonus for deferring their pay. Now out-of-work veterans said they didn't need their army pay in 1945; they needed it now, before their families starved. Thousands of men came to Washington to petition Congress to no avail, so the veterans, some with families, stayed in Washington. Newspapers started calling them the Bonus Army. These people had been living on the Washington Mall in shacks made of scrap wood and cardboard in an attempt to change Congress's mind.

Newspapers started calling the Bonus Army shelters Hoovervilles, after the president, which was only fair. The men had fought when their country asked them to. The least the nation could do was pay them for their service. Embarrassed by the increasing debacle on his front lawn, President Hoover ordered the real army, including cavalry and tanks, to push the Bonus Army out of town. Shots were fired, two veterans died, and hundreds more were hurt when the military attacked the homeless camp. Now people said Hoover couldn't get elected as town dogcatcher. In America one did not attack war veterans. Angela almost felt sorry for the Republicans who'd been smeared with Hoover's stupidity—almost. She'd been attacked by the police a time or two and she wouldn't wish it on anyone, nor was she going to waste pity on the men who ordered the attack.

The upshot was that Franklin Roosevelt had a clear path to the White House and he knew it. He'd been using his campaign speeches to lay out his plan to fix the economy. "A New Deal for Americans," he called it. Angela didn't care much what he called it—he was still a rich man playing a rich man's game for a rich man's job, and she wasn't dumb enough to think he really cared about American workers.

The three of them followed the crowds to the rotunda, where a large speaking platform stood. Several men sat upon the bunting-adorned stage, their coats unbuttoned and their top hats in their laps. A woman sat second from the left, a stout-bodied, stern-faced matron in a plain tweed coat and a slouched velvet hat.

"Who's the woman, do you think?" Marie asked.

Angela didn't know. Neither did Mamma. She sure didn't look like a rich man's wife.

A woman in front of them turned and answered. "That's Frances Perkins. They say Roosevelt is going to make her Secretary of Labor. Can you believe that? A woman in the cabinet!"

Angela agreed that a female cabinet member seemed entirely unbelievable.

"It's about time," Mamma said.

They waited about twenty minutes before one of the seated men, responding to some signal unseen, approached the podium to introduce and speak briefly about Roosevelt's political credentials. Then a small group of men came onstage, two men supporting a third between them. They left the middle man at the podium before taking their seats.

"Why, he can't hardly walk," Angela said. "I'd heard but didn't believe it."

Marie grabbed Angela's coat and shushed her. Roosevelt began to speak.

"My friends, it is my intention to be honest and to avoid all hypocrisy and sham. That a candidate would outline his plan for his presidency while campaigning is unprecedented, but these are unprecedented and unusual times," he said.

The crowd roared its approval. Angela remembered something Mamma once told her: "Beware of a man professing honesty, for he is surely about to tell you a lie."

Roosevelt went on to thank the man who introduced him and the people behind him before he started the body of his speech.

"It seems to me that no business which depends for existence on paying less than living wages to its workers has any right to continue in this country," he continued. "By business I mean the whole of commerce as well as the whole of industry; by workers I mean all workers, the white-collar class as well as the men in overalls; and by living wages I mean more than a bare subsistence level—I mean the wages of decent living."

"They always say 'men,' as if they don't know there are any

women workers," Angela said to Marie. The man next to her scowled but she paid him no mind.

"'Man' means everyone," Marie yelled back over the noise of the crowd.

Angela didn't agree, not one bit. Man meant men and anyone who said other wise was fooling themselves.

"Throughout industry, the change from starvation wages and starvation employment to living wages and sustained employment can, in large part, be made by trade unions," Roosevelt said. "Now the government will help in that great dream of the living wage. It is in our interest to do so because a decent living, widely spread among our millions of people, means prosperity for all. It is the only way to utilize the capacity of our industrial plants now standing closed or working at half power."

Marie bumped Angela's shoulder. "See? I think he's the real thing."

"It's just words," Angela said, bumping her sister back. "That's what they do—they talk. They never do anything but talk."

"On this idea, my first steps as president will be to put millions of men back to work," Roosevelt said. "The idea is simply for employers to hire more men to do the existing work by reducing the work hours of each man's week and at the same time paying a living wage for the shorter week."

"No employer and no group of less than all employers in a single trade could do this alone and continue to live in business competition. But if all employers in each trade now band themselves faithfully in these modern guilds—without exception—and agree to act together and at once, none will be hurt and millions of workers, so long deprived of the right to earn their bread in the sweat of their labor, can raise their heads again. The challenge is whether we can sink selfish interest and present a solid front against a common peril."

Angela could hardly believe her ears. The man had a plan. An honest to goodness plan. If she had to guess, it was based on the old 54–48 plank of the 1919 strikes, when workers asked for the wages they'd been paid for working fifty-four-hour weeks, while actually reducing their workweek to forty-eight hours. The people around her seemed to agree. Cheers erupted from the crowd each time Roosevelt paused.

"This law is also a challenge to labor. Workers, too, are here given a new charter of rights long sought and hitherto denied. But they know that the first move expected by the nation is a great cooperation of all employers, by one single mass action, to improve the case of workers on a scale never attempted in any nation. I am fully aware that wage increases will eventually raise costs, but I ask that managements give first consideration to the improvement of operating figures by greatly increased sales to be expected from the rising purchasing power of the public. That is good economics and good business. The aim of this whole effort is to restore our rich domestic market by raising its vast consuming capacity," Roosevelt concluded.

Angela allowed her heart to hope. Perhaps this economic disaster they were calling a Great Depression had taught the nation something. Or made them ready to hear the message socialists and anarchists had been trying to communicate for decades, that workers must be brought into American prosperity for America to prosper as a whole. If this rich man who'd be the next president of the United States really cared about the workers, really thought poverty was bad for the country, and really thought the government could help—well, then, she was with him.

Whatever worked, that had always been her motto, whether it was anarchists or mainstream politicians. She'd vote for this rich man, and if he made good on his talk, she'd do what she could to help.

Chapter Eleven

STARTING OVER AGAIN

"You gain strength, courage, and confidence by every experience in which you really stop to look fear in the face. . . . You must do the thing you think you cannot do."

—Eleanor Roosevelt, 1960

November 1933–February 1934

"It'll be a temporary assignment to start," David Dubinsky said, steepling his fingers together and leaning over his desk. "But once you've had some success, and I know you will, I'll make it permanent."

Has this man lost his mind? Probably not. Crazy men don't become the president of ILGWU. Except he had asked Angela to meet with him. Lowly organizers like her never met with union presidents.

"You want me to go to Baltimore? Me? Are you sure?" Angela asked.

"I don't make mistakes, Mrs. Camponeschi. Nor do I joke about job offers." He smiled at her to curb the severity of his words.

"It's Bambace," she said. "I took my maiden name back after the divorce."

She waited for him to object. Most of the union men she'd met didn't like that she was a woman, let alone a divorced woman who'd given up her husband's name. There'd been a lot of gossip about Dubinsky in both the Local 25 and the Local 22. Some people said he was a radical, while others said he was a reactionary. Angela was about to see which.

He looked down at some papers on his desk, his thick silver hair shining in the light of his desk lamp.

Angela's heart raced. *Did I just anger the union president?*

"I'm sorry, Mrs. Bambace. I'll make a note of that here," he said. "I suspect—ah, well, you are no doubt familiar with the previous president's beliefs."

Angela's shoulders slumped in despair. "Then you know why I left your union."

Morris Sigman was one of the reasons she left the ILGWU for Amalgamated. The former ILGWU president had led a purge of the union's leftists. And people said Dubinsky had lobbied for Sigman's presidency in 1925. Sigman lasted only three years as president, but he'd gathered around himself a cadre of reactionary men who liked to pretend workingwomen didn't exist.

Angela gripped her purse tightly in her lap, aware she was not being terribly polite to this man. The inter-union war of the mid-twenties had not been good for the ILGWU. In fact, she'd gone back to Amalgamated to get away from the infighting.

That, and under Sidney Hillman, Amalgamated took women workers and organizers more seriously than the ILGWU. Still, she'd returned to the fold after Sigman's resignation in 1928 opened the door for the return of Benjamin Schlesinger. A socialist, Schlesinger had been the union's president before Sigman, and his return to the post signaled an end to the war on the left. But Schlesinger died last summer, yet another victim of tuberculosis, which ran rampant amongst people who'd once worked long hours in poorly ventilated factories.

Dubinsky stood and walked around the desk to take a chair next to Angela. She noticed he wasn't much taller than Fiorello La Guardia. "It's not my union, Mrs. Bambace. It's our union. I intend to end the exclusion of women from the union's leadership. After Miss Pesotta's triumph in Los Angeles, no one can doubt the efficacy of female leadership."

Angela grinned. "Rose is quite a woman."

She'd known Rose Pesotta since 1919, back when she belonged to the Local 25. The ILGWU sent her to Los Angeles last year to organize the Mexican women in the city's needle trades. They'd started with fairly simple demands: the women would be allowed to join the union, they'd be guaranteed thirty-five hours of work each week, and the factories would be brought up to minimum safety standards. Owners played hardball, probably on the assumption that Mexican women wouldn't stand up for themselves. They'd found out otherwise. The women went out on strike in October and in spite of regular beatings from the Los Angeles Police, they'd stood firm. After twenty-six days, L.A.'s garment industry gave in to their demands. Rose Pesotta was out there now, establishing the Local 96.

Dubinsky nodded his agreement. "I want you to do for Baltimore what Pesotta did for Los Angeles. In many ways, they're similar jobs. Even though it's less than two hundred miles from New York, Baltimore is a southern city, with all the race problems of the South. You'll be organizing white and black workers."

Angela couldn't believe her ears. "We're going after black women?" she asked.

"If they work in the needle trades, we are," Dubinsky said.

"Won't that put them in danger?"

"It may. Them and you both." Dubinsky walked to the window. Dark gray clouds gathered over the buildings across the street. "It looks like snow," he said. He ran a hand through his hair. "It's not that different from Los Angeles's attitude toward Mexican women. I think Rose had luck there because they recognized her as an outsider. Oh, sure, she isn't Mexican, but as a Russian Jew she's not mainstream American. You're not either. That's one of the reasons I think you'll do well in Baltimore. Also, Philip Randolph speaks highly of you."

"You know Randolph?"

A few years before, Randolph had organized the railroad porters into the Brotherhood of Sleeping Car Porters, the first African American union. She'd met him in 1922 when he'd been running for some state office, she couldn't remember which. He'd come to an Amalgamated meeting to speak about the racial divide.

"Met him last spring," Dubinsky said, "at one of those meetings in Washington with Perkins."

"So you know Frances Perkins too?"

Dubinsky returned to his office chair. "I wouldn't say I know Madame Secretary, but I sat in a few meetings with her. Astounding woman. She's everything you've heard and more."

"Is it true she's going after a federal minimum wage? And a statute to make child labor illegal?"

Dubinsky beamed. "She is, and more. There's something in the wind about a federal retirement program. Something people pay into and then get back when they're too old to work. Social Security, she's calling it. Can you imagine that?"

Angela couldn't. Poor people in America—everywhere, really—usually worked until they died. "It's a wonderful idea. The conservatives will go crazy, saying the communists and socialists have taken over," she said.

Dubinsky laughed. "I expect you know she got her start here in New York."

"I thought she was from Boston. Didn't she go to one of those fancy girls' colleges?"

"She did. I didn't mean she was from New York, only that she got her start organizing in New York. She was here when the Triangle Shirtwaist Factory burned."

Angela could hardly believe her ears. "Me too," she said. "I was just a kid, but I grew up in East Harlem. I went with my mom and a neighbor to see the burned building, then down to Misery Lane, where I saw the bodies. It was terrible. And another neighbor took my sister and me to the funeral and procession. I've never forgotten it."

"Neither has Perkins, so you have that in common," he said, then looked at his watch and frowned. "I'm afraid I have another meeting. Will you do it? Will you go to Baltimore and organize a local union for us there?"

Angela stood. "I need to think about it. I have two sons and a mother to think of. They live in Queens."

Dubinsky stood and held out his hand. "Think fast, Mrs.

Bambace. This union needs you. More importantly, those workers in Baltimore need you. If you can do there what you did in New Jersey, you'll make history in the South—a lady organizer in a town they said couldn't be unionized."

Angela shook Dubinsky's hand and assured him he'd hear from her before the week was out. By the time she left the office and walked down the two flights of stairs to the sidewalk, she'd made up her mind: she'd take the job. She didn't know how she'd manage it with Mamma and the boys, and Luigi wouldn't like it, but she was going to take that job. After years of being angry with unions refusing to take women seriously, she couldn't very well turn down an opportunity like this. She stopped on the sidewalk and looked up. Snowflakes swirled down from the sky, the first of the season. She should get home before it got much worse. Instead, she turned and headed back into the building. She wouldn't keep Dubinsky in suspense.

The door opened with a loud click of the lock. Angela tugged the key out, reminding herself to buy a little bottle of olive oil. The stuff did wonders with sticky locks and squeaky hinges. She pushed open the door, stepped inside her new office, and nearly turned to leave. *It's cheap for a reason. And its address, 1 North Eutaw, couldn't be more perfect.* The linoleum floor was gray with grime, a pile of broken chairs littered one corner, and a blizzard of old paper covered the three desks. She flipped the light switch. Nothing. At least the heat was on. If only Mamma were here to help, instead of at home in Flushing with the boys. She relocked the door and walked two blocks down to a small corner market to buy supplies. A cold wind tugged at her stocking-clad legs. She'd thought Baltimore would be warmer than this, even though it was January. It was warmer than New York, but not by much.

Back at the office she unloaded a crate of cleaning supplies, including a mop, broom, and a packet of dishtowels. She was glad she'd worn her old dress. Six hours later, she'd hauled the papers, which turned out to be insurance invoices, to the basement incinerator and dragged the broken furniture out to the alley. She'd mopped the floor three times before it was clean, an undertaking made easier by the big sink in the bathroom at the back of the office. She used newspaper and vinegar to clean the front window, which now let in enough light to make the room seem downright cheerful.

One more trip to the market netted her a sandwich of capicola and fontina, a bottle of root beer, a notebook, and a box of pencils. While she ate she made three lists: office supplies, to-dos, and questions. Unions didn't go South much and the ILGWU didn't have even one office in Baltimore, nor in any other Southern city.

As she wrote, her excitement grew. She had a real chance to make her mark, to build something from the ground up, and if she succeeded it would make up for being away from Oscar, Philip, and Mamma. She'd give herself a year. If it worked, she'd get a bigger apartment, talk Luigi into moving to Baltimore, and have a spare room for the boys to visit. Maybe they could go to college in Baltimore. The city had excellent colleges, including Johns Hopkins and University of Maryland. Her boys would have the education she never did. Plus, Luigi said he'd come every weekend and look for a job in Baltimore. They could live together then, which would be lovely. He wasn't a perfect man, but there was no doubt about it—he was the love of her life.

She would succeed at this job, establish a vibrant ILGWU

shop, get a promotion, make more money, and send her boys to college. Angela's heart quickened at the thought. She bent her head to her to-do list and drew a line through "Turn on electricity." There'd be plenty of natural light until mid-October. First, she needed people to run Baltimore's newest union office.

Two weeks later, she'd hired four people. She'd found her office manager by putting a sign in the window. Ella didn't look old enough to be out of school and she was as sweet as the local ice tea, but she had the shop whipped into shape after her first week of work. Mr. Dubinsky pulled Nick and Eddie from a New York local and sent them to Baltimore to act as Angela's organizers. Nick Bonanno wasn't much older than Ella, but he was eager to learn union organizing from an old-hand New Yorker like Angela, or so he said. Eddie was less impressed with her. She overheard him telling Nick that women shouldn't have union jobs and he'd do better job of it. Angela wasn't surprised. The ILGWU didn't have many women in management positions and most men didn't want to work for a woman boss. She figured Mr. Dubinsky sent Eddie to test her resolve.

She'd also hired a driver. She had the budget for a full-time secretary, but not the operation to keep one busy full time, so she figured she'd use half the secretary salary to hire a driver. In New York everyone got around on the subways and trains, so she'd never learned to drive. But her new job came with a car and there were factories outside the city that were hard get to without one. So she'd had Nick park the car in front of the office and put a sign on it say, "Driver wanted." Jesse had stuck his head in the office soon after and asked about the driving job. He was tall and thin, and had a tendency to stoop. He also had a bad leg that made him limp, but he laughed at Angela's jokes and didn't mind working for a woman.

Eddie came half undone when he found out Angela hired a black driver. He didn't want Jesse in the front office, but Angela didn't care. She told Eddie that they weren't here to organize just the white folks, or to play along with segregation. Union organizing was about equality, and equality wasn't a thing only some people had. Either everyone was equal or no one was. Besides, Jesse had a quiet way about him that she found restful and he didn't mind that the job was only part-time.

For now, she had Nick and Eddie canvasing the factories in the north side of Baltimore, while Jesse drove her south early each morning to one factory or another. She'd stand outside the doors and catch the workers as they went in to work. She talked and handed out fliers, knowing most of them would end up in a trash can. Union organizing was like damning a fast river. You threw in rocks and they washed away. You threw in more and they washed away. But one day a rock stuck, and then another, and before you know it, you'd stopped the water. Or started a union.

Most of the workers were afraid to even talk to a union organizer, let alone go to a meeting or sign up.

"You going to pay my rent after I get fired?" one upset woman asked Angela.

Another one said, "Sure, I'd like to get paid more. But Mr. Mayfair's only got so much money. You union types get the wages jacked up and they'll have to let some of the workers go to pay for the rest of us."

When Angela tried to explain that it didn't work that way, the woman refused to believe her.

"Mr. Mayfair said so himself. And he'd know," the woman said.

"Listen," Angela argued, "I've been doing this for fifteen

years and I can tell you, all employers say something like that. Then the union comes in, wages go up, and somehow the shop keeps going."

The woman put her hands on her hips and glared at Angela. "Don't make no sense."

"Sure, it does," Angela said. "Workers are happier, they work harder, they quit less, do better work, all that. And maybe at the end of the day, they have enough left over to buy some of what they make. Everyone wins."

It wasn't an argument she'd had much success with, at least not yet, but she was building a damn. One day a woman would listen, then another, and they'd have a meeting, and before you know it the shop would be unionized. And once everyone saw nothing terrible happened, the second and third would go faster, if not easier. Nothing was easy when you were fighting for what was right.

Their first day out, they'd passed a roadside stand around lunchtime. Fabulous barbecued meat smells wafted out of the place, just a few hundred feet from the factory she'd been working that morning. After years of eating with a dozen or so seamstresses, she hated to eat alone, so she asked Jesse to come eat with her.

He jerked his head back and forth so hard his hat shifted, exposing his close-cut silver hair. "No, ma'am. I got my lunch right here," he said, reaching over the back seat and pulling out a dented lunch pail. "You go on in by yourself, Mrs. Bambace."

She'd tried to get him to call her Angela but he'd refused. Ella took her aside and explained how dangerous it would be if anyone heard Jesse calling a white woman by her first name. At the sight of his lunch pail, Angela resisted the impulse to thwack herself in the forehead. "You can't eat in that place, can you? And not with me, even if you could go inside."

"No, ma'am," he said with a tired smile. "You go on now. I'll be here waiting when you get back." He opened his lunch pail to expose a wrinkled apple and a thin sandwich on drying bread.

Angela walked into the cafe and ordered two rib specials. She asked the waitress to wrap them up so she could take them home. While she waited for her lunch, she looked out the window at Jesse sitting in the car. He was eating his apple and reading a hardback book. It reminded her of the first time he'd driven her. He'd been sitting in the car reading when she'd climbed into the front passenger seat. He'd scrambled out of the car like it was on fire, then peered inside and told her she had to get in back. She'd wanted to argue, to say she wasn't the sort of bigot who couldn't share the front of a car with a black man, but the look on his face told her this wasn't about her. She kept forgetting she was in the South now, and every time she forgot, she embarrassed Jesse.

She took the lunches out to the car, vowing to make no more mistakes with her driver. Jesse took one look at the food and broke into laughter. After that they had all their lunches like that. Sometimes lunch with Jesse was the best part of her day. They'd laugh and tell stories and have a high old time.

The first day of Angela's third week at the new office, she came in to find Jesse standing by the front door, holding a slip of paper.

"Telegram for you, Mrs. B," he said, handing it to her. "Western Union boy just came by, only a minute ago."

Angela tore open the envelope to find a message from Dubinsky.

Selden Coat Company ignoring Wagner Act.
Paying women half. Go see. 301 N. Calvert St.
DD

Angela held the telegram out to Jesse. "Isn't that just a few blocks away?" she asked.

He read the telegram and nodded. "Yes, ma'am. Doesn't the Wagner Act say bosses gotta pay ladies the same as men?"

"It sure does," she said.

Also known as the National Labor Relations Act, the law was part of President Roosevelt's New Deal plan to fight the Great Depression. The Act, which Roosevelt signed into law almost six months ago, also guaranteed workers a right to unionize. It was just like Roosevelt said in his stump speech: if workers made a living wage, they'd have money to spend at the grocery store and on clothes, and all of that spending got the economy rolling again. But factory owners didn't see it that way. They couldn't see that in the long run, a decently paid employee was good for everyone. In Angela's experience, the owning class had trouble seeing anything in the long run. Short-term profits, that's what they saw. And short-term profits could be found in paying workers the least amount possible.

"You want me to go home, Mrs. B?"

Angela looked up at Jesse. "No. Let's try that factory down on Mill Road this morning, the one I canvassed the other day. I can go over to this coat factory this afternoon."

Usually, she watched the office in the afternoons so Ella could go home to her children, but it wouldn't hurt to go out. No one ever came in the office anyway. Not yet.

Angela walked over to 201 N. Calvert Street just before 3:00. It was hard to tell when factories let out. Some of them started early and let out early so the women workers could be home when their kids got out of school. Others started later and ended later so they were open during daylight hours, thus saving on lighting bills.

The directory in the building's lobby said Selden was on the fifth and sixth floors. Angela knew from experience that the cutters and seamstresses would be on the lower floor and the finishing, shipping, and administrative offices would be on the highest floor. She climbed up the stairs and peered through a glass door. Rows of women sat at long tables sewing swaths of dark wool. Angela noticed that the tables were either all white or all black women; they didn't sit together. As usual, the cutting tables took on the far side of the room, near the windows. White men wielded large razorlike knives with deadly accuracy, cutting through multiple layers of fabric with each slashing cut. Angela had never seen a factory that hired female cutters. It was one way they justified paying men more, arguing that cutting was skilled labor while sewing was not. It was nonsense, of course. If operating a sewing machine and stitching dozens of garments for hours at a time wasn't skilled work, she'd like to know what was.

There was a young, blonde woman sitting at a small desk just inside the door. In Angela's experience, there was always a woman at the door. She'd be the one to handle the time cards, keeping track of who worked which days and for how long, and a dozen other small administrative jobs that kept a place like this going. And for all that she'd be paid no more than the seamstresses, sometimes even less. The shop's bookkeeper, on the other hand, would be male and make enough money to support his family in middle-class style. In all Angela's years of factory work, she'd figured this much out: if the job was done by a man, it was important, skilled work that paid accordingly; any job done by women was considered unskilled and paid a pittance.

Angela pulled open the door and poked her head in. "When's quitting time?" she asked the woman at the desk.

The woman pointed at the wall clock and said, "The bell goes in five minutes."

Angela smiled and thanked her before scurrying back down the stairs. She knew she had to start small. If you barged right in, the women, who wanted nothing more than to leave work and go home, felt trapped. But if you caught them on the sidewalk, they'd be feeling high-spirited with the freedom of being done for the day, and would be much more amenable to rebellion.

Angela waited outside, thankful for the January sunshine. Then a knot of women came out the building's front double doors. She waited. Every group had a leader or two and they were never the first women out the door—leaders stopped and talked, figuring out problems after their shifts ended. As women walked by, some ignored Angela, and others gave her quick sideways glances that said they knew she didn't belong there.

Then Angela spotted her: a tall, rawboned woman with dishwater blonde hair. Two women in the same age range flanked her while a gaggle of younger women came behind, like tender boats around the tall ships in Baltimore's harbor.

Angela stepped up to the tall woman. "Excuse me, could you spare a moment to talk? It's important," she said.

The woman reared back her head like she'd seen a dangerous animal, but then she smiled and stopped. "Sure. Watchoo up to?" Her voice came out rich and deep, like aged scotch, with a hint of West Virginia hill country.

Angela introduced herself, careful to keep the New York Italian accent out of her voice.

"Girls, we got ourselves a real-life union organizer," the woman said. The women laughed and squealed in faux dismay. "Now settle down and let's hear what Mrs. Bambace has to say. Oh, I'm Mrs. Macintosh," she said, sticking out a large-knuckled hand.

Angela took her hand, recognizing the needle scars on the woman's forefingers for what they were.

The other two older women introduced themselves as well, one as Miss Baumgartner and the other as Mrs. Graziano.

"I hear you all are paid less than the men," Angela said, giving everyone a flier announcing a meeting this coming Thursday afternoon.

Mrs. Macintosh nodded. "I been working here for nigh on five years. Just glad to have a job, mostly. But it ain't fair."

Miss Baumgartner and Mrs. Graziano agreed. The flock of young women behind them shifted around, but didn't say anything.

"It's against the law now that Roosevelt's the president," Angela said. "If you join the union, we can make them pay you the same as the men."

"The police don't care about us," Mrs. Macintosh said, and spat on the sidewalk. The other women gasped in shock.

Angela shook her head. "I didn't say the police. I said the law. It's against the law."

"But the police enforce the law, and they don't care what we get paid. We'll get fired," Mrs. Graziano said, more to Mrs. Macintosh than to Angela.

"No," Angela said. Her voice came out louder than she meant. "The president passed another law that says you can't fire people for unionizing. And you can't pay union women less. So if they fire you, we can sue them."

"Ha. Fat lot of good that does my family," Mrs. Macintosh said. "I still gotta pay the bills and the baby needs medicine for her ears. We all got bills." She gestured to the women gathered around her.

"I know. I do too," Angela said. "But we won't have to sue them. You wait and see. They know we can sue and they know we'll win, so they won't fight you. They won't fight us."

Angela stood on the street and talked to the Selden Coat Factory women for another twenty minutes, after which Mrs. Macintosh agreed to get some of the black women to talk next time.

It went pretty quickly after that. Each day she talked to another group of women and her groups gradually became larger. Angela thought organizing women was easier than organizing men. Women were more likely to be angry and more likely to take a chance with a union, maybe because they had less to lose than male workers. And she found that organizing black women was nearly effortless. No one had less to lose than a black woman who worked in a factory below the Mason-Dixon Line.

By Easter they had a union contract and a 25 percent pay raise. And no one lost their job. The factory owner, Mr. Mayweather, tried a workaround, offering the women a raise if they didn't join the union, but the gambit backfired on him. Mrs. Jefferson, an older woman who spoke for the black seamstresses, pointed out that if Mr. Mayweather could afford a raise without the union, he could afford a raise *with* the union. All the ladies agreed, especially after they figured out Mr. Mayweather was more afraid of losing his workforce than he was of paying them a fair wage.

Later, Angela would look back at the Selden Coat Factory as the turning point in her career. Before Selden, she'd been a mediocre shirtwaist seamstress who organized on the side. Selden made her a professional labor organizer, one who made her bones organizing a Southern city everyone said was not organizable. That she did it with a workforce one-third black and nearly all female only made her achievement seem all that much larger to the men who ran the union.

Angela understood that she'd succeeded, not in spite of the mixed workforce, but because of it.

Chapter Twelve

MARCH FOR DEMOCRACY

"A fascist is one whose lust for money or power is combined with such an intensity of intolerance toward those of other races, parties, classes, religions, cultures, regions, or nations to make him ruthless in his use of deceit and violence to attain his ends."

—Henry Wallace
Thirty-third US Vice President, 1946

March–April 1936

"Mamma, I'd like you to meet Dorothy Welch and Helen Miller," Oscar said. His smile looked more than a little uneven. He'd never brought a girl home before, and Angela supposed he technically still hadn't. Baltimore wasn't Oscar's home, though he and Philip came down on the train every other weekend to visit. She found a bigger apartment after Luigi moved in, one with a spare bedroom for the boys. After a year of bimonthly visits, they'd made some friends in the city. Oscar was talking about going to college in Baltimore after he graduated high school.

The girl closest to Oscar was a budding beauty who, at fifteen or sixteen, still retained an awkward coltishness common in girls that age. Her light brown hair framed her face in soft waves and her gray-blue eyes crinkled with pleasure. The girl next to her was shorter, darker, and less lithe, but just as happy looking. She'd bobbed her hair, marking herself as a girl rebel. These were girls who didn't have to quit school and work in the woolen mills or dressmaking factories. Happy, loved, well-fed girls.

Angela smiled at them. "Miss Welch, Miss Miller, how do you do? Oscar, ask your friends if they'd like to sit and if they need anything."

Oscar blushed while the girls smiled and said the appropriate polite things. "Mamma, Dorothy and Helen have a problem they think you could help them with."

These two? A problem? It hardly seemed likely. Angela sat forward and tried to act unsurprised. "What can I help you with, ladies?"

Dorothy glanced at her dark-haired friend, who nodded encouragingly.

"It's not so much our problem as it is a problem with the city," Dorothy said. She grabbed a small handful of her skirt, crumpled it, and let it go.

Angela kept her face straight, but not without effort. She could barely remember being this young and unsure. "Start at the beginning and see where your words take you," she said.

Dorothy firmed up her shoulders and gave a slight smile. "We both go to Western High School. You know, in Upton."

Angela did know. Upton was an old Baltimore neighborhood

and Western was the oldest all-girls public school in Baltimore. It had a reputation for readying its students for nearby Goucher College, another all-girls institution. If Angela had a daughter, she'd send her to Western and Goucher.

"Well, last year Father Evers gave a talk at our school. You know about him?"

Angela nearly upset her coffee cup. They'd been talking about Evers down at the ILGWU office just the other day. "I do know him. He's a German-American and the pastor at Zion Church. He's also a Nazi sympathizer."

"Yes, yes, he is," Helen said, leaning forward. "He pretends to be all nice, but he's scary."

"No," Dorothy said, shaking her head. "His ideas are scary. I think it's possible to have scary ideas and still be a good person, don't you, Mrs. Bambace?"

"Goodness, what a question. Perhaps. I've always thought actions count more than words. What did the pastor do to upset you so?"

"It's not just him," Dorothy said. "But let me get back to the beginning. He gave this speech at school and he said we all misunderstood Hitler and his followers. He said Hitler had given the Germans a sense of security they badly needed after the war."

"Not just that," Helen interjected. "He said that what was happening to the German Jews was their fault. That they were in the way of real German's economic success. Isn't that dumb? How could German war debt be the Jews' fault?"

"It's not about logic. Hate never is," Angela replied. "People like a scapegoat for trouble, someone to blame for their problems. And the someone is always an outsider group—immigrants, Catholics, anarchists, socialists, black people, or Jews, groups like that. You know there's a fair number of people in this country who don't like Jews."

"Well, a few of us girls got together after the talk and wrote a letter," Dorothy said. "Most of the girls wouldn't sign it, but some did. Then we gave the letter to Principal Lewis. He told us there was nothing wrong with Father Evers's speech, so we gave the letter to Betty Richard's dad. He's a reporter for the *Baltimore Sun*. And he asked Father Evers about it."

"Well, Father Evers said we were being supersensitive. Supersensitive!" In her indignation, Helen's voice climbed into registers only heard by dogs.

Angela leaned forward and patted Helen's knee. "You can't let it upset you so much. As a woman, you'll be accused of being oversensitive, hysterical, emotional, and worse. It's what men say when they want to dismiss female anger. It's also a tactic used by bullies to dismiss objections of the bullied. You'll run into it time and time again—at least, you will if you grow up to care about right and wrong.

"Of course I will," Helen nearly screeched. She caught herself and looked abashed. Oscar's and Dorothy's looks of astonishment raised a pink blush on her cheeks. "I'm sorry."

"Don't be," Angela said in a tone as reassuring as she could manage. *When did I become the wise old woman in the room?* "Passion is a rare commodity. You should be proud you have it. Both of you girls. But I don't understand what you want from me."

Dorothy glanced at Helen, then spoke. "It's presumptuous, but Oscar says you know people. Important people. He says you always fight for the right thing, no matter what."

Angela looked at Oscar in amazement.

"You do," he said with one of his wide grins. "Did you think me and Philip hadn't noticed? And you taught it to us."

"I guess I did." Angela felt her own cheeks blush. When had her son turned into a man? She wanted to tell him how much she loved him, but stopped herself. He'd find it excruciatingly embarrassing.

Dorothy shifted in her chair, then settled back in. "Well, now there's a Nazi flag flying at the German embassy."

Ah, life's coincidences. "We were discussing it yesterday down at the office," Angela said.

Helen touched Dorothy's arm. "And that ship. Don't forget the ship."

Before Dorothy could speak, Angela did. "You mean the German battle cruiser scheduled to dock in the Baltimore harbor next month? Yes, we'd heard."

"We?" asked Oscar.

"A lot of people, Oscar," Angela explained. "Rabbi Israel met with us last week, along with a young black fellow from the NAACP. He and the rabbi want the union's help planning an anti-Nazi rally."

Dorothy popped up to her feet. "That's just what we were going to ask you to help us with. Some kind of demonstration or parade or something so the good people of Baltimore don't feel outnumbered by the Nazi lovers."

Oscar laughed and leapt to his feet as well. "See? I told you she'd help."

Dorothy leaned over and planted a kiss on Oscar's cheek. "You're the bee's knees."

Oscar flushed red to the tips of his ears and collapsed back into his seat.

Angela pretended she'd seen nothing. She'd discovered in mothering boys that pretending to see nothing was usually the wisest course. Instead, she talked to the girls.

"I take it you and your friends at school would like to help?" Angela said. "If we have this march, we'll need to get a permit for it first. But if we do, we could use you to hand out fliers. A lot of fliers. But only if your parents say you can."

Both the girls bounced in their chairs and promised they'd round up two dozen girls to help. "Honestly, Mrs. Bambace, our moms will probably want to help too," Dorothy said. "Right, Helen?"

Helen nodded so enthusiastically that her curly hair looked like it had a mind of its own.

In the face of the girls' enthusiasm, Angela felt brighter than she had in months. Had she once been this way? She didn't think so. These girls had never been to Misery Lane, which, she supposed, was exactly what she'd been fighting for her entire life: for girls who wouldn't have to know how bad things could be.

The German warship *Emden* docked as planned in the second week of April. Jesse drove Angela down to the harbor to see what the fuss was about. He parked just down the block from the wharf.

"You go see, Mrs. B. I've seen enough foolishness in my day to last me a lifetime," he said.

"You don't want to go?" she asked.

He shook his head. "Too many angry white folks for the likes of me."

Angela breathed a sigh of relief. The crowd that gathered to see one of Hitler's ships wasn't the kind that would welcome a black man, especially a black man with a white woman.

She walked down the sidewalk to the two-story steel pier that held the *Emden*. The dockside crowd had adopted a carnival-going attitude, with giggling girls wearing their best dresses and flirting with blue-eyed sailors and a crowd of German and English speakers excited to see a ship bristling with guns. She'd read in the newspaper that the *Emden* was five hundred feet long and carried six hundred officers and sailors. And as the ship had approached Baltimore, the captain gave his crew a rousing speech celebrating Hitler's birthday.

There were nearly seventy thousand German-Americans living in the Baltimore area, some of them only recently arrived and others going back to the immigration waves of the early nineteenth century. Like the Italian immigrants in New York, many of them lived in German-speaking enclaves that resisted assimilation. Angela thought this sort of thing made sense for first-generation immigrants. Technically, she was a first-generation, having been born in Brazil, but she'd come to America before she turned two, so it seemed like home. Not so for the people who'd come here as adults. If she had found herself in a strange land as an adult, she'd want markets with familiar food and people who spoke the same language too.

But the children and grandchildren of immigrants generally thought of themselves as much more American than old country. Look at Oscar and Philip—for all that they were 100 percent Italian stock, they were also 100 percent American. But Italy and Germany's turn toward fascism in the last few years had encouraged culturally conservative immigrants to imagine they'd be better off in the home country. Angela had seen an interview in the newspaper where a German-American man called it a mistake that his father had moved to America.

Angela knew some Italians like that. Heck, she'd been married to one. Romolo had never acculturated to America. He spoke Italian, he ate Italian, and he worked for and with Italians.

Papà had been like that too, but Papà's problem was more that wherever he was, he thought the next place was better. When he was in Italy he thought Brazil would be better, and in Brazil he'd yearned for Italy, and when he returned to Italy he turned his eyes to America. But once here, he'd never been happy.

She bumped into a young couple who'd stopped to buy a cup of lemonade from a street vendor. After apologizing, Angela turned her eye to the ship causing all the commotion. It was frighteningly big. And it was flying a bright red, white, and black Nazi flag. The sight of it hit Angela like an unexpected punch in her midsection. She turned away from it and caught sight of a familiar man's face.

"Mrs. Bambace," the man said, his voice deep and melliflu-ous, as if he were older than his mid-twenties.

"Mr. Marshall," Angela replied with a smile, as polite as their exchange could be in this kind of public setting.

Thurgood Marshall was a Baltimore native, educated at Frederick Douglass High School and Howard University's School of Law. He came to prominence two years earlier when he brought a case against the University of Maryland for keeping black students out of law school. He'd won by pointing out the weakness in *Plessy v. Fergusson*'s "separate but equal" standard, that separate was *never* equal.

Angela first met Thurgood at a NAACP meeting. The ILGWU brought the legendary Philip Randolph, the man who'd organized a union for Pullman porters, to Baltimore last year. She'd introduced Philip that night, and met young Thur-good right beforehand. She'd heard through the grapevine that Thurgood was in charge of the NAACP's contributions to the anti-Nazi rally, but she hadn't yet spoken to him about it.

Thurgood looked over the crowd at the ship. "Scary, isn't it?" His voice was low and quiet.

"More than I thought it would be." She waved at the happy crowd and said, "Somehow this makes it worse."

"Worse than the mayor?" Thurgood spoke without taking his eyes off the ship.

Representatives of a dozen city churches and organizations—the rabbis, ACLU, NAACP, the Urban League, YMCA and YWCA, and the People's Unemployment League, as well as representatives of the ILGWU, including herself—had signed a document protesting the *Emden*'s arrival and presented it to the mayor's office, who dismissed the document as "too radical."

"The mayor is one man and he's more worried about votes than right and wrong," Angela said. They both knew German-Americans constituted a huge voting bloc in the city.

Marshall agreed. "This isn't all of Baltimore. There are good people here. You wait and see."

Angela hoped he was right. While she walked back to Jesse and the car, she worried. What happens when you throw a rally and no one comes? Or the wrong people show up? What happens then?

The morning of April 22, Angela rolled out of bed to find a leaden gray sky. She kissed Luigi's cheek, careful not to wake him up, and tiptoed into the kitchen. He'd been out late at a union meeting.

These days he worked with the Steel Workers Organizing Committee as part of the Congress of Industrial Organizations (CIO). They were having some success, which was saying something. Steel workers were harder to organize because steel companies were larger and more aggressive than textile companies, and therefore better at resisting worker unionization. Luigi spent a lot of time in Pennsylvania, where the worst of the mills were, but he always came home to Angela.

Her feeling of impending doom held while she made coffee and toast. She looked longingly at the bath before she dressed, wishing she had time for a leisurely soak. The march was scheduled for noon, so people could attend on their lunch hour, but there was lots to be done before then.

She walked two blocks from her house to her favorite trolley stop on Howard Street. The trolley took her past the city's Lexington Market, a vast commercial area that sold everything from sides of beef to French pastries. She often stopped there on her way home, enjoying the genial cacophony of all the voices hawking wares in dozens of languages as much as she did the food she purchased.

At Pratt Street she hopped off the trolley, waving goodbye to the conductor. She caught another trolley across town to Fells Point, a piece of land that jutted into the city's harbor. They had a permit to use the Thames Street Park for the start of the protest. After some brief speeches they'd march down Thames Street, which ran along the waterfront, to where the *Emden* was moored.

Angela arrived in the park to find volunteers erecting a temporary speaking platform. Policemen stood at the park's corners, watching and waiting. Angela made a note to speak to them. She'd found protests went a lot better when you made friends with the police. They were men with families who, by and large, didn't want violence any more than the protesters or strikers did.

Then she saw Helen and Dorothy. She hustled over to the

girls. "It's a school day. What are you two doing here?" Angela asked.

They grinned like schoolgirls on a holiday. "Our civics teacher talked Principal Lewis into excusing us," Dorothy explained.

"Betty, Mary, and Lucy are here too," Helen said, pointing behind her.

Angela waved the extra girls over and said to them, "I'm Mrs. Bambace. I'm sure Dorothy and Helen told you about me."

The girls admitted that they knew all about Oscar's mom, the union organizer.

"Here's the deal I'm going to make with you. I'm in no position to tell you to go home, but I won't have you in danger either." She gave them her steeliest glare. "See those men?" she asked, nodding at the policemen. "They're here to protect us. We have a permit and that means permission from the city for our protest and march."

"The mayor's fine with this?" Helen asked. She grinned at Angela, knowing she was being cheeky.

Angela chuckled. "You wouldn't think so, but he is. He signed the permit. I suspect he doesn't like Nazis in his city any more than we do, but he's worried about reelection. I suspect he's using this protest to test the water. You understand?"

The girls all nodded.

"Back to my original point. The police are here because they expect violence. Nazi supporters aren't afraid to get physical, nor are their brothers-in-arms, the Ku Klux Klanners. If there is violence, I want you girls to scram. Find a policeman, run away, whatever seems sensible at the time."

The girls agreed they'd run at the first sight of danger, but the gleam in their eyes told Angela they were having a grand adventure. She remembered how she'd felt when she and Marie went up to Lawrence to see Carlo Tresca—she'd thought that had been a great adventure too. Angela made a note to thank her mother the next time she saw her.

"Did you hand out all your fliers?" Angela asked.

"We have a few more," one of the new girls said, holding up a cotton bag.

"Pair up and hand out the rest. And be sure you're polite, even if someone is rude to you."

Angela watched the girls go, grateful for their volunteer help. And it wasn't just high school girls. Rabbi Israel used funds his congregation raised to print twenty thousand fliers, which they'd been handing out the last few days. The ladies in the rabbi's congregation did the bulk of the work getting the word out, though the high school girls had done their best.

The Zimmermans had introduced Angela to the rabbi right after she'd first moved to Baltimore, and she'd been glad they did. The rabbi was a moral force for labor organizations and had been for decades. The last few years he'd turned his community's energies toward the struggle for unemployment insurance.

When she'd first heard that the federal government might use tax dollars to help people who lost their jobs, she'd thought it would never get anywhere, not even with FDR in the White House. Then, lo and behold, last year's Social Security Act included a provision for funding just such a thing. The last time they'd talked, the rabbi told her he was working on school lunch programs for poor children. In a democracy, he'd told her, all children have the right not to be hungry at school.

As the morning progressed, the park began to fill with people, many of them carrying signs. She saw boards that read, "We're with the German People—Against Hitler," and "Don't

Let It Happen Here." A number of signs began with the word "Congratulations" and ended with "on Destroying Democracy, on Persecuting Labor Leaders, on Burning the Books, and on Persecuting Minorities." Angela knew some of the signs had been made at her office and others at the NAACP office, but most of them looked like the efforts of regular citizens.

Once the clock tower on the bank across the street tolled noon, they began. The rabbi introduced a man from the American League Against War and Fascism, a group made up mostly of pacifists. The speaker reminded the crowd of the George Armwood lynching only three years before, in 1933. Accused of assaulting a white woman, Armwood was beaten by the police, then taken from jail by a crowd, who hanged him and burned his body.

"Hate and economic crisis can turn workers into fascist material," the man said. Angela knew he was right. Hate was the first step toward fascism.

The next speaker was a representative of Baltimore's Finnish Federation. He read a letter of protest sent to the German ambassador and Hitler, asking for the release of all political prisoners. Angela assumed the crowd knew that "political prisoners" was code for "German Jews."

As far as Angela was concerned, the highlight of the protest speeches came when Elizabeth Gilman took the stage. A socialist who'd run for governor a few years before, Gilman played an important role among Baltimore's progressives.

Gilman talked about the pro-Nazi controversy of 1934, when Maryland celebrated the three hundredth anniversary of its founding. The parade for the anniversary was to be a "cast of thousands," celebrating the state's history of tolerance. Parade organizers asked the German delegation not to fly the Nazi flag in the parade. Rather than comply, the delegation withdrew from the parade and began a public campaign to discredit the event. Reverend Evers, of Western High School infamy, likened the banishment of the swastika to "severing the stripes from the stars in the flag of the United States." Gilman spoke eloquently about the dangers of pro-fascist clergy, pointing out that Evers had on several occasions made public statements blaming Jewish propaganda for turning America toward Anti-Nazism.

Angela snorted at this part of Gilman's speech. Most of the Germans she knew were hard-working, decent people who believed in democracy and tolerance. Some of the people in the park wore buttons that said "I'm German and I Hate Hitler."

Like Italian immigrants, ethnic Germans had a hard time in America during the Great War. Angela supposed all immigrants from countries America went to war with did. It wasn't fair, but what did Mamma always say? *Angela, whoever told you it would be fair?* She supposed mammas everywhere said that to their children.

As Gilman finished her speech, Angela caught Edward Lewis's eye and gave him the nod. Lewis, a tall, light-skinned black man, headed the city's branch of the Urban League. Lewis had a cadre of volunteers ready to get people moving down Thames Street when the time came.

In the end they didn't have any trouble, or not any worth speaking of. The police closed Thames Street for the five blocks between the park and the *Emden* and the marchers went right down the street. Angela thought it would be a good day to rob a bank because it looked like every policeman in Baltimore stood sentinel on Thames Street. Crowds of spectators lined the sidewalks, most of them cheering, some of them mocking. Hundreds joined them in their walk down the street.

The sun broke through the clouds as they reached the wharf, reminding Angela that there really was nothing as much fun, nor more empowering, as a peaceful protest. Surrounded by like-minded individuals, all of them different races, religions, and ages, all of them demonstrating their desire for a better world, a person could believe in freedom and justice for all.

The people in Germany certainly couldn't do this, nor the Italians under Mussolini. Angela was lucky she lived in a country where fascists hadn't taken the reins of power and where, hopefully, they never would. They were all lucky to live where you could protest and sometimes even win.

And wasn't that the promise of America? That in a democracy, people could fight for what they thought was right—and if they did, then little by little, they could win?

The next day, the *Baltimore Sun* reported that two thousand people had marched against fascism and another five thousand had watched from the sidelines. A small article on the newspaper's third page announced that Goucher College had canceled its dance for the *Emden*'s cadets. The piece also said the American Legion would cancel its reception for the German officers.

Five days after that, the *Emden* steamed out of the Baltimore harbor. Only a few people gathered to see the ship off.

Part V

1968–1972

Chapter Thirteen

PROTEST AND POLITICS

"If we work together, in our strength we can win whatever battles face us."

—Angela Bambace, 1972

August 1968

Angela read the letter and then the note. She smiled. Hubert Humphrey really was the nicest man. She picked up the phone and punched in the familiar numbers.

"Hello?" a young woman's voice answered.

"Mindy, it's your nanny," Angela said.

"Nanny! How are you? I miss you so much."

"I'm hoping we'll see each other soon. When do your fall classes start?"

"Not until September. Sometime the first week. I'm not sure. Why?"

"So you'll be home this summer?" Angela asked.

"Of course, Nanny," Mindy said. "Finals are the last week of May and then I'll take the bus home to Baltimore. Daddy says I can work for him this summer. He still thinks I want to be a doctor."

"You need to be who you need to be, baby. You should talk to your parents and explain. Find the thing you can do to make the world a better place and they'll accept it. You know they love you."

"I don't want to disappoint either of them," Mindy said. "And Daddy's got his heart set on me working at his hospital."

"And what do you want? Doesn't that matter?"

"Okay, Nanny. I'll think about it."

Angela thought she'd pushed her granddaughter enough for one day. Time for the real question. "So, how would you like it if the two of us took the bus back to Ohio in late August?"

"That would be oodles of fun, Nanny, but why? Are you going back to college?"

Angela laughed. "I can't go back if I've never been. No, I've received a letter from the National Democratic Committee asking me to be an alternate delegate at the convention. And Hubert Humphrey added a personal note—he really wants me there. It's in Chicago, August 23 to 28. I thought you could go with me before you start your fall semester."

"Really, Nanny? Could I?" Mindy asked.

Angela smiled at the excitement in Mindy's voice. "I think Hubert's just being nice because I'm so old, but I'd like go anyway."

"You're not old, Nanny."

"I'm almost seventy, my dear," Angela said with a chuckle. "So do you want to go? You go everywhere else with me, so why not Chicago?"

"We go to the movies and drool over Sean Connery. Or to your union things, or lunch with your ladies. Nothing like this," Mindy said. "The Democratic National Convention is going to be the protest event of the year. Maybe the decade. Of course I'll go. Wait until I tell my friends. They'll be positively green with envy."

Angela grinned into the phone. If anyone had told her how much she'd enjoy having grandchildren, she'd have skipped ahead to them first. And Oscar's daughter Mindy was such a character. Every time they were together, Angela felt decades younger.

"Speaking of the sexy Mr. Connery, did you hear?" Angela asked.

Mindy groaned into the phone. "How could he? I can't imagine anyone else as James Bond. It's just wrong."

"I heard he's sick of James Bond. Swears he'll never do another Bond movie. He's making a cowboy movie instead."

"Then we'll go see that, won't we, Nanny?"

"Yes, we will. And drool into our popcorn!"

Angela was still chuckling when she hung up the phone.

Angela slid the *Chicago Sun-Times* over to Mindy. "There's quite a panic among Mayor Daley's people," she said.

They were eating breakfast in the hotel cafe before going to the convention hall. Outside the sun was shining, as if determined to burn away the city's anger and violence.

"They say it's going to be the biggest protest ever," Mindy said, pushing away her plate and peering at the newsprint. "You'd think the Russians were attacking."

"It has ever been thus when the government encounters

leftist protests. You wouldn't remember the Palmer Raids. Or the Sacco and Vanzetti funeral parade."

"But this is the Democrats. They're not supposed to send the National Guard after people."

Angela frowned over her coffee cup. "I'm afraid Mayor Daley is a Democrat in the old Tammany Hall model, rather than the FDR model. He's an autocrat whose power comes from corrupt machine politics, and like all autocrats, he dislikes resistance. You know this stuff, kid."

Mindy sighed. "Can we go over to the park?"

Thousands of anti-war and free speech protesters had gathered in Chicago's Lincoln Park. The police regularly swept through it, arresting young people for gathering without a permit. Protesters pointed out that they'd applied for permits months ago but had been denied. An anti-war group even filed a lawsuit against the city, but the case failed when it came before a judge who'd once been Mayor Daley's law partner.

Angela shook her head. "I like a good protest as much as any woman, but this city is spoiling for another riot and I won't put you in the middle of that kind of chaos, if for no other reason than your parents would kill me."

The two women, one at the start of her life and the other nearing the end, appraised each other. They both knew Chicago experienced three days of rioting back in April in the wake of the Martin Luther King Jr.'s assassination. Violence escalated after Mayor Daley told the police to "shoot to kill" rioters. The rioters had responded with more violence, including arson, looting, and attacks on white and black people alike. Thirty-nine people died in the riot and thousands more were injured or had property destroyed.

Mindy sighed again. "Okay, Nanny."

"I know you don't like it, but yesterday Mayor Daley issued another 'shoot to kill' order if protesters don't vacate the park each night by eleven p.m.," Angela said.

Mindy shook her head. "I can't believe we live in a country where shooting protesters is a thing we do."

An image of a machine gun set up across the street from striking picketers popped into Angela's mind. She shook her head, jolting the image from her mind.

"Let's get going. The first day of a nominating convention is always fun," Angela said.

They had a long day at the International Amphitheater. Delegates argued among themselves all day, mostly about the Vietnam War and whether it was fair that Humphrey be a nominee. As the de facto nominee, Humphrey had run in no state primary elections, instead throwing his hat in the ring at the last minute. In the primaries, President Lyndon Johnson had run against Eugene McCarthy and Robert Kennedy. Kennedy's assassination in June and Johnson's announcement that he would not seek a second term had left the field wide open for McCarthy—until Humphrey declared his candidacy right before the convention. As Johnson's vice president, he represented old-style Democratic politics and a pro-war stance, while McCarthy ran on an "elect me and I'll end the war" platform.

When Angela and Mindy left the convention after 11:00 p.m., they could smell the tear gas from the student protest. Angela hustled her granddaughter into their hotel before the gas did them any damage.

The convention's second day went just as the first until news came that security guards had roughed up newsman Dan Rather inside the convention hall. Rather had tried to interview a Georgia delegate who'd been kicked off the convention hall floor when guards punched Rather and knocked him to the floor. News cameras caught the scuffle.

The next morning, Angela and Mindy learned that esteemed anchorman Walter Cronkite called the guards thugs on national television. The news anchor also warned his viewers that the biggest protest yet was scheduled for later that day. Over fifteen thousand people were expected in Grant Park to protest the Vietnam War and the Democratic Party's tacit approval of it.

Over a room-service breakfast, Mindy asked the question that had been on her mind for days: "Nanny, I thought you hated the war in Vietnam."

"I do," Angela said, setting down her coffee cup. "It's wrong—wrong for the Vietnamese, wrong for the American boys who have to fight over there, wrong for the parents on both sides who lose their children to a senseless war, wrong that the sons of poor white and black people are the ones doing the fighting. Wrong, wrong, wrong."

"Then why support Humphrey? I mean, you're a delegate for him and he's pro-war."

"It's not that simple, baby. It never is." Angela took a sip of her coffee before continuing. "While we Democrats tear ourselves apart over this war, the Republicans have already nominated Richard Nixon. He's firmly pro-war and he's vowed to crack down on civil rights protests of all types. He's an authoritarian and I think he's dangerous. Not that most Americans would agree with me."

Mindy frowned. "What does that have to do with Humphrey?"

"Because we live in momentous times, my girl. And people who care about freedom for everyone need to vote for the person who can beat Nixon. And I think that person is

Humphrey, not McCarthy. I like McCarthy's politics just fine, but he's too far left for American voters. The white Southern Democrats won't vote for him, so if we run him they'll vote for Nixon and we'll lose the election."

Angela watched her granddaughter think. She could tell Mindy didn't like her reasoning.

"I'm not much of an idealist, honey," Angela continued. "I've always supported whichever party or person I thought could get the job done. Because in the end that's all that matters. Ideas are just ideas. Action makes people's lives better. Without action, we'd have no equality. You see?"

Mindy chewed on her lower lip. "Then what about all those protesters? Are they doing the wrong thing?"

"Absolutely not," Angela said, a bit more forcefully than she'd intended. "Without radicals there can be no middle ground. Radicals make moderate change appear reasonable by changing the conversation. We wouldn't be having this conversation right now if it weren't for the protesters. The nation wouldn't be having a conversation about the limits of free speech and the morality of the war if it weren't for the protesters. Remember, dear, it's not democracy if people can't protest."

Angela got up and looked out the hotel window. "It's peaceful out there now. Maybe it'll be fine. They say that Yippie concert in New York went really well. There wasn't any violence at all. When I read about it, it reminded me of an anti-Nazi protest we had in Baltimore years ago, before the war."

"I didn't know you had music festivals back then, Nanny," Mindy joked.

"No, silly, not the music, but the peacefulness. We expected the pro-Nazi people and the Ku Klux Klan to give us a hard time—or the police, even—but in the end the police kept everything peaceful. It was a good day. Like that Yippee concert in New York."

"Yip Out, Nanny. They called it a Yip Out."

The Yippies, or Youth International Party, led by Abbie Hoffman, planned a music festival in New York meant to be a warmup for a similar event in Chicago to be held in the park near the convention center. The NYPD had allowed a wide range of behavior at the Central Park event, to say the least, and their latitude had been rewarded with a peaceable day.

"Well, whatever they called it, it went a lot better than this business in Chicago," Angela said, motioning out the window.

Mindy joined her grandmother at the window. "To be fair, I don't think they wanted a peaceful demonstration here. The leaders said they were going to put LSD in the city water, for goodness' sake."

Prior to the Chicago convention, Yippies published fliers and articles threatening a wide variety of violent acts, from throwing nails on the roadways to cause traffic jams to contaminating city water with hallucinogenic drugs like LSD. The idea was to use this "street theater" to prove no one could influence political bigwigs into ending the war.

Angela laughed. "I can't imagine where they thought they'd get enough drugs to make a difference in a water system as large as Chicago. What a horrifying idea."

Mindy shook her head. "They wanted to shock people and it worked."

"It sure did." Angela looked at her watch. "We should get going. Are you absolutely sure you want to come? It's nominating day and things are going to get hairy, inside the convention center and outside too. You could stay here."

"Nanny!" Mindy turned toward her grandmother, her face red. "How can you say such a thing?"

Angela shrugged. "You're my grandchild and my job is to love you and keep you safe. It's not safe out there and I'm not sure it'll be much safer inside the convention center."

"I'm a grown woman, Nanny. How about I keep *you* safe from the hooligans?"

"Are you calling me a little old lady?" Nanny threw a damp towel at Mindy, who batted it away with a laugh.

"I would never, ever do that. At least not to your face," Mindy said.

They laughed and joked all the way to the hotel lobby. But one glance out the glass doors reminded them there wasn't anything funny out there. Not today.

They'd been walking for less than a minute when Angela's eyes began to burn. The tear gas was thicker today. She took a deep breath and regretted it. Her lungs screeched in protest. Beside her, Mindy sneezed. Angela dug in her purse, pulled out a crumpled handkerchief, and handed it to her granddaughter. They walked past policemen wearing riot gear. Somewhere in the distance, an ambulance wailed.

"Nanny!" Mindy tugged on Angela's purse strap and surreptitiously pointed to their left. "Is it really him?"

Angela glanced to her left, where the line for non-delegate convention attendees stretched down the sidewalk. A knot of people stood around one of the men in line. Two women squealed as the crowd shifted.

"It's Paul Newman," Mindy said, nudging her nanny.

"I heard he was coming. He's been campaigning for Eugene McCarthy since last winter, back when no one took a Minnesota congressman seriously as a presidential candidate. Some people even said it was Newman's superstar support that turned McCarthy into a viable presidential contender."

Mindy sighed. "And he was just fabulous in *Cool Hand Luke*."

Angela chuckled. "If by fabulous you mean super sexy, I agree."

"Nanny!" Mindy's look of delight belied her shocked tone. "Can we meet him?"

"He's here for McCarthy, not Humphrey, so he's not with our delegates."

"Everybody knows that, Nanny, but you know everyone."

"How would I know a big shot Hollywood star like Paul Newman?" Angela asked.

"'Cause you're you," Mindy said with a grin. "Humphrey lets you call him Hubert. And you know Thurgood Marshall and he's on the Supreme Court now."

"Well, there's a lot of space between the Supreme Court and *Cool Hand Luke*, my dear. Still, let's meander over there and see what happens."

Their efforts to get closer to the handsome movie start got them nowhere, though they got close enough to confirm his eyes really were as blue as everyone said. Newman was with the playwright Arthur Miller, which impressed Mindy not one bit, but Angela thought seeing the man who'd written *The Crucible* was pretty swanky. Though ostensibly about the Salem witch-craft trials, *The Crucible* was really a dramatic statement against the anti-leftist crusade undertaken by the House Un-American Activities Committee and Senator Joseph McCarthy, who was no relation to Newman's Eugene McCarthy, back in the 1950s.

The nominating night proved a long one. The mood in the

convention center swung from partylike ebullience to tense hostility as a number of Bobby Kennedy's delegates made a bid to nominate his younger brother Teddy. Bobby's assassination, they insisted, had unfairly prevented the anti–Vietnam War segment of the party from winning the nomination.

At one point the Maryland contingent of Humphrey delegates heard a rumor that McCarthy was going to throw his support behind Teddy. With the noise on the convention floor at an earsplitting roar, Angela and the others scrambled to find out if the rumor was true. It turned out not to be, but they had a good sixty minutes of heart-wrenching anxiety before they figured it out.

Screaming, sign-waving delegates—some for Humphrey, some for McCarthy, and a few for the dark horse candidate George McGovern—made communication nearly impossible. Sensing imminent defeat, the Humphrey delegates forced a ballot vote on the principle that the McCarthy/Kennedy movement couldn't be allowed any more time to organize.

The tactic worked. Amid boos and catcalls, the roll call began. When Illinois threw all 172 of its votes to Humphrey, the convention center erupted into a wild mix of cheers and boos. When the balloting ended, Humphrey had won 1759 votes to McCarthy's 601 and Kennedy's 12.75.

Angela watched the balloting with trepidation. She hated the Vietnam War as much as any of the young people protesting in Chicago's parks, and Humphrey's victory signaled a defeat of an anti-war plank in the party platform. But Hubert was a good man, and like she'd told Mindy, he had a better chance of beating Nixon than any other candidate. Still, they'd have more war, no matter who won the presidency. Thinking about the death that would follow made Angela sick with dread.

The convention wore on into the night. The balloting for vice president took forever, though Senator Edmund Muskie from Maine won on the first ballot. Afterward, the speeches started.

Mindy tugged at Angela's arm. "I smell tear gas," she said.

Angela agreed. The faint scent made her stomach roil. If they could smell it inside the convention hall, how bad must it be outside? Knowing it would be hours before Humphrey spoke and unable to risk the near-certain violence that would come when the main body of convention-goers left the safety of the convention, Angela grabbed Mindy and headed for the exit. They walked right past Paul Newman on their way out.

Outside, the air was thick with tear gas. They staggered toward their hotel only to find a melee of armed National Guardsmen, Chicago policemen, and unarmed protesters between them and the hotel's front doors. Unarmed civilians littered the ground while ambulance attendants scrambled between them.

Angela grabbed Mindy's arm and pulled her down the block toward the hotel's rear entrance. There they found a cluster of hotel employees helping guests inside. They rode the elevator in silence.

Once inside their hotel room, they returned to the window. The scene outside was a nightmarish conglomeration of whirling red, blue, and yellow police and ambulance lights set against the darkness. Even from three stories up, with the windows closed, they could hear protesters chanting, "Hell no, we won't go."

The morning newspapers disagreed about the events outside the convention hall. The Chicago newspaper praised Mayor Daley's no-nonsense stance toward the demonstrators and commended the police for controlling the crowd. The *New York Times* noted that the police and National Guard had been more violent than the protesters, though the paper blamed everyone present for the violence and injuries. The police arrested 668 people and over 400 demonstrators were treated for tear gas exposure.

Angela and Mindy checked out of the hotel that day and took a bus to Oberlin, Ohio, where Angela met her grand-daughter's friends and toured their college campus. Afterward, she rode the bus home. She arrived in Maryland eight days after Humphrey's vice presidential nomination.

By the time Angela made it to Baltimore, the press had come to an agreement. They were calling the violence outside the convention center the Chicago Police Riot. In December, a month after Richard Nixon won the presidential election, the federal government's National Commission on the Causes and Prevention of Violence issued its report on the convention riot. In a section titled "The Chicago Police Riot of 1968," the report said that while protesters had harassed and provoked the police and military, it condemned Mayor Daley for calling out the National Guard and ordering them to violently suppress the protest. The report also said the police had been indiscriminate in their attacks on civilians and condemned Daley's failure to prosecute them for criminal acts.

Angela thought about sending a copy of the report to Mindy, but decided not to. The girl had enough on her mind and it didn't matter—she'd seen enough of the riot to know what it was. They both had.

Chapter Fourteen

WHO MORE SPECIAL THAN WE?

"Angela was amazing—feisty, strong-willed and courageous. She drank, she smoked and she cared more about people than anyone I've ever known."
—Tim 'Slim Man' Camponeschi

September, 1968

Angela surveyed her refrigerator. It was so much easier to pick up Chinese from Jimmy Wu's. Jimmy was a better cook than she was. Or maybe it was that he could cook more things. But she'd done that last Sunday. She'd really only mastered three dishes, including an Italian red ragù that Mamma used to make. She'd throw all sorts of things into it, from meatballs to chunks of pork. Her grandkids called it roadkill stew, which wasn't far off the mark. But it was still hot outside, too hot for heavy red sauce.

She'd make *Pasta e Piselli*. The grandkids loved it and she could make it at the last minute. She peered into the refrigerator vegetable drawer. *Good.* She had tomatoes and there were peas in the freezer. She just needed a couple heads of cauliflower. Should she pick up some veal cutlets too? Breaded cutlets were her third specialty, if such a plain thing could be considered a specialty at all. She ruefully remembered her attempts at gnocchi when she'd first been married. No wonder poor old Romolo ate most of his meals at the restaurant back then.

After the divorce, she hadn't cooked much. Mamma did it, and most of the laundry too. Angela sighed as she closed the refrigerator door. Mamma died back during World War II, during those bad years when Philip had been overseas with the army and Luigi had moved back to New York to manage the Theatrical Costume Workers' Union. He'd commuted between New York and Baltimore on the weekends for a few years, but she'd been alone during the week, missing Mamma and her boys.

She blew out a breath. *Enough of this sad stuff. You better get to the market or dinner will be late.*

Angela returned from the market carrying two bulging net bags. She heaved the bags onto the kitchen table with a groan. Cauliflower was easy to carry, but three bottles of Chianti really cut into her old fingers. But the kids and grandkids were coming—and when the Bambaces got together, the wine flowed like water. Pulling her battered cutting board from behind the toaster, Angela began cutting up cauliflower and tomatoes. She put each in a separate bowl and set them aside before starting in on the garlic and onions. She used nearly a whole head of garlic, though Oscar always said she used too much. He could make it any way he wanted at his house, but at her house the *Pasta e*

Piselli would taste like Mamma's did. And her grandson Tim said you could never have too much garlic.

She grinned at the thought of Tim. Like his sister Mindy, he was artistic, but his thing was music. Fourteen years old and already so talented. Mamma would have liked to know they had a couple of artists in the family.

She heard the front door thunk open.

"Mamma?" Oscar called out.

"In here." Angela wiped her hands on her apron and turned toward the door to the dining room just as Oscar walked in. She smiled as she always did when she saw one of her grown-up sons. "Where's Lorraine and the kids?" she asked.

Oscar kissed Angela on the cheek, then stood back and grinned at her. "They'll be here soon. I came straight from the lawyer's office. I have good news."

She nearly laughed aloud. "Did you do it?"

He nodded. "Ken and I signed the papers this morning."

She threw herself into his arms. "Oh, Oscar, I'm so proud of you. You're doing such a good thing for so many people."

"Well, it was your idea," he said.

"I know. But you didn't have to listen to your mother. And you gave up a lucrative practice to do it." She handed him a straw-covered bottle of Chianti and watched him open it.

She'd gone to Oscar over a year ago to ask for his help. So many of her garment workers had bad eyes. It was an occupational hazard for people who spent years leaning over machines in bad light, peering at thread, needles, and seams. But they couldn't afford glasses, let alone eye exams, and union insurance didn't cover eye stuff. A few years before, Oscar had founded a hospital just for poor people, pioneering the practice of preadmission tests so patients didn't have to pay for longer hospital stays than necessary. She'd figured that a man who could do that could help her figure out the eye insurance problem. And, boy, had he.

"I was ready for a new adventure, Mom. Hospital administration isn't as much fun as it sounds. And Ken was keen to try it."

Ken was Kenneth Blum. He and Oscar had put together a plan for an insurance company that would provide prepaid eye exams and glasses for ILGWU members across the nation.

Oscar poured himself two glasses of wine and handed one to Angela. "Ken says we'll get the other unions too, because no one has eye coverage and in this day and age people expect it, especially for their kids."

"You're going to do a lot of good, darling."

"And make a ton of money, according to Ken, so don't pat me on the back too much."

She tipped her wine glass at Oscar. "That's not why you're doing it and you know it."

He chuckled. "Well, how many times did you say it to me and Philip? 'Work hard and always do the right thing, boys.' We didn't have much choice with you as our mom. Speaking of which, is Philip coming?"

Angela shook her head. "No."

Oscar frowned and sighed. "I was just getting used to him being back."

Angela nodded. Philip spent most of last year in Puerto Rico, where he'd been working as director of a Peace Corps camp. He'd been back to Baltimore for only a few weeks when Hubert Humphrey asked him to join his speechwriting staff. Philip was her funny son and he had a good touch with writing.

"The campaign is in Seattle right now and heading for Salt

Lake City," Angela said. "He called last night and told me this story about a heckler in Seattle who yelled at Hubert about how he should be tried for war crimes. You know, on account of Hubert's support of the war. So Hubert decided to break with Johnson about the war. He's going to say he wants a ceasefire."

Oscar sat down his wine with a thump. "And Phil's going to write the speech?"

"He and two other guys." She grinned at her son. "He's pretty excited."

A thump at the front door and a gaggle of voices interrupted them. Lorraine and the grandkids had arrived.

Angela leaned back in her chair and hollered into the kitchen, where the two youngest grandchildren, Johnny and Lisa, were eating dinner. "You kids eat your pasta or I'm gonna shove it down your throats," she said.

A chorus of laughter and squeals rang out. Lisa yelled, "Yeah, and you're not gonna give us any dessert either."

"I won't! Not this time."

More mock groans rose in the air.

Johnny called out, "Nanny ate a banany and it came out her fanny."

"Knock it off in there," Oscar hollered, but he ruined the effect by laughing. It was an old exchange and one the family found hugely fun. Grandma threatened violence and the kids talked back, often in rhymes.

Philip's second-oldest son, Tim, grinned across the table at his older brother, Scott. "I'm glad I graduated to the big table," Tim said. Scott saluted him with his fork. A piece of pasta flew off the fork and dropped onto the tablecloth.

"Hard to see the difference between the two," Lorraine observed.

"The big table has wine," Oscar said and lifted his glass.

With Oscar's kids Mike and Mindy both away at college—medical school and Oberlin College, respectively—they had more room at the dining room table these days. Scott was sixteen and Tim was fourteen, and Angela thought that was old enough for the adult table and wine with dinner. Of course, it left the two eleven-year-olds unsupervised in the kitchen, but kids needed to get out from under their parents' watchful eyes from time to time. Unlike the house she'd grown up in, this one tolerated a lot of noise and folly.

"You keep coming by the office after school to help me and I'll let you sit at the head of the table," Angela said, handing Tim the pasta bowl. Teenaged boys were bottomless pits.

"Glad to help, Nanny. Gotta make that cabbage—I have my eye on a new guitar," Tim said. He filled his plate and handed the bowl to his mother.

"Well, we have about a billion election mailings and they gotta go out. If you come by tomorrow, I'll take you to lunch."

"At the Oyster Bar? Pete's going to get jealous if you keep showing up with another man," Tim joked.

Philip ruffled Tim's hair. "Is old Pete still doting on Nanny?"

Tim laughed. "You should see it. She cocks an eyebrow and he comes running over with another bourbon Manhattan."

"Poor Pete. These days, I have to turn him down. More than one Manhattan and I don't want to go back to work."

"When are you going to retire, Mom?" Oscar asked, grinning at Lorraine. Lorraine had the sense to act like she hadn't heard the question.

"Retire? Why should I retire?" Angela picked up her spoon

and pretended to examine her reflection in it. "Are you saying I'm old?"

"No, Nanny! Never," Tim exclaimed. Everyone at the table laughed. "You'd smack anyone who ever said that."

Lorraine patted Tim on the arm. "Oscar does have a point, Mom. You've done it all. You're the ILGWU's first female vice president, and before that you organized the entire Upper South Department."

"A region they said couldn't be organized, by the way," added Oscar. "You said it yourself—you started with zero union members and now you have thousands."

"Fifteen thousand," Angela said. "So, you think the work is done?"

Oscar shook his head. "It's never done. But maybe it's time for someone else to do it."

"We'll see," Angela said, and changed the topic to Oscar's new venture in optical insurance. She had a few more good years in her. Female union vice presidents weren't common enough that she could afford to quit too soon, and not before the men got used to working with women in positions of authority.

Angela listened as the talk swirled around her, so proud of her family. Both her boys went to the University of Maryland. Oscar earned his medical degree and went to work in public health before moving back to Baltimore to become a surgeon. He married Lorraine along the way and they had three children: Michael, Mindy and Johnny.

Philip did just as well. After he graduated from high school, he went off to the war as an MP and nearly scared her to death every day he was gone. She remembered the cheery letters she used to write him and how hard she'd worked to pretend she wasn't worried. In some ways both her boys had emulated her and their Uncle Shelley, though they rarely saw him. Shelley was an army doctor who'd served in both World War II and the Korean War. Her little brother lived out west now and didn't seem interested in either her or Marie's families; he was busy with his own life. Unlike Shelley, Philip came back from the army and went to law school right across town. He was her comedian, while Oscar was her philosopher.

From across the table Tim called, "Hey, Nanny, you heard from Aunt Marie and Uncle Nino lately?"

A groan rose from the table. Angela ignored it, not blaming them. No one liked Nino. He'd turned into a cranky old man and a bully who pushed around his wife and daughters.

"Is he still working on his translation of *Don Quixote*?" Scott asked. Nino had retired fifteen years ago and since then he'd been working on his book. Whenever Angela or one of the kids visited, he'd hole up in his office for hours, but the book was never any closer to being done. It had become something of a family joke.

Angela shrugged. "Marie didn't say. Last time we spoke, she mostly talked about their new goats."

More groaning around the table. "Like the old goat she already has isn't bad enough," Tim said.

Everyone laughed. Angela knew she should correct them. Children should respect their elders, but Nino was a mean old man who'd isolated his family when he moved them to a farm in western Massachusetts. He roamed the property shooting small animals, then got drunk and yelled at his wife. Why Marie put up with it, Angela would never understand.

"Settle down or I'll send you to stay with him," Angela said, trying to keep a straight face. "Uncle Nino will straighten out each and every one of you."

Oscar gestured for a straw-covered Chianti bottle. "Did you hear what he did to Mindy last time we visited? He killed a couple chickens in front of her and Marie cooked them for dinner. Poor, tender-hearted Mindy could hardly look at the dinner table, and that was before Nino showed her how to crack open the chicken leg bones and suck out the marrow. I thought she'd have a screaming fit, but she took it like a champ." More groans and laughter circled the table.

"Mindy's tougher than people think," Angela said. "Did she talk to you?"

Oscar nodded and looked at his wife. "She doesn't want to be a doctor. She said she talked to you about it. Lorraine and I both told her you were right—she should be what she wants to be, not what we want."

Lorraine pushed herself away from the table and began picking up plates. "She says she wants to be an artist or maybe help animals," she said.

Angela rose to help Lorraine, but Oscar waved her back into her seat. "I got it, Mom. And I'll put the rug rats in the kitchen to wash dishes."

"Hey, don't call us rats," Johnny called.

Angela sat at the table and watched her family. Tim saw her and chucked a pea at her. Angela laughed and threw one back. Tim winked. "Wanna drink some wine later, Nanny?"

She laughed again. A few weeks ago Oscar brought a case of wine by the house and left it in the basement. That night she and Tim drank two bottles of it—though she'd drunk way more of it than her teenage grandson. That wine had been incredible. A week later Oscar discovered the missing bottles. He sat the two of them down in the living room and yelled at them. "That was a full case of 1954 Chateau Mouton Rothschild. Do you have any idea how expensive it was? It's special. Or it was before you drank it."

She'd looked at her son and then her grandson and said, "Who more special than we?"

Oscar stared at her and then started to laugh. They'd all laughed until Oscar told them what the bottles cost. Still, wasn't that what special wine was for? You were supposed to drink it with people you love. Why not? Life was short and hard. An old lady might as well drink special wine and throw peas while she could.

Their squealing brought Oscar and Lorraine back into the room to put an end to the pea imbroglio. They talked and laughed into the night.

Epilogue

So much has been said. So many speeches. All complimentary. Mostly exaggerated.

Yes, it was tough going for a while.

Yes, my work was difficult and discouraging.

But I know that there are a number of labor leaders here who met with the same stubbornness and lack of understanding of our dream, the one dream we all share. It was hard and it was tough, but we knew one day soon the workers would come to the realization that what we preached made sense and so, little by little, they became curious and wanted to know just what the word union meant.

The women who had been receiving less pay for the same work as men decided to stand up and challenge this discrimination. The employer, fearful of losing his workers, agreed to give equal pay to all. This was the beginning, and little by little we won, but we knew our work had just begun.

The dream is a dream no more. It is a reality. We won our battles, though we must not let up for a minute for fear of slipping back.

But the dream is achieved, the reality is here—you can feel it, you can touch it, you can see it.

And if we share credit for this, we can share a bit of blame too. The last election showed us we cannot be divided. We must stick together. If we join hands, no one can beat us. If we work together, in our strength we can win whatever battles face us.

So I leave my work with this fervent hope and prayer that we join together tonight determined to be a united labor movement for the good of all Americans and for the achievements we can win through unity and strength. Let the union flags unfurl and together we will build a brave new workers' world.

TAKE A BOW, ANGELA

Though these days few people have heard of Angela Bambace, her life's work stands as a testament to the kind of difference a person can make by working at the local level to make people's lives better. The awards enumerated below suggest just that the people of her time appreciated Bambace's commitment to a wide variety of causes.

December 1955—Honored by Baltimore Federation of Labor & the Baltimore Industrial Union Council for "selfless devotion to the labor movement."

May 1963—Received an AMITA from Italian American Awards, the first labor leader to be so honored.

June 1963—Certificate of achievement in combatting crime and delinquency by Maryland Crime Investigations.

July 1963—Designated Outstanding Citizen of Baltimore by Mayor Theodore McKeldin.

November 1963—Histadrut (National Committee for Labor Israel) award for Outstanding Service.

November 1963—Certified Distinguished Citizen of Maryland for "the betterment of the Baltimore Community," by Governor Marvin Mandel.

January 1965—Honored by Histadrut for sponsoring an ILGWU scholarship for vocational training for young Israelis.

November 1966—Selected as first female recipient of Baltimore Community Relation's Committee annual honoree.

November 1967—Appointee, Mayor's Task Force for Equal Rights in Education.

April 1972—Honored by Citizens Awards for service to human rights and achieving constructive change.

November 1972—Designated Outstanding Citizen of Baltimore by Mayor William D. Schaefer for "significant contributions to the welfare of the people," on the occasion of her retirement.

December 1972—Honored by Virginia Local 201.

January 1973—Appointed Trustee for Board of Trustees, Community College of Baltimore.

April 1973—Awarded Distinguished Marylander by Americans for Democratic Action.

July 1973—Appointed member of Maryland Commission on the Status of Women (four-year term) by Governor Marvin Mandel.

December 1973—Honored by Community Action Agency of Baltimore for serving "beyond the call of duty to further the goals of community action."

DRUMROLL, PLEASE

First and foremost, I thank Angela's grandchildren Tim Camponeschi and Mindy Camponeschi. Both were generous and kind, answering multiple emails and providing invaluable information about their fabulous grandmother. Chapter 14 is based on Tim's blog, which you can find at his website www.slimman. com, and a series of long emails and phone calls with Mindy. I thank both of you most heartily.

The librarians at the University of Minnesota, Immigration History Research Center Archives, who copied the majority of Angela Bambace's papers for me for a shockingly small fee.

Robert Barbera, founder of the Mentoris Project, gave the go-ahead for this book after I talked to him about adding more women to the publication list. I deeply appreciate Mr. Barbera allowing me the freedom to pick an Italian-American woman like Angela, who is far from famous and an unlikely biography topic. Publishers with vision are hard to come by these days and I thank everyone at Mentoris, including Ken Lazebnik, Natalie Barbera Nunez, and Karen Richardson, for their hard work and thoughtful kindness. Alyssa Bluhm did a stellar job with the copyediting.

Grateful thanks to my officemate, writing partner, and friend Rosanne Welch, for getting me the gig, and to her lovely husband, Douglas Welch, for his free tech help.

Paul Lamphier read the manuscript and found a number of errors. All writers should have such fathers. And last, but not least, thanks to my husband, Leo Burke, who shifted for himself while his wife ignored him to write, write, and write some more.

ABOUT THE AUTHOR

Peg A. Lamphier has a doctorate in American history she uses to write nonfiction monographs, encyclopedias, and a small pile of novels. A native Montanan (go Bobcats!), she lives in the mountains of Southern California with five dogs, six tortoises, a huge cat, three canaries, one daughter (who's away at college), one husband (who is around *all* the time), and a collection of vintage ukuleles that she plays with more enthusiasm than talent. When she's not writing, Peg teaches interdisciplinary education at California State Polytechnic–Pomona and American women's history at Mount San Antonio Community College. For more, see www.peglamphier.com.

ALSO BY PEG A. LAMPHIER

Kate Chase and William Sprague:
Politics and Gender in a Civil War Marriage

Spur Up Your Pegasus:
Family Letters of Salmon, Kate and Nettie Chase, 1844-73
(with James P. McClure and Erika M. Kreger)

Women in American History: A Social, Political and Cultural
Encyclopedia with Document Collection [4 volumes]
(with Rosanne Welch)

The Lincoln Special
Kate Warne Civil War Spy Series, Book 1

The Great Show
Kate Warne Civil War Spy Series, Book 2

Rebel Belles
Kate Warne Civil War Spy Series, Book 3

Deadly Delights & Vampires:
The Perils of Petronella Crabtree, Journal 1

Soldier, Diplomat, Archaeologist:
The Bold Life of Louis Palma di Cesnola

NOW AVAILABLE FROM THE MENTORIS PROJECT

America's Forgotten Founding Father
A Novel Based on the Life of Filippo Mazzei
by Rosanne Welch

A. P. Giannini—The People's Banker
by Francesca Valente

A Boxing Trainer's Journey
A Novel Based on the Life of Angelo Dundee
by Jonathan Brown

Building Heaven's Ceiling
A Novel Based on the Life of Filippo Brunelleschi
by Joe Cline

Building Wealth
From Shoeshine Boy to Real Estate Magnate
by Robert Barbera

Christopher Columbus: His Life and Discoveries
by Mario Di Giovanni

Dreams of Discovery
A Novel Based on the Life of the Explorer John Cabot
by Jule Selbo

The Faithful
A Novel Based on the Life of Giuseppe Verdi
by Collin Mitchell

Fermi's Gifts
A Novel Based on the Life of Enrico Fermi
by Kate Fuglei

First Among Equals
A Novel Based on the Life of Cosimo de' Medici
by Francesco Massaccesi

God's Messenger
The Astounding Achievements of Mother Cabrini
A Novel Based on the Life of Mother Frances X. Cabrini
by Nicole Gregory

Grace Notes
A Novel Based on the Life of Henry Mancini
by Stacia Raymond

Harvesting the American Dream
A Novel Based on the Life of Ernest Gallo
by Karen Richardson

Humble Servant of Truth
A Novel Based on the Life of Thomas Aquinas
by Peggy O'Reilly

Leonardo's Secret
A Novel Based on the Life of Leonardo da Vinci
by Peter David Myers

The Making of a Prince
A Novel Based on the Life of Niccolò Machiavelli
by Maurizio Marmorstein

Marconi and His Muses
A Novel Based on the Life of Guglielmo Marconi
by Pamela Winfrey

No Person Above the Law
A Novel Based on the Life of Judge John J. Sirica
by Cynthia Cooper

Ride Into the Sun
A Novel Based on the Life of Scipio Africanus
by Patric Verrone

Saving the Republic
A Novel Based on the Life of Marcus Cicero
by Eric D. Martin

Soldier, Diplomat, Archaeologist
A Novel Based on the Bold Life of Louis Palma di Cesnola
by Peg A. Lamphier

The Soul of a Child
A Novel Based on the Life of Maria Montessori
by Kate Fuglei

FUTURE TITLES FROM THE MENTORIS PROJECT

Alessandro Volta, a Biography
Rita Levi-Montalcini, a Biography
and
Novels Based on the Lives of:
Amerigo Vespucci
Andrea Doria
Andrea Palladio
Antonin Scalia
Antonio Meucci
Artemisia Gentileschi
Buzzie Bavasi
Cesare Beccaria
Father Eusebio Francisco Kino
Father Matteo Ricci
Federico Fellini
Frank Capra
Galileo Galilei
Giuseppe Garibaldi
Guido d'Arezzo
Harry Warren
Laura Bassi
Luca Pacioli
Maria Gaetana Agnesi
Peter Rodino
Pietro Belluschi
Saint Augustine of Hippo
Saint Francis of Assisi

For more information on these titles and
The Mentoris Project, please visit
www.mentorisproject.org.

Made in the USA
Las Vegas, NV
07 February 2021